A TRACE OF HOPE

(A KERI LOCKE MYSTERY—BOOK 5)

BLAKE PIERCE

BOOKS BY BLAKE PIERCE

THE MAKING OF RILEY PAIGE SERIES
WATCHING (Book #1)

RILEY PAIGE MYSTERY SERIES
ONCE GONE (Book #1)
ONCE TAKEN (Book #2)
ONCE CRAVED (Book #3)
ONCE LURED (Book #4)
ONCE HUNTED (Book #5)
ONCE PINED (Book #6)
ONCE FORSAKEN (Book #7)
ONCE COLD (Book #8)
ONCE STALKED (Book #9)
ONCE LOST (Book #10)
ONCE BURIED (Book #11)
ONCE BOUND (Book #12)
ONCE TRAPPED (Book #13)

MACKENZIE WHITE MYSTERY SERIES
BEFORE HE KILLS (Book #1)
BEFORE HE SEES (Book #2)
BEFORE HE COVETS (Book #3)
BEFORE HE TAKES (Book #4)
BEFORE HE NEEDS (Book #5)
BEFORE HE FEELS (Book #6)
BEFORE HE SINS (Book #7)
BEFORE HE HUNTS (Book #8)
BEFORE HE PREYS (Book #9)

AVERY BLACK MYSTERY SERIES
CAUSE TO KILL (Book #1)
CAUSE TO RUN (Book #2)
CAUSE TO HIDE (Book #3)
CAUSE TO FEAR (Book #4)
CAUSE TO SAVE (Book #5)
CAUSE TO DREAD (Book #6)

CHAPTER ONE

When Detective Keri Locke opened her eyes, she immediately knew something was off. First of all, she didn't feel as if she had been asleep for long. Her heart was racing and she felt clammy all over. It was more like she'd passed out than been sleeping for a long time.

Second, she wasn't in bed. Instead, she was flat on her back on the couch in her apartment living room and Detective Ray Sands, her partner and, as of late, her boyfriend, was leaning over her with a concerned expression on his face.

She tried to speak, to ask him what was wrong, but her mouth was dry and nothing came out but a hoarse crack. She couldn't remember how she got here or what had happened before she lost consciousness. But it must have been something huge for her to react that way.

She saw in Ray's eyes that he wasn't sure what to say. That wasn't like him. He wasn't one to beat around the bush. A six-foot-four African-American LAPD cop and former professional boxer who'd lost his left eye in a fight, he was direct in almost everything he did.

Keri tried to push up on her arms to get to a more elevated position but Ray stopped her, gently resting a hand on her shoulder and shaking his head.

"Give yourself a moment," he said. "You still look a little unsteady."

"How long was I out?" Keri croaked.

"Not quite a minute," he answered.

"*Why* was I out?" she asked.

Ray's eyes widened. He opened his mouth to reply but stopped, clearly at a loss.

"What is it?"

"You don't remember?" he asked incredulously.

Keri shook her head. She thought she heard a buzzing in her ears but then realized that it was another voice. She glanced over to the coffee table and saw her phone resting there. It was on and someone was speaking.

"Who's on the phone?" she asked.

"Oh, you dropped it when you collapsed and I put it there until I could revive you."

"Who is it?" Keri asked again, noting that he had avoided her question.

"It's Susan," he said reluctantly. "Susan Granger."

Susan Granger was a fifteen-year-old prostitute whom Keri had rescued from her pimp last year and gotten placed in a girls' home. Since then, the two had become close, with Keri acting as a kind of mentor for the damaged but spirited young girl.

"Why is Susan calli—?"

And then the memory hit her like a wave crashing down on her entire body. Susan had called to tell Keri that her own daughter, Evie, who had been abducted six years ago, was to be the central participant in a grotesque ceremony.

Susan had learned that tomorrow night at a house somewhere in the Hollywood Hills, Evie was going to be auctioned off to the highest bidder, who would be allowed to have his way with her sexually before killing her in some sort of ritualistic sacrifice.

That's why I passed out.

"Hand me the phone," she ordered Ray.

"I'm not sure you're up for this yet," he said, obviously sensing that she could now remember everything.

"Give me the goddamn phone, Ray."

He handed it over without another word.

"Susan, are you still there?" she said.

"What happened?" Susan demanded, her voice borderline panicky. "One minute you were there and then nothing. I could hear something happening but you didn't answer."

"I passed out," Keri admitted. "It took me a moment to regroup."

"Oh," Susan said quietly. "I'm sorry I did that to you."

"It's not your fault, Susan. I was just taken by surprise. It's a lot to process at once, especially when I'm not feeling a hundred percent."

"How are you doing?" Susan asked, the concern in her voice almost palpable.

She was referring to Keri's injuries, sustained in a life-and-death fight with a child abductor only two days ago. She had only been released from the hospital yesterday morning.

The doctors had determined that the bruises on her face, where the abductor had punched her twice, along with a badly bruised chest and swollen knee, weren't enough to keep her another day.

The abductor, a deranged zealot named Jason Petrossian, had gotten the worst of it. He was still hospitalized under armed guard. The girl he'd kidnapped, twelve-year-old Jessica Rainey, was recovering at home with her family.

"I'll be okay," Keri said reassuringly. "Just some bumps and bruises. I'm glad you called, Susan. No matter how bad the news, knowing this is better than not knowing. Now I can try to do something about it."

"What can you do, Detective Locke?" Susan said, her voice rising as the words tumbled out of her. "Like I said, I know Evie is the Blood Prize at the Vista. But I don't where it's happening."

"Slow down, Susan," Keri said firmly as she pulled herself to a sitting position. Her head felt a little dizzy and she didn't protest as Ray put a steadying hand on her back as he sat down beside her on the couch. "We'll figure out how to find her. But first I need you to tell me everything you know about this whole Vista thing. Don't worry about repeating yourself. I want every detail you can recall."

"Are you sure?" Susan asked hesitantly.

"Don't worry. I'm okay now. I just needed a moment to take all this in. But I'm a Missing Persons detective. This is what I do. Just because I'm looking for my own daughter doesn't change the job. So tell me everything."

She pushed the speakerphone button so Ray could listen too.

"Okay," Susan said. "As I told you before, there's a club of rich johns who have pop-up sex parties in the Hollywood Hills. They call them Hill House Parties. The house is filled with girls, almost all underage prostitutes like I was. They usually have them every few months and most of the time, they only give a few hours' notice, usually via text. Am I making sense?"

"Absolutely," Keri said. "I remember you telling me about this. So remind me about the Vista event."

"The Vista is like their biggest party of all. It only happens once a year and no one knows when. They like to give a little more notice for that one because no one wants to miss it. That's probably why my friend heard about it already even though it's not until tomorrow night."

"And the Vista is different from the other Hill House Parties, right?" Keri prodded, knowing Susan was reluctant to revisit the particulars and giving her permission to do it.

7

"Yeah. At all the other parties, the john pays for whatever girl he likes and just does whatever he wants with her. Guys can be with anyone they want and a girl can be used all night by anyone. But the Vista is different. On that night the organizers pick one girl—she's usually special in some way—and make her the Blood Prize."

She stopped talking and Keri could sense she didn't want to continue, didn't want to hurt the woman who'd rescued her and helped her see a future for herself.

"It's okay, Susan," Keri insisted. "Go on. I need to know everything."

She heard the girl give a deep sigh on the other end of the line before continuing.

"So the event starts around nine at night. For a while it's just like a regular Hill House party. But then they bring in the girl who has been chosen as the Blood Prize. Like I said, there's usually something different about her. Maybe she's a virgin. Maybe she was just abducted that day so she's been on the news. Once it was former child star who got hooked on drugs and ended up on the streets."

"And this year it's Evie," Keri prodded.

"Yeah, there's a girl named Lupita from my hooking days in Venice who I keep in touch with. She still works the streets and she overheard some guys talking about how they were using the lady cop's daughter this year. They're using the nickname 'mini-pig' to describe her."

"Very creative," Keri muttered bitterly. "And you said they picked her because I'm getting too close?"

"Right," Susan confirmed. "The powers that be were tired of moving her around. They said she's become a liability with you constantly on the hunt for her. They just want to finish her off and dump her body somewhere, so you know she's dead and will stop looking. I'm so sorry, Detective."

"Go on," Keri said. Her body was numb and her voice sounded like it was coming from somewhere far away, outside of herself.

"So it's basically an auction. All the big spenders will bid on her. Sometimes it gets into the hundreds of thousands. These guys are competitive. Plus there's the fact that by punishing her, it's like they're reaching out and hurting you. I'm sure that'll up the cost. And I think they're all turned on by how it ends."

"Remind me of that part," Keri asked, closing her eyes in preparation. She sensed Susan's hesitation but didn't press, letting the girl gather herself to say what had to be said. Ray edged a little closer to her on the couch and moved his arm from her back, wrapping it around her shoulder.

"Whoever wins the auction is taken to a separate room while the Blood Prize is prepared. She's bathed and put in a fancy dress. Someone does her makeup, movie-star style. Then she's taken to a room where the guy gets to have his way with her. The only rule is he can't hurt her face."

Keri noticed that Susan's voice had grown hard, as if she was turning off the part of herself that felt emotion so she could get through this. Keri didn't blame her. The girl went on.

"I mean, he can do things to her, you know. He just can't hit her or slap her above the neck. She's got to look right for the big event later. They don't mind if her mascara is streaky because she's been crying. That adds to the drama. Just no bruises."

"What happens next?"

"The guy has to be finished a little bit before midnight because that's when the final sacrifice happens. They put her in a fresh dress and strap her down so she can't move too much. She can wriggle a little. They like that. But not too much."

Despite her eyes being closed, Keri sensed Ray stiffening beside her. He seemed to be holding his breath. She realized she was doing the same thing and forced herself to exhale when she heard Susan pause to swallow.

"The guy puts on a black robe and a hood to hide his identity," she continued. "That's because the thing is shown on TV in the main room where everyone else is. I think it's recorded too. Obviously none of these guys want video evidence of them murdering a teenage girl.

"When they're both prepped, the guy comes in and stands behind her. He delivers some prepared line, I don't know what. Then he's handed a knife and, right at the stroke of midnight, he slits her throat. She dies, right there on camera. Everybody recites something. Then they turn the TV off and the party resumes. That's pretty much it."

Keri finally opened her eyes. She felt a tear trickle down her cheek but refused to wipe it away. She liked the way it almost burned her skin, like a wet flame.

As long as she could keep that flame of righteous fury alive in her heart, she was sure she could keep Evie alive too.

CHAPTER TWO

For a long time, no one spoke. Keri didn't think she could. Instead, she let the rising tide of rage fill her up, making her blood boil and her fingers tingle.

Finally Ray cleared his throat.

"Susan, this is Detective Locke's partner, Ray Sands. Can I ask you a question?"

"Of course, Detective."

"How do you know all this? I mean, were you at one of these parties?"

"Like I told Detective Locke, I was taken to a Hill House Party once when I was about eleven. I was never brought back but I know girls who have been. One of my friends was taken twice. And you can imagine how word spreads. Any girl who's been in the life in LA knows all the details about the Vista. It's become almost an urban legend. Pimps sometimes use it to keep their girls in line. 'Talk back and you might be the Blood Prize this year.' Only this legend is actually true."

Something in Susan's tone—the mix of fear and sadness—snapped Keri out of her silence. This young girl had made so much progress in recent months. But Keri feared that asking her to return, even just in memory, to the dark place she'd inhabited for years was unfair and cruel. Susan had shared everything she could, at the cost of her own emotional well-being. It was time to let her try to be a kid again.

The adults had to take over now.

"Susan," she said, "thank you so much for telling me all this. I know it wasn't easy for you. With the information you've given us, I think we've got a great start at finding Evie. I don't want you to worry about this anymore, okay?"

"I could check around some more," the girl insisted.

"No. You've done enough. It's time to get back to your new life. I promise to check in with you. But for now I need you to focus on schoolwork. Maybe read a new Nancy Drew book we can talk about next week. We've got it from here, kiddo."

They said goodbye and Keri hung up. She looked over at Ray.

"You think we've got a great start at finding Evie?" he asked skeptically.

"No, but I couldn't tell her that. Besides, it may not be great. But it's a start."

*

Keri and Ray sat in Ronnie's Diner, both lost in thought. The morning rush at the nondescript joint in Marina del Rey had ended and most of the customers in the place were enjoying a leisurely breakfast.

Ray had insisted they leave the apartment and Keri had agreed. She had dressed more casually than usual, in a long-sleeved shirt and faded jeans, with a light jacket to protect against the crisp January morning.

She wore a baseball cap, pulled down low over the top half of her face. She let her dirty-blonde hair, normally pulled back in a professional ponytail, intentionally hang loose to swallow her face and hide the bruises she knew would make others stare.

She hunched down in their booth as she sipped coffee, further hiding her already modest frame. Keri, almost thirty-six years old, was an unimposing five foot six. Recently, she'd taken to wearing more form-fitting attire, as she'd cut down on the drinking and gotten back into solid shape. But not today. This morning, she was hoping to go unnoticed.

It was nice just to get out after two days of doctor-ordered bed rest. But Keri was also hoping that a change of scenery would give her a fresh perspective on how to find Evie. And it had worked to some degree.

By the time their food arrived they'd agreed not to formally involve their team, the Missing Persons Unit of LAPD's West Los Angeles Pacific Division, in the search. The unit had been helping Keri look for her daughter on and off for years, to no avail. There was no reason to assume the outcome would be any different without new evidence to go on.

But there was another reason to keep a low profile. This was truly Keri's last chance to find her daughter. She knew the exact time that Evie would be in a certain part of LA—the Hollywood Hills at midnight tomorrow—even if she didn't have the specific location yet.

But if the team started poking around and word got out that they knew about the Vista event, the people who had Evie might cancel the event or just kill her early to avoid complications. Keri needed to keep things quiet.

Unspoken but understood between the partners and new couple was another wrinkle. They couldn't be sure they weren't being monitored by the person they most needed to keep in the dark—Jackson Cave.

Last year Keri had taken down a serial child abductor named Alan Jack Pachanga, ultimately killing him while rescuing a teenage girl. And while Pachanga was no longer a problem, his lawyer was.

Jackson Cave, the man's attorney, was a big-time corporate lawyer with a fancy downtown high-rise office. But he had also made something of a career of representing the dregs of society. He seemed to have a particular affinity for child predators. He claimed much of it was pro bono work and that even the worst among us deserved quality representation.

But Keri had uncovered information that seemed to link him to a vast network of child abductors, a network she suspected he was profiting from and helping to direct. One of the abductors in the network was a man who went by the title of the Collector.

Last fall, when Keri learned that the Collector was Evie's abductor, she lured him into a meeting. But the Collector, whose real name was Brian Wickwire, discovered her ruse and attacked her. She ended up killing him in their fight, but not before he swore she would never find Evie.

Unfortunately, she had no evidence that could prove Jackson Cave's connection to the man who'd taken her daughter or the larger network he seemed to run. At least none that she'd obtained legally.

In desperation, she'd once broken into his office and found a coded file that had proven helpful. But the fact that she'd stolen it made it inadmissible in court. Besides that, the connections between Cave and the network were so well-hidden and tenuous that proving his involvement would be nearly impossible. He hadn't reached his position of power atop the Los Angeles legal world by being sloppy or careless.

She even tried to convince her ex-husband, Stephen, a wealthy Hollywood talent agent, to help pay for a private investigator to follow Cave. A good investigator was well beyond her means alone. But Stephen refused, essentially saying he thought Evie was dead and Keri was delusional.

Of course Jackson Cave had no such financial limitations. And once he realized that Keri was on to him, he started having *her* surveilled. Both she and Ray had found bugs in their homes and cars. Each of them now did regular bug sweeps of everything from their clothes to their phones to their shoes before discussing anything sensitive. They also suspected even their LAPD office was monitored and acted accordingly.

That's why they sat in a loud diner, wearing clothes they'd swept for recording devices, making sure no one at nearby tables seemed to be listening in, as they formulated their plan. If there was one person they didn't want to know they were aware of Vista, it was Jackson Cave.

In her multiple verbal confrontations with him, it had become clear to Keri that something had changed in Cave. He may have originally viewed her as merely a threat to his business, another obstacle to overcome. But no longer.

After all, she'd killed two of his biggest earners, stolen files from his office, cracked codes, and put his business, and perhaps his freedom, at risk. Of course, she was doing it all to find her daughter.

But she sensed that Cave had come to see her as more than merely an opponent, some chick cop desperate to find her kid. He seemed to consider her almost as his nemesis, as some sort of mortal enemy. He didn't just want to defeat her anymore. He wanted to destroy her.

Keri was sure that was why Evie was to be the Blood Prize at the Vista. She doubted that Cave knew where Evie was being held or who was holding her. But he surely knew the people who knew the people who knew those things. And he had almost certainly instructed, at least indirectly, that Evie be the sacrifice at tomorrow's party as a way to break Keri beyond repair.

There was no point in tailing him or formally interrogating him. He was far too clever and careful to make any mistakes, especially since he knew she was on to him. But he was behind all of it—of that Keri was certain. She'd just have to find another way to solve this.

With a renewed sense of resolve she looked up to find that Ray was watching her closely.

"How long have you been staring at me?" she asked.

"A couple of minutes, at least. I didn't want to interrupt. You looked like you were doing some seriously deep thinking. Have any epiphanies?"

"Not really," she admitted. "We both know who's behind this but I don't think that helps us much. I need to start fresh and hope to track down some new leads."

"You mean 'we,' right?" Ray said.

"Don't you have to go in to work today? You've been off for a while taking care of me."

"You've got to be kidding, Tinker Bell," he said with a smile, alluding to their massive size disparity. "You think I'm just going to go into the office with everything going on? I'll use every sick, personal, and vacation day I have if it comes to that."

Keri felt her entire chest warm over with delight but tried to hide it.

"I appreciate that, Godzilla," she said. "But with me still being on suspension because of the IA investigation, we might need you to take advantage of some of those official police resources you have access to."

Keri was technically on suspension while Internal Affairs investigated the circumstances surrounding her killing of Brian "The Collector" Wickwire. Their supervisor, Lieutenant Cole Hillman, had indicated that it would likely be wrapped up soon in her favor. But until then, Keri had no badge, no department-issued weapon, no formal authority, and no access to police resources.

"Was there something particular you thought I should be looking into?" Ray asked.

"Actually, yes. Susan mentioned that one of the past Blood Prize girls was a former child actress who became an addict and ended up on the streets. If she was raped and murdered, especially by having her throat slit, there should be a record of it, right? I don't remember it being on the news but maybe I missed it. If you could track that down, maybe the forensic workup included DNA from the semen of the man who assaulted her."

"It's possible no one ever thought to even check for DNA," Ray added. "If they found this girl dead with her throat cut, they might not have felt the need to do anything further. If we can figure out who she was, maybe we can have more testing done, put a rush on it and ID who she was with."

"Exactly," Keri agreed. "Just remember to be discreet. Involve as few people as possible. We don't know how many ears our lawyer friend has in the building."

"Understood. So what do you plan to do while I pore over old records of murdered teenage girls?"

"I'm going to interview a possible witness."

"Who's that?" Ray asked.

"Susan's prostitute friend, Lupita—the one who said she overheard those guys talking about the Vista. Maybe she'll remember more with a little help."

"Okay, Keri, but remember to go a little easy. That area of Venice is rough and you're still not at full strength. Besides, at least for now, you're not even a cop."

"Thanks for the concern, Ray. But I think you know by now. Going easy just isn't my style."

CHAPTER THREE

As Keri pulled up in front of the Venice address Susan had texted her, she forced herself to forget about the lingering pain in her chest and knee. She was entering potentially dangerous territory. And since she was not officially on the job right now, she had to be on extra high alert. No one here would give her the benefit of the doubt.

It was only mid-morning and as she crossed Pacific Avenue in this seedy stretch of Venice, her only company was tattooed surfers, oblivious to the cold and headed to the ocean just a block away, and homeless men huddled in the doorways of not-yet-open businesses.

She arrived at the rundown apartment complex, walked through the open front door, and walked up three flights of stairs to the room where Lupita was supposedly expecting her. Business didn't usually pick up until after lunch so this was a good time to stop by.

Keri approached the door and was about to knock when she heard noise from inside. She checked and found the door unlocked and quietly opened it, peeking her head in.

On the bed in the unadorned room was a brunette girl who looked to be about fifteen. On top of her was a naked, wiry man in his thirties. Covers hid the particulars, but he was thrusting down aggressively. Every few seconds he would slap the girl in the face.

Keri fought the strong urge to march in and rip the guy off her. Even without the badge, it was her natural inclination. But she had no idea if this was a john and the activity taking place was standard operating procedure.

Sad experience had taught her that sometimes coming to the rescue was counterproductive in the long run. If this was a client and Keri interrupted, the guy might get upset and complain to Lupita's pimp, who would take it out on her. Unless a girl was willing to leave the life for good, as Susan Granger had, stepping in, while following the law, might only make things worse for her in the big picture.

Keri stepped into the room a bit more and caught Lupita's eye. The frail-looking girl with curly dark hair gave her a familiar look, a mix of pleading, fear, and wariness. Keri knew almost immediately what it meant. She needed help but not too much help.

This clearly was a john, maybe a new, unexpected last-minute one, because he was here when Lupita had agreed to meet Keri. But she'd been told to service him anyway. It was likely that the slapping was unexpected. But she wasn't in a position to object in case her pimp had given permission.

Keri knew how to handle it. She stepped forward quickly and quietly, pulling a rubber baton from the inside pocket of her jacket. Lupita's eyes got big and Keri could tell the john had noticed. He was just starting to turn his head to look behind him when the baton connected with the rear of his skull. He fell forward, collapsing on top of the girl, unconscious.

Keri held her finger to her lips, indicating for Lupita to stay quiet. She stepped around to the side of the bed to make sure the john really was out cold. He was.

"Lupita?" she asked.

The girl nodded.

"I'm Detective Locke," she said, neglecting to say that for now, she wasn't technically a detective. "Don't worry. If we're quick, this doesn't have to be a problem. When your pimp asks, here's what happened: a short guy in a masked hood came in, knocked out your john, and stole his wallet. You never saw his face. He threatened to kill you if you made a sound. When I leave this room, you count to twenty, then start screaming for help. There's no way you can be blamed. Got it?"

Lupita nodded again.

"Okay," Keri said as she rifled through the man's jeans and pulled out his wallet. "I don't think he'll be out more than a minute or two so let's cut to the chase. Susan said you overheard some guys talking about the Vista happening tomorrow night. Do you know who was talking? Was one of them your pimp?"

"Uh-uh," Lupita whispered. "I didn't recognize the voices. And when I looked out in the hall they were gone."

"That's okay. Susan told me what they said about my daughter. What I want you to focus on is the location. I know they always hold this Vista thing in the Hollywood Hills. But were they any more specific than that? Did they mention a street? Any landmarks?"

"They didn't mention a street. But one of them was complaining that it was going to be more of a hassle than last year because it was gated. In fact, he said 'the estate is gated.' So I'm assuming it's more than just a house."

"That's really helpful, Lupita. Anything else?"

"One of them said he was bummed because they wouldn't be close enough to see the Hollywood sign. I guess last year, the house was right near it. But this time they'll be too far away, in a different area. Does that help?"

"Actually it does. That means it's probably closer to West Hollywood. It narrows it down. That's really helpful. Anything more?"

The man on top of her groaned softly and started to stir.

"I can't think of anything," Lupita muttered, barely audible.

"That's all right. This is more than I had before. You've been a big help. And if you ever decide you want to get out of the life, you can reach out to me through Susan."

Lupita, despite her situation, smiled. Keri took off her cap, pulled a black hood out from her pocket, and put it on. It had small slits for her eyes and mouth.

"Now remember," she said in a deep voice intended to hide her own, "wait twenty seconds or I'll kill you."

The man on top of Lupita was coming to, so Keri turned and hurried out of the room. She rushed down the hall and was halfway down the stairs when she heard the screams for help. She ignored them and made her way to the front door, where she pulled off the hood, stuffed it back in her pocket, and put on her cap.

She rifled through the guy's wallet, and, after taking out the cash—all of twenty-three dollars—she tossed it in the corner by the door. As casually as possible, she walked back across the street to her car. As she got in, she could hear the shouts of angry men, headed toward Lupita's room.

When she was clear of the area, she called Ray to see if he'd had any luck with his lead. He picked up after one ring and she could tell from his voice that it hadn't gone well.

"What's wrong?" she asked.

"It's a dead end, Keri. I've gone back ten years and can't find any record of a former child star who was found with her throat slit. I did find a record of a former child actress named Carly Rose who fell on hard times and went missing as a teen. She'd be about twenty now. It could easily be her. Or she could have just overdosed in a subway tunnel and never been found.

Hard to know. I also found records of other girls between eleven and fourteen who meet a similar description—throats slit. Bodies just left in dumps or even on street corners. But usually they're girls who were on the streets for a while. And they're really spread out over time."

"That actually makes sense to me," Keri said. "These people probably had no compunction about dumping the bodies of girls who worked the streets or had no family. But they wouldn't want to draw attention by leaving the bodies of girls from good homes who were recently abducted or a girl who was well known. Those might initiate real investigations. I bet those girls were burned, buried, or dumped in the ocean. It's the ones no one would follow up on that they just dumped anywhere."

Keri chose to ignore the fact that she'd said all of that so matter-of-factly. If she lingered on it, she'd be bothered by how inured she'd become to these kinds of atrocities.

"That fits," Ray agreed, sounding equally unfazed. "It might also explain the gap in years. If they used a street prostitute one year, then used a few kidnapped suburban kids before returning to another teen hooker, it would be harder to establish a pattern. I mean, if a teen hooker showed up once a year with her throat slit, that might generate interest too."

"Good point," Keri said. "So there wasn't anything to go on then."

"Nah. Sorry. You have better luck?"

"A little," she said. "Based on what Lupita said, it sounds like the location may be in West Hollywood, on a gated estate."

"That's promising," Ray noted.

"I guess. There are a thousand of those up in those hills."

"We can have Edgerton cross-reference them to see if the property titles match up to anyone we know. With dummy companies, it's probably a long shot. But you never know what that guy will come up with."

It was true. Detective Kevin Edgerton was a genius when it came to anything tech. If anyone could suss out a meaningful connection, it was him.

"Okay, let him have at it," Keri said. "But have him do it under the radar. And don't give him too many details. The fewer people who know what's going on, the less chance someone inadvertently leaks something that tips off the wrong people."

"Understood. What are you going to do?"

Keri thought for a moment and realized she didn't have any new leads to follow up. That meant she had to do what she always did when she hit a brick wall—start fresh. And there was one person she realized she definitely needed a fresh start with.

"Actually," she said, "can you ask Castillo to call me, but have her do it outside, using her cell?"

"Okay. What are you thinking?" Ray asked.

"I'm thinking it's about time I reacquainted myself with an old friend."

CHAPTER FOUR

Keri waited anxiously in her car, eyeing the clock as she sat outside the offices of *Weekly L.A.*, the alternative newspaper where she had asked Officer Jamie Castillo to meet her. It was also where her friend, Margaret "Mags" Merrywether, worked as a columnist.

Time was starting to run short. It was already 12:30 on Friday, roughly thirty-six hours from when her daughter was going to be raped and ritualistically murdered for the pleasure of a group of wealthy soul-sick men.

Keri saw Jamie walking down the street and shook the dark thoughts from her head. She needed to stay focused on how to prevent her daughter's death, not obsess on the awfulness of how it might unfold.

As she had requested, Jamie was wearing a civilian coat over her uniform to draw less notice. Keri waved at her from the driver's seat, getting her attention. Jamie smiled and headed for the car, her dark hair blowing in the bitter wind despite being pulled back in a ponytail. She was taller than Keri by a few inches and more athletic too. She was a Parkour enthusiast and Keri had seen what she could do under duress.

Officer Jamila Cassandra Castillo wasn't yet a detective. But Keri was sure that once she made it, she'd be a great. In addition to her physical skills, she was tough, smart, relentless, and loyal. She'd already put her own safety and even her job on the line for Keri. If she wasn't already partners with Ray, Keri knew who her next choice would have been.

Jamie got in the car gingerly, wincing involuntarily, and Keri remembered why. While on the hunt for the suspect who gave Keri her current injuries, Jamie had been in the proximity of a bomb that went off at the guy's apartment. It had killed one FBI agent, badly burned another, and left Ray with a chunk of glass in his right leg, something he hadn't mentioned since. Jamie had ended up with a concussion and some serious bruises.

"Weren't you just released from the hospital today?" Keri asked, incredulous.

"Yep," she said with pride in her voice. "They let me go this morning. I went home, changed into my uniform, and made it in to work ten minutes late. Lieutenant Hillman cut me some slack though."

"How are your ears?" Keri asked, referring to the hearing loss Jamie had suffered in the moments after the bomb blast.

"I can hear you fine right now. I get some intermittent ringing. The doctor says that should go away in a week or two. No permanent damage."

"I can't believe you're working today," Keri muttered, shaking her head. "And I can't believe I'm asking you to go above and beyond on your first day back."

"It's no problem," Jamie assured her. "I needed to get out for a bit. Everyone was treating me like a porcelain doll. But I do have to get right back or I'd hang out. I brought what you asked for, though."

She pulled a file out of her bag and handed it to Keri.

"Thanks."

"No problem. And before you ask, I used the 'general' username ID when I searched the database, so it won't be tracked to me. I assume there's a reason you didn't want me using my own ID. And I further assume there's a reason you didn't volunteer anything about why you asked for this stuff?"

"You assume correctly," Keri said, hoping Jamie would leave it at that.

"And I assume you're not going to tell me what's going on or let me help in any way?"

"It's for your own good, Jamie. The less you know the better. And the less anyone knows you helped me, the better for what I'm doing."

"Okay. I trust you. But if you find that at some point down the road you do need help, you have my number."

"I do," Keri said, giving Castillo's hand a squeeze.

She waited until the officer had returned to her car and pulled out into the street before getting out of her own. Gripping the file Castillo had given her tightly to her body, Keri hurried up the steps and into the *Weekly L.A.* building, where Mags, and hopefully some answers, were waiting for her.

*

Two hours later, there was a knock on the door of the conference room where Keri had set up shop and had been

22

poring over documents. The large table in the center of the room was covered in papers.

"Who is it?" she asked. The door opened slightly. It was Mags.

"Just checking in," she said. "I wanted to see if you could use any help, darling."

"Actually, I could use a little break. Come on in."

Mags stepped inside, shut and locked the door behind her, made sure the blinds were still fully closed so no one could see in, and walked over. Once again, Keri marveled at how she had become friends with what was essentially the live-action version of Jessica Rabbit.

Margaret Merrywether was over six feet tall, even without the high heels she usually wore. Statuesque, with milky-white skin, ample curves, flaming red hair matched by her ruby red lips, and bright green eyes, she seemed like she'd stepped out of the pages of a high-fashion magazine for Amazon women.

And that was all *before* she opened her mouth to reveal an accent that suggested Scarlett O'Hara, only slightly undercut by a tart tongue that was more Rosalind Russell in *His Girl Friday*. Only that mildly biting tone hinted at Margaret's (Mags to her friends) alter ego. It turned out she also went by the pseudonym "Mary Brady," the alternative paper's muckraking columnist who had brought down local politicians, uncovered corporate malfeasance, and called out dirty cops.

Mags was also a happily divorced mother of two, made even wealthier after she parted ways from her banker ex-husband. Keri had met her while working a case and after some initial suspicion that her whole persona was some elaborate form of performance art, a friendship had blossomed. Keri, who didn't have many friends outside of work, was happy to be the boring one for once.

Mags sat down in the seat beside Keri and looked at the collage of police documents and newspaper clippings spread out on the table.

"So, my dear, you asked me to collect copies of every article the paper had ever written on Jackson Cave. And I see that you asked someone in the department to do the same with everything they have on him. Then you locked yourself in here for two hours. Are you ready to tell me what's going on?"

"I am," Keri said. "Just give me a moment first."

She got up, pulled a bug detector out of her bag, and proceeded to sweep the entire conference room. Mags raised her eyebrows but didn't seem stunned.

"You know, darling," she began, "I'm hardly one to tell you you're being overcautious. But I have this sort of thing done professionally twice a week."

"I have no doubt," Keri said. "But thanks for humoring me. This was given to me by a techie friend I trust."

"Someone in the department?" Mags asked.

"No, he's actually a mall security guard. It's a long story but let's just say the guy knows his stuff and he owed me a favor, so when I asked for a recommendation for a good bug detector, he gave me this as a gift."

"That sounds like a long story I might like to hear when we have a bit more time," Mags said.

Keri nodded absentmindedly as she continued to sweep the room. Mags smiled and waited patiently. When Keri was done and found nothing, she sat back down.

"Okay, here it is," she said and launched into her history with Cave, much of which Mags was already familiar with.

In fact, her friend had even recently helped her lure out information from an assassin-for-hire with a connection to Cave. He was a man known only as the Black Widower, a mystery figure who drove a black Lincoln Continental without plates.

Months earlier, Keri had watched on security camera footage as he casually killed the man who'd been holding Evie, shoved Evie into his trunk, and disappeared with her into the night, all, Keri suspected, on the orders of Cave.

Somehow, Mags had managed find a way to anonymously reach out to the Black Widower. It turned out that he was happy to pass on a lead about Evie's whereabouts for a hefty price. He seemed to have no loyalties, which worked out well for Keri in that instance because his information ultimately led to her learning of the existence of the Vista event.

But while some of the particulars, like the Black Widower connection, were old news to her, Mags said nothing. She didn't interrupt once, although she pulled out a notepad and took occasional notes. She listened intently, from the beginning all the way up to the call from Susan Granger this morning about Evie being the Blood Prize at the Vista.

When she was sure Keri was done, she asked a question.

"I understand your predicament, Keri. And I'm horrified for you. But I still don't understand. Why are you staring at hundreds of papers about Mr. Cave?"

"Because I'm at my wits' end, Mags. I have no more leads. I have no more clues. The only thing I know for certain is that Jackson Cave is somehow involved in my daughter's case."

"You're certain?" Mags asked.

"Yes," Keri said. "I don't think he was initially. He probably had no idea that one of his abductors' victims was my daughter. After all, I wasn't even a detective at the time. I was a college professor. Her disappearance is the *reason* I became a cop. I don't even know at what point I really attracted his interest. But at some point he must have pieced together that the kid the lady detective was searching for was abducted by someone he had commissioned."

"And you think he sought out her location?" Mags asked. "You think he knows where she is now?"

"Those are two very different questions. I'm sure that at some point he did investigate her location. It would have been in his interest to know her circumstance. But that would have been well before I started to sniff him out. Once he suspected I was looking into him, I have no doubt he made sure that he couldn't be connected to her. He knows that if I thought he could lead me to Evie, I'd follow him day and night. He probably worries that I'd kidnap him and torture him to get her location."

"Would you?" Mags asked, more curiously than accusingly.

"I would. A million times over I would."

"Me too," Mags whispered.

"So I don't think that Jackson Cave knows where my daughter is or who has her. But I do think he knows individuals who know individuals who know where she is. I think he could find out her current location if he was so inclined. And I think that he could direct her to be at a specific location at a particular time if he wanted. That's what I think is going on. I think Evie is the Blood Prize because he wants her to be. And somehow, his wishes have been conveyed to the people who can make it happen."

"So you want to follow that trail?"

"No," Keri said. "The maze from him to her is too complicated for me to figure out, even if I had unlimited time, which I obviously don't. That's a rabbit hole I won't go down. But I started to realize, all this time I've only been looking at Jackson Cave as an opponent, the mastermind who is keeping me from my daughter, this malevolent force out to destroy my family."

"He's not?" Mags asked, sounding surprised and almost offended.

"He is. But that's not how he sees himself. And that's not what he always was. I realized that I have to forget my preconceptions to learn who this guy is and what makes him tick."

"Why do you care what makes him tick?"

"Because I can't beat him if I don't understand how he thinks, what his motives are. And if I don't understand what's really important to him deep down, I'll never get leverage over him. And that's what I really need, Mags—leverage. This guy isn't going to volunteer any information to me. But if I can determine what matters most to him, maybe I can use that to get my daughter back."

"How?"

"I have no idea…yet."

CHAPTER FIVE

When Ray walked into the conference room three hours later, Keri still didn't have leverage. But she did think she had a better sense of who Jackson Cave was.

"Lovely to see you, Detective Sands," Mags said when he entered bearing submarine sandwiches and iced coffees.

"Good to see you too, Red," he said as he tossed the sandwiches on the table.

"Well, I do declare," she replied huffily.

Keri wasn't sure when Ray had started calling Margaret Merrywether "Red" but she got a kick out of it. And despite her reaction now, Keri was pretty sure Mags didn't mind either.

"I brought the guy's financials and property records," Ray said. "But I don't think they're going to be the answer. I reviewed them with Edgerton and he couldn't find anything hinky. But for a guy with that kind of money and power, that alone is actually kind of hinky."

"I agree," Keri said. "But hinky isn't enough to act on."

"He wanted to bring in Patterson but I told him to hold off for now."

Detective Garrett Patterson went by the nickname "Grunt Work," and for good reason. He was the second best tech guy in the unit behind Edgerton, and while he lacked Edgerton's intuitive gifts for finding unseen connections within complex information, he had another skill. He loved to pore over the minutiae of records to find that small but crucial detail that others missed.

"That was the right call," Keri said after a moment. "He might uncover something with the property records. But I worry that he couldn't help but tell Hillman or accidentally cast too wide a net and set off warning lights. I don't want to involve him unless we have no other choice."

"It may come to that," Ray said. "That is, unless you've cracked the Cave code in the last few hours."

"I wouldn't say that," Keri admitted. "But we have uncovered some surprising stuff."

"Like what?"

"Well, for starters," Mags piped in, "Jackson Cave wasn't always a complete asshole."

"That is a surprise," Ray said, unwrapping a sandwich and taking a big bite. "How so?"

"He used to work in the D.A.'s office," Mags replied.

"He was a prosecutor?" Ray asked, nearly choking on his food. "The defender of rapists and child molesters?"

"It was a long time ago," Keri said. "He joined the D.A. right out of law school at USC—worked there for two years."

"Couldn't hack it?" Ray wondered.

"Actually, his conviction rate was pretty amazing. He apparently didn't like to plead down often so he took most cases to trial. He got nineteen convictions and two hung juries. Not one acquittal."

"That is good," Ray acknowledged. "So why did he switch teams?"

"That took some digging," Keri said. "It was actually Mags who figured it out. You want to explain?"

"It would be my great pleasure," she said, looking up from the sea of pages in front of her. "I suppose a lifetime of doing tedious research pays off from time to time. Jackson Cave had a half-brother named Coy Trembley. They had different fathers but grew up together. Coy was three years older than Jackson."

"Was Coy a lawyer too?" Ray asked.

"Hardly," Mags said. "Coy was in trouble with the law throughout his teens and twenties—mostly petty stuff. But when he was thirty-one, he was arrested for sexual assault. Basically he was accused of forcing himself on a nine-year-old girl who lived down the street."

"And Cave defended him?"

"Not officially. But he took a nine-month leave of absence from the prosecutor's office right after the arrest. He wasn't Trembley's attorney of record and his name isn't on any of the legal documents filed with the court in the case."

"I hear a 'but' coming," Ray said.

"You hear correctly, dear," Mags declared. "*But* for tax purposes, his declared job during that time was 'legal consultant.' And I've compared the language in the briefs in Trembley's case. Some of the phrasing and logic are very similar to more recent Cave cases. I think it's fair to assume he was secretly assisting his brother."

"How'd he do?" Ray asked.

"Quite well. Coy Trembley's case ended in a hung jury. Prosecutors were debating whether to retry him when the little girl's father showed up at Trembley's apartment and shot him five times, including once in the face. He didn't make it."

"Jeez," Ray muttered.

"Yeah," Keri agreed. "It was around that time that Cave gave his notice to the D.A.'s office. He was off the grid for three months after that. Then he suddenly reemerged with a new firm that dealt mostly with corporate clients. But he also did a little white collar defense stuff and increasingly as the years went by, pro-bono work for folks like his half brother."

"Wait," Ray demanded incredulously. "Am I supposed to believe this guy became a defense lawyer to honor the memory of his dead brother or something, to defend the rights of the morally grotesque?"

Keri shook her head.

"I don't know, Ray," she said. "Cave almost never spoke about his brother over the years. But when he did, he always maintained that Coy was falsely accused. He was pretty adamant about it. I think it's possible that he started his practice with noble intentions."

"Okay. Let's say I give him the benefit of the doubt on that. What the hell happened to him then?"

Mags picked up from there.

"Well, it's pretty clear that the guilt of most of his early pro-bono clients was highly dubious. Some of them seem to have just been picked out of lineups or pulled off the street. Occasionally he got them off; usually he didn't. Meanwhile, he was going around making speeches at civil liberties conferences—good speeches actually, very passionate. There was even talk that he might run for office someday."

"Sounds like an American success story so far," Ray said.

"It was," Keri agreed. "That is, until about ten years ago. That's when he took on the case of a guy who didn't fit the profile. He was a serial child abductor who apparently did it professionally. And he paid Cave handsomely to represent him."

"Why did he all of a sudden take on that case?" Ray asked.

"Not a hundred percent clear," Keri said. "His corporate work hadn't really taken off yet. So it could have been a financial decision. Maybe he didn't view this guy as being as objectionable as others. The charges against him were for abduction for hire, not assault or molestation. The guy basically kidnapped kids and sold them to the highest bidder. He was, to use a generous description, a 'professional.' Whatever the reason, Cave took this guy on, got him acquitted, and then the floodgates opened. He started taking all manner of similar clients, many of whom were less...professional."

"Around the same time," Mags added," the corporate work picked up. He moved from a storefront in Echo Park to the downtown high-rise office he has now. And he's never looked back."

"I don't know," Ray said skeptically. "It's hard to see the through line from civil libertarian fighting for the least among us to remorseless legal shark representing pedophiles and possibly coordinating a child sex slave ring. I feel like we're missing a piece."

"Well, you're a detective, Raymond," said Mags snarkily. "By all means, detect."

Ray opened his mouth, about to fire back, before realizing that he was being teased. All three of them laughed, glad for the chance to break the tension they hadn't realized had been building up. Keri jumped back in.

"It has to be related to that serial abductor he represented. That's when everything changed. We should look into that more."

"What do you have on him?" Ray asked.

"His case just kind of dead ends," Mags said, frustrated. "Cave represented the man, got him off, and then that guy dropped off the radar. We haven't been able to find anything on him since."

"What was the man's name?" Ray asked.

"John Johnson," Mags answered.

"That sounds familiar," Ray muttered.

"Really?" Keri said, surprised. "Because there's almost nothing on him. It looks like it was a false identity. There's no record of him existing after he was acquitted. It's like he left that courtroom and then completely disappeared."

"Still, the name rings a bell," Ray said. "I think it was before you joined the force. Did you try pulling up a mug shot?"

"I started to," Keri said. "There are seventy-four John Johnsons in the database who had mug shots taken the month of his arrest. I didn't have a chance to go through them all."

"Mind if I take a look?"

"Go ahead," Keri said, punching up the screen and sliding her laptop over to him. She could tell he was on to something but didn't want to say it out loud yet in case he was wrong. As he scrolled through the images, he spoke almost absent-mindedly.

"You both said it was like he dropped off the radar, like he'd disappeared, right?"

"Uh-huh," Keri said, watching him closely, feeling her breathing quicken.

"Almost like...a ghost?" he asked.

"Uh-huh," she repeated.

He stopped scrolling and stared at an image on the screen before looking up at Keri.

"I think that's because he is a ghost; or more accurately, 'The Ghost.'"

Ray turned the screen so that Keri could see the mug shot. As she stared at the image of the man who first sent Jackson Cave down his dark path, a cold shiver went down her spine.

She knew him.

CHAPTER SIX

Keri tried to control her emotions as a shot of adrenaline coursed through her system, making her entire body tingle.

She recognized the man staring back at her. But she didn't know him as John Johnson. When they'd met, he'd gone by the name Thomas Anderson, but everybody referred to him as The Ghost.

They'd spoken only twice, each time at the Twin Towers Correctional Facility in downtown Los Angeles, where he was currently being incarcerated for crimes not unlike those John Johnson had been acquitted of.

"Who is it, Keri?" Mags asked, half concerned, half annoyed by the long silence.

Keri realized she had been mutely staring at the mug shot for the last few seconds.

"Sorry," she replied, shaking herself back into the moment. "His name is Thomas Anderson. He's being held at county lockup for the abduction and sale of children, mostly to out-of-state families who didn't meet adoption qualifications. I can't believe it didn't occur to me that Johnson and Anderson could be the same guy."

"Cave deals with a lot of abductors, Keri," Ray said. "There's no reason you should have made that connection."

"How do you know him?" Mags asked.

"I stumbled across him last year when I was looking through case files about abductors. At one point, I thought he might have taken Evie. I went to Twin Towers to interview him and it became clear pretty quickly that he wasn't the guy. He even gave me a few leads that helped me ultimately hunt down the Collector. And now that I think about it, he's the first person who mentioned Jackson Cave to me—he said Cave was his lawyer."

"You'd never heard of Cave before that?" Mags asked.

"No, I'd heard of him. He's notorious to Missing Person cops. But I'd never met one of his clients or had reason to think about him as anything other than a generalized scumbag until

32

Anderson made me more aware of him. Until I met Thomas Anderson, Jackson Cave was never on my radar."

"And you don't think that's a coincidence?" Mags asked.

"With Anderson, I'm not sure anything is a coincidence. Isn't it strange that he gets off scot-free as 'John Johnson' but then gets arrested doing the same abduction thing using his real identity, Thomas Anderson? Why didn't he use a fake identity again? I mean, the guy was a librarian for over thirty years. He basically ruined his life by using his real name."

"Maybe he thought Cave could get him off a second time?" Ray suggested.

"But here's the thing," Keri said. "Even though Cave was technically his defense attorney, at his last trial, the one at which he was convicted, Anderson defended himself. And supposedly, he was great. Word was he was so convincing that if the case wasn't iron-clad, he would have gotten off."

"If this guy was such a genius," Mags countered, "how was the case against him so strong in the first place?"

"I asked him the same thing," Keri replied. "And he agreed with me that it was odd that someone as clever and meticulous as him would get caught like that. He didn't come right out and say it but he essentially hinted that he meant to get convicted."

"But why on God's green earth!" Mags asked.

"That is an excellent question, Margaret," Keri said, closing the laptop. "And it's one I intend to address with Mr. Anderson right now."

*

Keri parked her car in the massive structure across from the Twin Towers and made her way to the elevator. Sometimes if she had to visit in the day, the massive county lockup facility was so busy that she had to go all the way to the uncovered tenth floor of the structure to find a parking spot. But it was almost 8 p.m. and she found a spot on the second floor.

As she crossed the street, she went over her plan. Technically, because of her suspension and the IA investigation, she didn't have authorization to meet with a prisoner in an interrogation room. But that wasn't common knowledge yet. She was hoping her familiarity with the prison staff would allow her to bluff her way through.

Ray had offered to come along to smooth her path. But she worried that would lead to questions, potentially getting him in trouble. Even if it didn't, he might be required to sit in on the interview with Anderson. Keri knew the guy wouldn't open up under those circumstances.

As it turned out, she needn't have worried.

"How's it going, Detective Locke?" Security Officer Beamon asked as she approached the lobby metal detector. "I'm surprised to see you up and moving after the run-in with that psycho earlier this week."

"Oh, yeah," Keri agreed, deciding to use her earlier confrontation to her advantage, "me too, Freddie. Looks like I was in a prize fight, right? I'm actually still officially on leave until I'm in better shape. But I was getting a little stir-crazy around the apartment so I thought I'd check on an old case. It's informal so I didn't even bring the gun and shield. Still cool if I interview someone even if I'm off the clock?"

"Of course, Detective. I just wish you'd take it a little easy. But I know you won't. Sign in. Get your visitor badge and head to the interrogation level. You know the drill."

Keri did know the drill and fifteen minutes later she was seated in an interrogation room, waiting for the arrival of inmate #2427609, or Thomas "The Ghost" Anderson. The guard had warned her that they were getting ready for lights out and it might take a little extra time to collect him. She tried to stay cool as she waited but knew it was a losing battle.

Anderson always seemed to get under her skin, as if he was secretly peeling back her scalp to reveal her brain and read her thoughts. Oftentimes, she felt like she was a kitten and he was holding one of those laser pen lights, sending her scampering in random directions at his whim.

And yet, it was his information that sent her down a road that had gotten her closer to finding Evie than anything else had. Was that by design or just luck? He'd never given her any indication that their meetings were anything other than happenstance. But if he was that far ahead of the game, why would he?

The door opened and he stepped through it, looking much as she remembered. Anderson, in his mid-fifties, was on the shorter side, about five foot eight, with a square, well-built frame that suggested he used the prison gym regularly. The manacles on his muscled forearms looked tight. Still, he appeared leaner than she remembered, as if he'd missed a few meals.

His thick hair was parted neatly but much to her surprise, it was no longer the jet black she remembered. Now it was mostly a salt-and-pepper combination. At the edges of his prison jumpsuit, she could still see portions of the multiple tattoos that lined the right side of his body all the way up his neck. His left side was still unblemished.

As he was directed to the metal chair across the table from her, his gray eyes never left her. She knew he was taking her in, studying her, sizing her up, trying to learn as much as he could about her situation before she said a word.

After he was seated, the guard took a position by the door.

"We're fine, Officer...Kiley," Keri said, squinting at his nametag.

"Procedure, ma'am," the guard said brusquely.

She glanced over at him. He was new...and young. She doubted he was on the take yet but she couldn't afford for anyone, corrupt or clean, to hear this conversation. Anderson smiled slightly at her, knowing what was coming. This would probably be entertaining for him.

She stood up and stared at the guard until he sensed her eyes on him and looked over.

"First of all, it's not ma'am. It's Detective Locke. Second, I don't give a rat's ass about your procedure, newbie. I want to talk to this inmate in private. If you can't accommodate that, then I need to talk to *you* in private and it's not going to be a comfortable chat."

"But..." Kiley started to stammer as he shifted from foot to foot.

"But nothing, Officer. You have two choices here. You can let me speak to this inmate privately. Or we can have that chat! Which is it gonna be?"

"Maybe I should get my superviso—"

"That's not on the list of choices, Officer. You know what? I'm deciding for you. Let's step outside so I can chat you up a little. You'd think taking down a religious zealot pedophile would give me a pass for the rest of the week but I guess now I have to instruct a corrections officer as well."

She reached for the door handle and started to pull when Officer Kiley finally lost what was left of his nerve. She was impressed at how long he'd lasted.

"Never mind, Detective," he said hastily. "I'll wait outside. Just please use caution. This prisoner has a history of violent incidents."

"Of course I will," Keri said, her voice now all buttered honey. "Thank you for being so accommodating. I'll try to keep it brief."

He stepped out and shut the door and Keri returned to her seat, filled with a confidence and energy that had been lacking only thirty seconds earlier.

"That was fun," Anderson said mildly.

"I'm sure," Keri replied. "You can bet I expect some valuable information in return for providing you with such quality entertainment."

"Detective Locke," Anderson said in a tone of mocked indignation, "you offend my delicate sensibilities. It's been months since we've seen each other and yet your first instinct upon seeing me is to demand information? No hello? No how are you?"

"Hello," Keri said. "I'd ask how you are, but it's clear you're not great. You've lost weight. The hair has gone gray. The skin near your eyes has gotten saggy. Are you ill? Or is something weighing on your conscience?"

"Both actually," he admitted. "You see, the boys in here have been treating me a little rough lately. I'm no longer in the popular crowd. So I have my dinner 'borrowed' occasionally. I get an unrequested rib massage now and then. Also, I have a touch of the cancer."

"I didn't know," Keri said quietly, genuinely taken aback. All the physical signs of wasting away made more sense now.

"How could you?" he asked. "I didn't advertise it. I might have told you at my parole hearing in November but you weren't there. I didn't get it, by the way. Not your fault though. Your letter was lovely, thank you very much."

Keri had written a letter on Anderson's behalf after he'd helped her before. She didn't advocate for his release but she had been generous in her description of his assistance to the force.

"You weren't surprised you didn't get it, I gather?"

"No," he said. "But it's hard not to hope. It was my last real chance to get out of here before the sickness takes me. I had dreams of wandering on a beach in Zihuatanejo. Alas, it's not to be. But enough small talk, Detective. Let's get down to why you're really here. And remember, the walls have ears."

"Okay," she started, then leaned in and whispered, "do you know about tomorrow night?"

Anderson nodded. Keri felt a surge of hope rise in her chest.

"Do you know where it's happening?"

He shook his head.

"I can't help you with the where," he whispered back. "But I might be able to help you with the why."

"What good will that do me?' she demanded bitterly.

"Knowing why might help you find out where."

"Let me ask you a different why," she said, realizing her anger was getting the best of her but unable to contain it.

"All right."

"Why are you helping me at all?" she asked. "Have you been guiding me all along, since I first met you?"

"Here's what I can tell you, Detective. You know what I did for a living, how I coordinated the theft of children from their families to be given to other families, often for massive fees. It was a very lucrative business. I was able to conduct it from a distance using a false name and live a happy, uncomplicated life."

"As John Johnson?"

"No, my happy life was as Thomas Anderson, librarian. My alter ego was John Johnson, abduction facilitator. When I was caught, I turned to someone we both know to ensure that John Johnson was exonerated and that Thomas Anderson was never connected to him. This was almost a decade ago. Our friend didn't want to do it. He said he only represented those mistreated by the system and that I was, and this is funny to think about now, a cancer on that system."

"That is funny," Keri agreed, not laughing.

"But as you know, I can be convincing. I persuaded him that I was taking children from wealthy, undeserving families and giving them to loving families without the same resources. Then I offered him an enormous amount of money to get me acquitted. I think he knew I was lying. After all, how could these low-income families afford to pay me? And were the parents who lost their children all really terrible? Our friend is very smart. He had to have known. But it gave him something to hold on to, something to tell himself when he took six figures in cash from me."

"Six figures?" Keri repeated, disbelieving.

"As I said, it's a very lucrative business. And that payment was just the first. Over the course of the trial, I paid him about half a million dollars. And with that, he was on his way. After I was acquitted and resumed work under my own name, he even started helping me facilitate the abductions to these 'more deserving' families. As long as he could find a way to justify the transactions, he was comfortable with them, even enthusiastic."

"So you gave him that first bite of forbidden fruit?"

"I did. And he found that he liked the taste. In fact, he discovered that he had a taste for a great many things he hadn't been aware that he might like."

"What exactly are you saying?" Keri asked.

"Let's just say that somewhere along the way, he lost the need to justify the transactions. You know that event tomorrow night?"

"Yes?"

"It was his brainchild," Anderson said. "Mind you, he doesn't partake. But he realized there was a market for that sort of thing and for all the smaller, similar festivities throughout the year. He filled that niche. He essentially controls the upscale version of that...market in the Los Angeles area. And to think that before me, he was working out of a one-room office next to a doughnut shop representing illegal immigrants being randomly charged with sex crimes by cops looking to make quotas."

"So you developed a conscience?" Keri asked through gritted teeth. She was disgusted but she wanted answers and worried that being too overt with that disgust might shut Anderson down. He seemed to sense how she felt but proceeded anyway.

"Not yet. That's not what did it for me. It happened much later. I saw this story on the local news about a year and a half ago about a female detective and her partner who rescued this little girl who was kidnapped by her babysitter's boyfriend, a real creep."

"Carlo Junta," Keri said automatically.

"Right. Anyway, in the story, they mentioned that this detective was the same woman who had joined the police academy a few years earlier. And they showed a clip from an interview after her academy graduation. She said she'd joined the force because her daughter was abducted. She said that even though she couldn't save her own daughter, maybe by being a cop, she could help save some other family's daughter. Does that sound familiar?"

"Yes," Keri said softly.

"So," Anderson continued, "because I worked in a library and had access to all kinds of old news footage, I went back and found the story from when this lady's daughter was abducted and her news conference right afterward when she pleaded for her daughter's safe return."

Keri flashed back to the news conference, which was mostly a blur. She remembered speaking into a dozen microphones jammed in her face, begging the man who had snatched her daughter in the middle of a park, who had tossed her in a van like a rag doll, to return her.

She remembered the scream of "Please Mommy, help me" and the bobbing blonde pigtails getting farther away as Evie, only eight at the time, disappeared across the green field. She remembered the bits of gravel that were still embedded in her feet during the news conference, trapped there when she ran barefoot through the parking lot, chasing after the van until it left her in the dust. She remembered it all.

Anderson had stopped talking. She looked at him and saw that his eyes were rimmed with tears, just as hers were. He pressed on.

"After that, I saw another story a few months later where this detective rescued another kid, this time a boy grabbed while he was walking to baseball practice."

"Jimmy Tensall."

"And a month later, she found a baby girl that had been snatched right out of a carrier at the supermarket. The woman who stole her had a fake birth certificate made and was planning to fly with the baby to Peru. You caught her at the gate as she was about to board the plane."

"I remember."

"That's when I decided I couldn't do it anymore. Every transaction reminded me of that news conference where you were begging for your daughter's return. I couldn't keep it at arm's length anymore. I got soft, I guess. And right around then, our friend made a mistake."

"What was that?" Keri asked, feeling a tingly sensation that only came when she sensed something big about to be revealed.

Thomas Anderson looked at her and she could tell he was wrestling with some kind of big internal decision. Then his brow unfurrowed and his eyes cleared. He seemed to have made up his mind.

"Do you trust me?" he asked quietly.

"What the hell kind of question is that? No friggin' w—"

But before she had finished the sentence, he had pushed away the table that separated them, swung the manacles on his wrists around her neck, and pulled her to the ground, sliding back into a corner of the interrogation room.

As Officer Kiley burst into the room, Anderson used her body as a shield, keeping her in front of him. She felt a sharp prick at her neck and glanced down to see what it was. It looked like a shaved-down toothbrush handle. And it was pressed against her jugular.

CHAPTER SEVEN

Keri was totally bewildered. A moment earlier, Anderson had been tearing up at the thought of her missing daughter. Now he was holding a razor-sharp piece of plastic to her throat.

Her first instinct was to make a move to break his grip. But she knew it wouldn't work. There was no way she could do anything before he'd be able to jam the plastic spike into her vein.

Besides, something about this wasn't right. Anderson had never given her any sense that he had malice toward her. He seemed to actually like her. He seemed to want to help her. And if he really had cancer, this was a fruitless exercise. He said himself that he'd be dead soon.

Is this way of avoiding the agony, his version of suicide by cop?

"Drop it, Anderson!" Officer Kiley screamed, his weapon pointed in their general direction.

"Put your gun down, Kiley," Anderson said surprisingly calmly. "You're going to accidentally shoot the hostage and then your career will be over before it's even started. Follow procedure. Alert your superior. Get a negotiator over here. It shouldn't take long. The department always has one on call. Someone can probably be in this room in ten minutes."

Kiley stood there, uncertain how to proceed. His eyes darted back and forth between Anderson and Keri. His hands were shaking.

"He's right, Officer," Keri said, trying to match Anderson's soothing tone. "Just follow standard procedure and this will all work out. The prisoner isn't going anywhere. Step outside and make sure the door is locked. Make your calls. I'm okay. Mr. Anderson isn't going to hurt me. He clearly wants to negotiate. So you need to bring in someone who has authorization to do that, okay?"

Kiley nodded but his feet remained rooted in place.

"Officer Kiley," Keri said, this time more firmly, "step outside and call your supervisor. Right now!"

That seemed to snap Kiley out of it. He backed out of the room, closed and locked the door, and grabbed the phone on the wall, never letting them out of his sight.

"We don't have much time," Anderson whispered in Keri's ear as he relaxed the plastic pressing against her flesh slightly. "I'm sorry about this but it's the only way I could be sure we could speak in complete confidence."

"Really?" Keri whispered back, half furious, half relieved.

"Cave has people everywhere, in here and out there. After this, I'm done for sure. I won't last through the night. I might not last the hour. But I'm more worried about you. If he thinks that you know everything I know, he might just have you eliminated, regardless of the consequences."

"So what do you know?" Keri asked.

"I told you Cave made a mistake. He came to me and said he was worried about you. He had done some checking and found out that one of his guys had kidnapped your daughter. As you found out, it was Brian Wickwire—the Collector. Cave didn't order it or know about it. Wickwire operated on his own a lot and Cave would often help facilitate moving the girls after the fact. That's what he did with Evie and he never gave it a second thought."

"So he wasn't targeting her?" Keri asked. She had suspected as much but wanted to be sure.

"No. She was just some cute blonde girl that Wickwire thought he could fetch a nice price for. But after you started rescuing girls and generating headlines, Cave went back through his records and saw that he was connected to her abduction through Wickwire. He was worried you'd eventually find your way to him and he asked me to help stash Evie somewhere well-hidden and to keep him out of it. He didn't want to know."

"He was covering his tracks even before I suspected he was involved?" Keri asked, marveling at Cave's foresight.

"He's a clever guy," Anderson agreed. "But what he didn't realize was that he was asking the exact wrong person for help. He couldn't have known. After all, I'm the one who corrupted him in the first place. Why would he suspect me? But I made up my mind to help you. Of course, I did it in a way that I thought would keep me protected."

Just then Kiley opened the door a crack.

"Negotiator's on his way," he said, his voice quavering. "He'll be here in five minutes. Just stay calm. Don't do anything crazy, Anderson."

42

"Don't you make me do anything crazy!" Anderson screamed back at him, pulling the toothbrush back up to Keri's neck and inadvertently poking her skin. Kiley quickly shut the door again.

"Ow," she said." I think you drew blood."

"Sorry about that," he said, sounding surprisingly sheepish. "It's hard to maneuver splayed out on the floor like this."

"Just rein it in a little, okay?"

"I'll try. There's just a lot going on, you know? Anyway, I talked to Wickwire and told him to place Evie at a location somewhere in LA where she'd be well taken care of, in case we needed her later on. I wanted to make sure she didn't leave the city. And I didn't want her to go through... more than she had to."

Keri didn't respond but they both knew there was nothing he could do about the years prior to that, and the horrors her daughter must have suffered in that time. Anderson continued quickly, clearly not wanting to linger on the thought any more than she did.

"I didn't know what he did with her but it turned out he put her with the older guy you eventually found out she was staying with."

"If you had decided to help me, why didn't you just find out her location and get her yourself?"

"Two reasons," Anderson said. "First, Wickwire wasn't going to give up her location to me. It was prized info and he kept it closely guarded. Second, and I'm not proud of this, I knew that I'd get arrested if I came to you with your daughter."

"But you got arrested intentionally anyway a few months later for child abductions," Keri protested.

"I did that afterward, when I realized I had to take drastic action. I knew that eventually you'd research child abductors and traffickers and find your way to me. And I knew that I could set you on the right path without making Cave suspicious of me. As to getting arrested intentionally, that's true. But you may recall that I defended myself in court. And if you check the court record closely, you'll discover that both the prosecutor and the judge made several errors, errors I baited them into, that would almost certainly lead to my conviction being overturned. I was just waiting until the right time to appeal the case. Of course that's all moot now."

Keri looked up and saw a commotion outside the window of the room. She could see multiple officers passing by, at least one of whom was carrying a long gun. He was a sniper.

"I don't mean to be cold but we need to wrap this up," she said. "There's no telling if someone out there has an itchy trigger finger or if Cave has ordered one of his minions to put you down as a precaution."

"Quite right, Detective," Anderson agreed. "Here I am blathering on about my moral conversion when what you want to know is how to get your daughter back. Am I right?"

"You are. So tell me. How do I get her back?"

"I genuinely don't know. I don't know where she is. I don't believe Cave knows where she is. He might know the location of the Vista event tomorrow night but there's no chance he'll attend. So it's pointless to have him followed."

"So you're saying I have no hope of getting her back?" Keri demanded, disbelieving.

Have I been through all this for that answer?

"Likely not, Detective," he admitted. "But maybe you can get him to *give* her back."

"What do you mean?"

"Jackson Cave used to consider you an annoyance, an obstacle to running his business. But that has changed in the last year. He's become obsessed with you. He not only thinks you are out to destroy his business. He thinks you want to destroy him personally. And because he has twisted reality to make himself the good guy, he thinks you are the bad guy."

"He thinks *I'm* the bad guy?" Keri repeated, incredulous.

"Yes. Remember, he manipulates his moral code as he sees fit so that he can function. If he thought he was doing evil things, he couldn't live with himself. But he's found ways to justify even the most heinous of acts. He told me once that the girls in these sex slave rings would be starving on the streets if not for him."

"He's gone mad," Keri said.

"He's doing what he can to look himself in the mirror each morning, Detective. And these days, part of that means believing that you are on a witch hunt. He views you as the enemy. He sees you as his nemesis. And that makes him very dangerous. Because I'm not sure what lengths he'll go to in order to stop you."

"So then how can I get a guy like that to *give* Evie back to me?"

"If you went to him and convinced him that you're not after him, that all you want is your daughter, maybe he'd relent. If you could persuade him that once you had your daughter safe in your arms you would forget about him forever, maybe even leave the police force, he might be convinced to lay down his arms. Right now he thinks you want his destruction. But if he could be made to believe that you don't want him, that you only want *her*, perhaps there's a chance."

"You think that would really work?" Keri asked, unable to hide the skepticism in her voice. "I just say 'give me my daughter back and I'll leave you alone forever' and he goes for it?"

"I don't know if it will work. But I know that you're out of options. And you have nothing to lose by trying."

Keri was turning the idea over in her head when there was a knock on the door.

"The negotiator's here," Kiley yelled. "He's coming down the hall now."

"Wait a minute!" Anderson yelled. "Tell him to stay back. I'll tell him when he can come in."

"I'll tell him," Kiley said, though his voice indicated he was desperate to hand over communication as soon as possible.

"One last thing," Anderson whispered in her ear, even more quietly than before if that was possible. "You have a mole in your unit."

"What? West LA Division?" Keri asked, stunned.

"In your Missing Persons Unit. I don't know who it is. But someone is feeding information to the other side. So watch your back. More than usual, I mean."

A new voice called out from the other side of the door.

"Mr. Anderson, this is Cal Brubaker. I'm the negotiator. May I come in?"

"Just one second, Cal," Anderson called out. Then he leaned in even closer to Keri. "I have a feeling this is the last time we'll talk, Keri. I want you to know that I think you're a very impressive person. I hope you find Evie. I really do. Come in, Cal."

As the door opened, he brought the toothbrush back up to her neck but didn't actually touch the skin. A pot-bellied man in his mid to late forties with a mop of bushy gray hair and thin, circular-framed glasses that Keri suspected were just for show eased into the room.

He was wearing blue jeans and a rumpled lumberjack-style shirt, complete with the red and black checkerboard pattern. It was borderline laughable, like the "costumed" version of what a nonthreatening hostage negotiator might look like.

Anderson glanced at her and she could see that he felt the same way. He seemed to be fighting the urge to roll his eyes.

"Hi, Mr. Anderson. Can you tell me what's bothering you this evening?" he said in a practiced, unaggressive tone.

"Actually, Cal," Anderson replied mildly, "while we were waiting for you, Detective Locke talked some real sense into me. I realized I was just letting myself get a little overwhelmed by my situation and I reacted...poorly. I think I'm ready to surrender and accept the consequences of my choices."

"Okay," Cal said, surprised. "Well, this is the most painless negotiation of my life. Since you're making things so easy on me, I have to ask: are you sure there's nothing you want?"

"Maybe a few small things," Anderson said. "But I don't think you'll take issue with any of them. I'd like to make sure Detective Locke gets taken straight to the infirmary. I accidentally poked her with the point of the toothbrush and I'm not sure how hygienic it is. She should get it cleaned up right away. And I'd appreciate it if you had Officer Kiley, the gentleman who brought me in here, cuff me and take me wherever I'm headed. I have a feeling some of those other guys might be a little rougher than needed. And maybe, once I drop the pointy object, you could ask that sniper to clear out. He's making me a bit nervous. Reasonable requests?"

"All reasonable, Mr. Anderson," Cal agreed. "I'll do my best to accommodate them. Why don't you start the ball rolling by dropping the toothbrush and letting the detective go?"

Anderson leaned in close so only Keri could hear him.

"Good luck," he whispered almost inaudibly before dropping the toothbrush and lifting his arms high so that she could slip under the manacles. She slid away from him and slowly got to her feet with the aid of the overturned table. Cal reached out his hand to offer assistance but she didn't take it.

Once she was standing upright and felt steady she turned to face Thomas "The Ghost" Anderson for what she was certain would be the last time.

"Thanks for not killing me," she muttered, trying to sound sarcastic.

"You bet," he said, smiling sweetly.

As she stepped toward the interrogation room door, it opened wide and five men in full SWAT gear burst in, tearing past her. She didn't look back to see what they did as she stumbled out the door and into the hallway.

It looked like Cal Brubaker had been true to at least part of his word. The sniper, leaning against the far wall, with his gun at his side, had stood down. But Officer Kiley was nowhere in sight.

As she walked down the hall, escorted by a female officer who said she was taking her to the infirmary, Keri was pretty sure she could hear the sound of gun butts slamming into human bone. And while she didn't hear any subsequent screaming, she did hear grunting, followed by deep, ceaseless moaning.

CHAPTER EIGHT

Keri hurried back to her car, hoping to leave the parking structure before anyone noticed she was gone. Her heart was beating in time with her shoes, pounding hard and fast on the concrete.

Her trip to the infirmary had been a gift from Anderson. He knew that after a hostage situation, she was sure to face hours of interrogation, hours she didn't have to spare. By demanding she be allowed to go to the infirmary, he was ensuring her a window in which she would have little supervision and possibly be able to leave before being cornered by a bunch of Downtown Division detectives.

That's exactly what she had done. After a nurse had cleaned up the small puncture wound on her neck and bandaged it, Keri had feigned a brief post-hostage-crisis panic attack and asked to use the bathroom. Since she wasn't an inmate, it was easy to slip out after that.

She made her way down in the elevator with the janitorial staff who got off at 9 p.m. Security Officer Beamon must have been on break because there was some new guy manning the lobby and he didn't give her a second look.

Once out of the building, she started across the street to the parking structure, still expecting some detective to come racing outside after her demanding to know why she'd been interrogating a prisoner when she was on suspension. But she heard nothing.

In fact, she was completely alone with her footsteps and heartbeat as all the off-duty janitors headed down the street to the bus stop and metro station. Apparently none of them drove to work.

It was only when she had reached the second floor of the stairwell that she heard the sound of other shoes below. They were loud and heavy and they seemed to come out of nowhere. She would have noticed them earlier if they'd been walking before. They couldn't have come from across the street. It was almost as if someone had been waiting for her arrival to start moving.

She headed toward her car, about halfway down the row on the left. The footsteps followed and it became clear now that it wasn't one set of shoes but two, both clearly belonging to men. Their gaits were thick and lumbering and she could hear one of them wheezing slightly.

It was possible that these men were detectives but she doubted it. They likely would have identified themselves already if they wanted to question her. And if they were cops with ill intent, they wouldn't be approaching her in the Twin Towers parking structure. There were cameras everywhere. If they were on Cave's payroll and meant her harm, they would have waited until she was off city property.

Keri slid her hand down involuntarily to her gun holster before remembering that she'd left her personal weapon in the trunk. She had wanted to avoid questions from security and decided that carrying her personal piece into a city jail might not accomplish that goal. For the same reason, her ankle pistol was in the same place. She was unarmed.

Feeling her pulse quicken, Keri ordered herself to remain calm, not to speed up her pace to alert these guys that she was on to them. They had to know. But maintaining the illusion might give her time. Same for looking over her shoulder—she refused to do it. That was certain to set them running after her.

Instead, she casually glanced in the windows of some of the shinier SUVs, hoping to get a sense of who she was dealing with. After a few cars, she was able to size them up. Two guys, both wearing suits: one big, the other huge with a belly that tumbled over his belt. It was hard to gauge age but the bigger one looked older as well. He was the wheezer. Neither were holding guns but the fat one had what looked to be a Taser and the younger one was clutching some kind of nightstick. Apparently someone wanted her taken alive.

Trying to appear nonchalant, she pulled her keys from her purse, sliding the pointy ends between her knuckles facing outward as she hit the button to unlock her car, now only twenty feet away. The two men were still about ten feet from her but there was no way she could get to her car, open the door, get in, close the door, and lock it before they caught her, even at their size. She silently cursed herself for parking head-in.

The beep her car made seemed to startle the fat one and he stumbled a bit. After that, Keri knew that pretending she didn't notice them at this point would seem more suspicious than turning around, so she stopped abruptly and spun quickly, taking them by surprise.

"How's it going, guys?" she asked sweetly, as if discovering two hulking dudes right behind her was the most natural thing in the world. They both took another couple of steps before awkwardly pulling up five feet from her.

The younger guy appeared to be at a loss. The older guy started to open his mouth to speak. Keri's senses were tingling. For some reason, she noticed he had missed a patch of hair on the left side of his neck the last time he'd shaved. Almost without thinking, she pushed the alarm button on her car remote. Both men glanced involuntarily in that direction. That's when she moved.

She lunged forward quickly, swinging her right fist, the one with the exposed keys, at the left side of his face. Everything began to move in slow motion. He saw her too late and by the time he started to raise his left arm to try to block the punch, she had made contact.

Keri knew it was a direct hit because at least one of the keys went pretty deep before hitting resistance. The screaming started almost immediately as blood gushed from his eye. She didn't pause to admire her handiwork. Instead, she used her forward momentum to dive forward, slamming her right shoulder into his left knee even as he was already crumpling to the ground.

She heard a sickening pop and knew that his knee ligaments were being torn violently apart as he fell to the ground. She forced the sound from her brain as she tried to roll smoothly back up to a standing position.

Unfortunately, throwing herself against such a massive person had rattled her body from head to toe, re-aggravating the pain of the injuries she suffered only days earlier. Her chest felt like it had been whacked with a frying pan. She was pretty sure she'd slammed her injured knee on the concrete parking structure floor as she dived and the collision had left her right shoulder throbbing.

More immediately troubling than any of that was that smashing into the guy had slowed her movement enough for the younger, fitter guy to regain his senses. As Keri came out of her roll and tried to recover her balance, he was already moving toward her, his eyes blazing with an intense mix of fury and fear, the nightstick in his right hand starting its downward swing.

She realized that she wasn't going to be able to avoid it completely and turned her body so that the blow landed on her left side rather than her head. She felt the brutal smash against the ribs on her left torso just below the shoulder, followed by a stinging pain that radiated outward from the point of impact.

The air left her body as she collapsed to her knees in front of him. Her eyes had gone watery immediately upon being hit but she still managed to make out an ominous sight directly in front of her. The younger guy's feet had started to rise onto his toes, his heels leaving the ground.

It took less than a fraction of a second for Keri to process what that meant. He was rising up, lifting the nightstick over his head so that he would be able to bring its full force down on hers for a knockout blow. She saw his left foot start to come forward and knew that meant he was starting the downward motion.

Ignoring everything—her inability to breathe, the pain ricocheting from her chest to her shoulder to her ribs to her knee, her blurry vision—she dove forward, directly at him. She knew she didn't have much momentum pushing off from her knees but she hoped it was enough to prevent a direct hit on the top of her skull. As she did, she thrust her right hand, the one still clutching the keys, in the general direction of the guy's crotch, hoping to make any kind of contact.

It all happened at once. She felt the stick hit her upper back at the same time she heard the grunt. The whack stung her but only for a second as she realized the man had lost his grip on the stick almost immediately after making contact. She heard it hit the concrete and roll off into the distance as she collapsed to the floor.

Glancing up, she saw the man doubled over, both hands clutching at his groin area. He was cursing loudly and without end. At least for the moment, he seemed oblivious to her. Keri looked over at the fat man, who was several feet away, still rolling on the ground, screaming in agony, both hands covering his left eye, seemingly unaware of his knee, which was bent in an inhuman direction.

Keri gulped in a deep breath of air, the first in what felt like forever, and forced herself into action.

Get up and move. This is your chance. It may be your only one.

Ignoring the pain she felt everywhere, she pushed herself up off the hard ground and half-ran, half-limped to her car. The younger guy glanced up from his crotch and made a token attempt to reach out and grab her. But she steered well clear of him and stumbled toward her car, got in, locked, it, started it, and pulled out without even looking in the rearview mirror. Part of her hoped the young guy was back there and that she'd hear a thud as she slammed into him.

She hit the gas and tore around the corner of the second floor and down to the first. As she approached the exit booth, she was amazed to see the younger guy stumbling down the stairs and shuffling in the direction of her car.

She could see the horror on the face of the booth attendant, who was looking back and forth between the hunched over man shambling in his direction and the tire-screeching car careening to the same spot. She almost felt bad for him. But it wasn't enough to prevent her from speeding through the exit, slamming into the wooden gate, and sending chunks of it flying off into the night.

*

She spent the night at Ray's place. For one thing, it didn't seem safe to go back to hers. She didn't know who had come after her. But if they were willing to attack her in a camera-filled parking lot across from the jail, her apartment didn't seem like such a heavy lift. Besides, the way she felt, Keri wasn't in any condition to fend off additional attackers tonight.

Ray had drawn a bath for her. She'd called him on the way over so he knew the basics of the situation and mercifully wasn't peppering her with questions while she tried to regroup. As she lay in the water, letting its warmth ease her aching bones, he sat in a chair beside the tub, intermittently coaxing her to sip spoonfuls of broth.

Eventually, after drying off and putting on a pair of his pajamas, she felt well enough to do a postmortem. They sat on his couch in the living room, lit only by a half dozen candles. Neither of them commented on the fact that both their weapons rested on the coffee table in front of them.

"It just seems so brazen," Ray said, referring to the boldness of the parking structure attack, "and kind of desperate."

"I agree," Keri said. "Assuming these were Cave's flunkies, it makes me think he was really concerned that Anderson spilled all the beans in that interrogation room. But what I don't get is, if he was willing to go that far, why didn't he just have those guys shoot me in the back and get it over with? What was with the Taser and the nightstick?"

"Maybe he wanted to find out what you know, see who else knows it, before getting rid of you. Or maybe it's not Cave at all. You said Anderson told you there's a mole in the unit, right? Maybe someone else didn't want that information getting out."

"I guess that's possible," Kari admitted, "although he was so quiet when he said that part that I almost couldn't hear him. It's hard to imagine that even in a bugged room, anyone caught it. To be honest, I'm still having trouble even processing that bit of information."

"Yeah, me too," Ray agreed. "So where do we go from here, Keri? I stayed in that conference room with Mags for another couple of hours but we didn't learn anything really new. I'm not sure how to proceed."

"I think I'm going to take Anderson's advice," she replied.

"What, you mean go see Cave?" he asked, incredulous. "Tomorrow's Saturday. Are you just going to show up at the front door of his home?"

"I'm not sure what other choice I have."

"What makes you think it's going to do any good?" he asked.

"It may not. But Anderson's right. Unless something breaks soon, I'm out of options, Ray. Evie is going to be murdered on closed circuit television in twenty-five hours! If talking to Jackson Cave—appealing to him for my daughter's life—has even a chance of working, then I'm going to try it."

Ray nodded, clasping her hand in his and wrapping his huge arms around her shoulder. He was gentle but she winced in pain nonetheless.

"Sorry," he whispered quietly. "Of course—we'll do whatever it takes. But I'm going with you."

"Ray, I'm not holding out much hope that this will work. But he's definitely not going to say anything if you're standing there next to me. I have to do this alone."

"But he might have tried to have you killed tonight."

"Probably just maimed," she said with a weak smile, trying to lower the temperature. "Besides, he won't do that if I show up at his house. He won't be expecting me. And it'd be too risky. What kind of alibi would he have if something happened to me while I was at his home? He might be delusional but he's not stupid."

"Fine," Ray relented. "I won't go with you to the house. But you better believe I'll be close by."

"Such a good boyfriend," Keri said, snuggling up closer to him, despite the discomfort that moving caused. "I'll bet you've got a black-and-white outside patrolling the neighborhood to make sure your little lady sleeps safe through the night."

"How about two?" he said. "I'm not letting anything happen to you."

"My knight in shining armor," Keri said, yawning despite her best efforts. "I can still recall the days when I was a criminology professor at LMU and you would come and speak to my students."

"Simpler times," Ray said quietly.

"And I also remember the dark days after Evie was taken, when I started drinking scotch instead of water, when Stephen divorced me for sleeping with everything that moved, and the university dumped me for corrupting one my students."

"We don't have to hit every pothole on memory lane, Keri."

"I'm just saying, who was it that pulled me out of that pit of self-loathing, dusted me off, and got me to apply to the police academy?"

"That would be me," Ray whispered softly.

"That's right," Keri murmured in agreement. "See? Knight in shining armor."

She rested her head on his chest, allowing herself to relax, to ease into the rhythm of his breathing as he slowly inhaled and exhaled. As her lids became heavy and she drifted off into sleep, one last coherent thought passed through her head: Ray hadn't actually ordered two police cars to patrol the neighborhood. She'd checked out the window as she'd changed earlier and counted at least four units. And that was just what she could see.

She hoped it was enough.

CHAPTER NINE

Keri gripped the steering wheel tightly, trying not to let the sharp curves of the mountain road make her more nervous than she already was. It was 7:45 a.m., just over sixteen hours until her daughter was supposed to be ritually sacrificed in front of dozens of wealthy pedophiles.

She was driving through the winding Malibu hills on a chilly but clear and sunny January Saturday morning to the home of Jackson Cave. She hoped to convince him to return her daughter safely to her. If she couldn't, this would be the last day of Evie Locke's life.

Keri and Ray had woken up early, just after 6 a.m. She hadn't been very hungry but Ray had insisted she force down some scrambled eggs and toast to go with her two cups of coffee. They were out of the apartment by seven.

Ray spoke briefly to one of the patrol officers outside, who said that none of the units had reported any suspicious activity during the night. He thanked them and sent them on their way. Then he and Keri got in their cars and drove separately to Malibu.

At that hour on a Saturday morning, the normally clogged Los Angeles roads were virtually empty. Within twenty minutes, they were on the Pacific Coast Highway, catching the last remnants of the sunrise over the Santa Monica Mountains.

By the time Keri was white-knuckling it up Tuna Canyon Road high in the Malibu hills, the splendor of the morning had given way to the grim reality of what she had to do. Her GPS indicated she was close to Cave's place so she pulled over. Ray, who was right behind her, eased up next to her.

"I think it's right up past the next bend," she said through the open car window. "Why don't you go ahead and set up a little further down the road. He's the type of guy who will have surveillance cameras all around so we don't want to be driving up there together."

"Okay," Ray agreed. "The cell service is really spotty up here so once you're done I'll just follow you back down the hill and we can debrief at that diner we passed at the PCH turnoff. Sound good?"

"Sounds like a plan. Wish me luck, partner."

"Good luck, Keri," he said sincerely. "I really hope this works."

She nodded, not really able to think of a meaningful reply at that moment. Ray gave her a little smile and drove on ahead. Keri waited another minute, then eased her foot onto the gas pedal and made the last curve before Cave's house.

When it came into view, she was surprised to find it looked modest compared to other homes in the area, at least from the street. The place had a bungalow appearance to it, almost like an elaborate version of something one might find at a South Seas resort.

Then again, she knew this wasn't even Cave's main Los Angeles residence. He had a mansion in the Hollywood Hills, which was much more conveniently located to his downtown high-rise office. But it was common knowledge that he liked to spend his weekends at his Malibu "retreat," and she'd checked around to make sure that was where he'd be this morning.

Keri pulled into the short gravel driveway just off the road and hopped out. She walked slowly up to the security gate, taking in the impressive privacy measures Cave had employed. The house might not be massive but the safety precautions were. The gate itself was wrought-iron and easily fifteen feet high, with curled spikes that pointed outward toward the street.

A twenty-foot, ivy-covered stone wall surrounded the property as far as the eye could see, with what appeared to be three additional feet of electrified fencing above that. She counted at least five cameras mounted on the walls and attached to high branches of several trees just inside the property.

Keri pushed the "call" button on the keypad next to the gate and waited.

"May I help you?" a middle-aged female voice asked.

"Yes, Keri Locke here to see Jackson Cave."

"Does Mr. Cave know you're coming, Ms. Locke?" the voice asked.

"I doubt it," Keri said. "But I suspect he'll still be willing to see me."

"Just a moment, please."

Keri stood by the gate for another thirty seconds, staring at the ocean in the distance, listening to the wind whistle through the leaves of the trees. She hadn't seen a single car pass by in the time she'd been there.

"Please come in," the voice finally said as the heavy gate slowly creaked open.

Keri drove her car just inside the gate, parked, and walked toward the front door of the bungalow. As she got closer, she saw that her initial impression of the place had been wrong.

What had appeared to be an unassuming one-story cottage on a cliff overlooking the Pacific was actually a multi-tiered home built into the cliff itself. From where she stood, she could see at least three floors and an indoor/outdoor pool, but it was possible there were even more below.

The front door opened and Jackson Cave stepped out to greet her. Apparently he was just finishing up a call as he was putting his phone in his in pants pocket. It was not quite 8 a.m. on a Saturday morning and yet he looked immaculate. His thick black hair, with sunglasses nestled softly in it, was already slickly combed back like he was channeling Gordon Gekko in *Wall Street*.

He wore tight, light blue jeans, a black sweater rolled up to his elbows to reveal his wiry, tanned forearms, and laceless black loafers. He smiled at her with his disturbingly white teeth, which made his over-bronzed face seem even more unnatural. His smile always came across as a sneer but that might just have been for her. Maybe he had a more genuine smile for other people. Somehow she doubted it.

"Detective Locke," he said, spreading his arms wide in welcome, "had I known you'd be stopping by, I would have prepared breakfast."

His voice dripped with all its usual smarm, but she noticed something she rarely saw in his piercing blue eyes—uncertainty. He didn't have any idea why she was here. She had him off-balance.

She was tempted to come back at him with a snarky reply. It was her default position. She was as good at getting under his skin as he was at infuriating her. But that wasn't the goal today. She needed to appeal to, if not his sympathy, at least his self-interest.

She needed to persuade him that if he was able to return Evie to her, she would leave him be. She needed to convince him that she was not his enemy; that she was not, as Anderson had put it, the "bad guy."

"Thank you, Mr. Cave," she said, trying to sound pleasant but not unctuous. "That's very kind. But I actually already ate—pounded back two coffees too."

"Ah, well come in then," he said, visibly surprised by her innocuous reply. He'd clearly been expecting something more biting. "You can tell me what brought you so far west so early on a weekend morning."

He held the door open for her and she stepped inside a vast living room that was as warm and welcoming as Cave was not. The Polynesian-themed design with bamboo-style paneling was charming, as was the wicker-inspired furniture and the open indoor fire pit. The entire room was windowed with views of the ocean and mountains in every direction.

"This place is gorgeous," she marveled despite herself.

"Thank you," he said. "I designed it in conjunction with a hotel magnate client from Fiji. He builds private estates in this style over there. This is a hut to him."

"If I were you, I'd live here all the time," Keri said, meaning it.

"Bit of a commute though," he said, unable to keep the sarcasm from dripping into his voice.

Keri bit back the urge to suggest he just have a helipad built. It would be counterproductive and it was possible he already had. Instead, she looked around the parts of the house that were visible. The kitchen was massive, with a center island larger than her entire apartment kitchen. Part of a dining room could be seen off in a corner with a table that looked to be made of marble.

She saw a hallway that must have led back to the bedroom wing and thought she heard voices coming from that direction. A Hispanic woman in her forties with her hair tied back in a bun opened a sliding door and stepped inside from the small deck.

"Can I get you anything to drink?" she asked, and Keri recognized the voice from the gate intercom.

"No thank you. I'm good."

She smiled and then turned to Cave.

"Mr. Cave, I was going to go back and make sure your other guest is doing all right?"

"That's fine, Gracie," he said as she headed for the hallway. He turned to Keri. "Please sit down. I had a client over for dinner last night. It got late so I let him stay in the guest room overnight. I think he's just starting to stir."

"Ah, I thought I heard something back there," she said as she sat in one of the wicker chairs.

"He might have been talking in his sleep. Or maybe it was his stomach growling."

He cackled at that last line. Keri didn't get it. He seemed to realize he had breached the decorum of the moment and snapped back into character almost immediately.

"Well, Detective Locke," he said, more reserved now as he sat down opposite her, "I have to say, this has been our least...combative conversation in recent memory. Care to end the suspense and tell me why we're both minding our P's and Q's?"

Keri took a deep breath.

This is it. The sink or swim moment. Make it a good one, Keri.

"Okay, Mr. Cave. I'm going to tell you why I'm here. But when I do, I'd like you to open yourself up to the possibility that what I'm saying is true, that my intentions are genuine, and that I don't have any kind of angle."

"Are you suggesting, Detective Locke, that you haven't always been forthright in your dealings with me?" he asked almost coquettishly, leaning in. He clearly didn't buy what she was selling.

"I am. I'm telling you that I haven't always been straight with you, just as you haven't always been totally honest with me. We've been playing this game for a while, now, Jackson. But it's a really dangerous game. And I'm tired of playing. I just want to go home. And here's the thing. I want to take my little girl home with me."

Cave pulled back suddenly at the words "little girl" and the playful smile disappeared from his lips.

"I have no idea what you're talkin..." he started but Keri held up her hand.

"It's okay," she said, making sure to keep her voice calm and free of blame. "I'm not accusing you of anything. I think we got off on the wrong foot way back when. You represented Alan Pachanga, a child abductor who had kidnapped a missing girl I was after. As you know, my daughter, Evie, was abducted as well."

Cave flinched but didn't speak. Keri considered that a good sign and continued before he changed his mind.

"And I think I poured all my vitriol about losing her onto you because you were defending a man who kidnapped children and my daughter was kidnapped. That wasn't fair to you. You were just doing your job, after all. I think I fixated on you for a while as being part of my problem, blaming you for everything that was going wrong in my life, when it wasn't really about you at all. You were just someone to project my own fears and frustrations on, you know?"

Cave settled back into his chair, letting her words sink in. The creak of the wicker was almost comforting as it broke what was otherwise complete silence. He was squinting at her, almost as if there was a glare coming off her. Keri didn't know what to make of it. Finally he spoke.

"I have to say, this comes as a surprise to me, Detective," he said, his voice a mixture of suspicion and bewilderment. "And you'll have to forgive me if I'm a bit skeptical. After all, for the last year, you've been hounding me, interfering with my business, casting aspersions on my character. I have reason to believe you may have even committed a crime by breaking into my offices and stealing confidential files. And now you're telling me that you've had this epiphany and that you see that I'm not really so bad and you've misjudged me?"

"No, I wouldn't go that far," Keri admitted. "We're laying our cards on the table here, right, Jackson? I don't think I've misjudged you. I know the kind of people you work for and I'm not a fan. I know what your business is. We can at least be honest with each other about that. What I'm saying is the fact that you defend people I find reprehensible doesn't mean you are responsible for the abduction of my daughter or anything that's happened to her since. They can be separate things. And I want you to know that I lost sight of that for a while. But I see it now."

"And what gave you this sudden insight?' he asked, acid-tongued, not realizing that even asking the question suggested vulnerability.

Keri took another deep breath. This was her last card to play. If it didn't work, if he didn't fold, she feared she was done for.

"Coy Trembley," she said quietly.

"Who?" he asked, though his eyes grew wide with recognition.

"Your half-brother, Coy Trembley."

"How do you know about him?" he demanded, looking around the empty room of his secluded mountain retreat as if someone might overhear.

"I was doing research on you and I came across the case. I figured out what happened, Jackson. Once I understood that case, the accusations he faced, what ultimately happened to him, it made it a lot easier for me to understand why you do what you do."

"You're working me," he said unconvincingly.

"No, Jackson. I get it. I understand that you saw your brother wrongfully accused of a terrible crime and decided to dedicate yourself to ensuring that didn't happen to other people. As the mother of an abducted girl, I hope you realize that not all those who are accused are innocent. But I also have to accept that you're doing this because, in and among the guilty, *are* some innocents. And there aren't very many people willing to put themselves on the line to defend them. You're one of those people, Jackson. And I respect that, even though it's hard. Sometimes it's really hard, especially when the guilty go free. You can see why it's hard for me, right?"

"I know it can't have been easy for you all these years," he conceded.

"Thank you for that," she said. "I think that's the first step here—for us to stop seeing each other as the enemy. I mean, sure, professionally, we're on opposite sides. But I had to stop thinking of you—the person, Jackson—as the bad guy and just start seeing you as a man doing his job to the best of his ability."

"I am trying to do my job," he said.

"I know that. I just lost sight of it for a while. And I hope that you can stop seeing *me* as the bad guy. I'm not your enemy. I don't want to bring you down. I accept that I will win some cases and lose some and that you and your law firm will exist independent of that. My focus is no longer going to be on you. Hell, I'm not even sure I'm going to stay on the force much longer."

"What do you mean?" he asked.

"The truth is, I'm kind of burned out, Jackson. I did this all to help people, sure. But it was also a way to find my daughter. If I could just do that, the rest of it would just kind of fade away, you know. Because I know she's still out there and all I want is to be with her again. Part of me would like to try to go back to just being a mom, making lunches and volunteering in art class. If I had that, being a cop wouldn't seem so important anymore."

Cave looked at her closely. He seemed to be studying her. Beyond that, she couldn't read his expression. She couldn't tell if he believed her or not or if he even cared.

"So what exactly is it you're asking of me, Detective Locke?" he said.

"I'm asking if you could put the word out. I know you have many clients who know many people. I'm hoping one of them might know where Evie is and might be willing to convey to whoever has her to simply drop her off at the closest precinct or bus station or whatever. I just want my daughter back. I won't investigate who took her. I won't open a case. Hell, I'll even turn in my badge if that'll make a difference. I'm asking you to please let people know that. Tell anyone you think might know anyone who knows anyone who knows anything about where she might be. Wouldn't it be nice to be on the same side for once, Jackson?"

A clatter from the hallway grabbed their attention. Gracie was assisting an obese man in his sixties wearing a robe far too small for him into the living room. His purple briefs were poking out below the belt and a bird's nest of mottled chest hair was exposed above. He looked half-awake and hung over. At least now Keri understood Cave's joke about the growling stomach.

His small remaining tufts of gray hair stood up like mini-Mohawks atop his head. His face was ashen and he had deep creases in his face and multiple chins. His eyes were tiny black dots. He looked vaguely familiar. When he saw Keri, his eyes widened a bit and he made a clumsy attempt to cover himself up.

"Detective Locke," Cave said, assuming the vocal stylings of a dinner party host, "this is Herbert Wasson, the chairman of the Wasson Media Group. Herb, this is Detective Keri Locke of the LAPD."

"Nice to meet you," Wasson mumbled. "Didn't expect others."

"It's all right," Keri said. "I was just going anyway."

"I'll walk you out," Cave said and they both stood up.

"Nice to meet you too," Keri said to Wasson as she headed toward the door.

"Yeah," the man replied. He seemed to want to say something else but couldn't think of anything appropriate and instead plopped down on the loveseat with his legs splayed out.

"Thank you for stopping by, Detective," Cave said, now officially back in controlled mode.

"Thanks for hearing me out, Jackson," she said, trying to keep the personal connection alive. "And let's both try to remember to see each other not as the enemy but as two people just trying to get by. I think it would lower both our blood pressures a lot, don't you think?"

"You'd be surprised what a consistent regimen of long-distance running can do for your blood pressure, Detective. I swear by it."

"I'll keep that idea in mind," Keri said as warmly as she could. "Thanks, Jackson. And please don't forget what I said about reaching out to people you know. I'd really appreciate it. I'm just looking for a fresh start, you know?"

"I know you are," he replied, his voice even, his eyes cold. "Thanks again for stopping by, Detective."

"Please, call me Keri."

"Okay then. Now be careful heading back down the hill. Some of those turns are really sharp, Detective."

He closed the door before Keri could respond. As she walked back to her car one thing was clear. She hadn't sold him. He still viewed her as the enemy. And her daughter was still destined to pay for it.

CHAPTER TEN

Keri should have sensed something was wrong earlier.

But she was lost in thought on the drive back down the hill. All she could think about was how Cave had called her "Detective" right after she'd said he could call her Keri. She thought of how his eyes had gone cold, as if he'd intentionally squeezed the humanity out of them.

As she navigated the sharp twists and turns of the switchback road, she wondered if she'd ever connected with any part of him, if there'd ever been a chance that he might return Evie to her. It had seemed for a half moment that he might. But then it was gone. And she was certain she'd never get that moment back. She refused to think about what that meant for her daughter.

As she banked sharply left, Keri realized she was riding the gas way too hard and pumped the brakes. The speed limit sign read "20" and she'd been pushing forty, far too fast even when her head was clear. The car behind her slowed down too, as if chastened by her return to sanity.

She looked farther in the distance of her rearview mirror but didn't see Ray. That wasn't a shock. It was hard to see too far back with all these hairpin turns. And she'd been going so fast that it would have been hard for him to keep up anyway. But the car behind her was doing a pretty decent job of it.

And that's when the feeling that something was off hit her. She looked at the car in the mirror again, and though she couldn't place it, something about it felt familiar. It was scratching an itch in the back of her head that she just couldn't quite reach.

Now that she thought about it, it was also the only other car she'd seen on the road since she'd left Cave's place. And there was the strange, simple fact that it was so close. Cars rode each other's bumpers all the time in LA, even in the mountains. But this wasn't that. The car behind her didn't seem like it was riding close behind in an attempt to pass her. It seemed like it just wanted to stay close, to keep her in sight, to not lose her.

Keri tried to get a good look at the driver but the sun visor was down and all she could tell was that the person was wearing black. She was surprised that whoever it was could even see out the front with the visor in the way.

She banked hard right at the next curve and got a good look at the body of the car in her side view mirror. That's when the itch in the back of her head tumbled to the center of her brain.

The vehicle was a black Lincoln Continental, and even with the curves and the speed, she could see it had no front license plate. Her mind flashed back to the security footage she'd seen months earlier, as a man in a ski mask got out of a similar-looking car with no plates, snuck up along the driver's side of a van, and put a bullet in the head of the driver.

After that, he'd dragged a teenage girl out of the back of the van and forced her into his trunk before driving off. The girl was Evie. The man who'd been shot had been keeping her in his home for over a year. And the shooter was the infamous Black Widower, assassin-for-hire.

This was the mystery man that Mags had told her cleaned up the messes of the rich and powerful, including Jackson Cave. He was also the man who, for thousands of dollars, had anonymously given Keri a lead on Evie's potential whereabouts. He didn't seem picky about his clients, as long as he got paid and kept his identity secret from everyone. Apparently this morning, Cave had hired him again.

Keri glanced at her GPS and saw that it was still a good two miles before she would reach the diner at the bottom of the hill where she was supposed to meet up with Ray, who was still nowhere to be found behind her. Her phone still had no signal.

A creeping sense that the situation was about to escalate came over her. Cave had obviously decided that not only would he not be making peace with her, he was going to ensure that she couldn't cause him any more trouble, ever. And this time he wasn't sending two suited goons. He was sending a professional killer.

What worried Keri most about this situation was that she wasn't prepared for it at all. If the Black Widower was behind her now, did that mean that he'd been at Cave's house when she was there? Was she just unlucky that he was already there to discuss some pending assignment to take someone out—maybe her?

He had to have been close by. It wasn't like he could have zipped out to Malibu on a whim if Cave had called him ten minutes prior. Was he the person who Cave had been on the phone with when she arrived? Or had he simply followed her and Ray all the way out here from the city?

Keri forced those questions out of her head to focus on the more immediate problem. The Black Widower was behind her. And that meant that while she was in that beautiful living room, politely asking Jackson Cave to spare her daughter's life, a professional assassin had been outside, using his skills to prepare to eliminate her. And until just now, she'd been oblivious to it. Had he tampered with her car while she was inside? How long had he been tailing her before he'd gotten this close behind her? Was he preparing to ram her from behind at the next turn?

As she rounded out of the latest curve into a brief straightaway, she saw a turnout area off to the right and decided to take matters into her own hands. Without signaling to warn him, she pulled over to allow the Lincoln to pass her, taking her foot off the accelerator. Looking in the rearview mirror, she saw that the Lincoln had slowed as well.

At least he's not planning to ram me.

Keri pressed on the brake, hoping to force him to pass her or stop completely. But nothing happened. She pumped harder but it only took her a fraction of a second to process that this was the Black Widower's doing. He had sabotaged her brake line and simply waited for a good time to blow it. Since she'd made him, this was apparently it.

The end of the turnout was coming up fast and she yanked the steering wheel hard to the left to get back on the road. Nothing happened. The wheel had locked in place, likely the Black Widower's doing as well. She was headed for the cliff edge at twenty-five miles an hour and there was nothing she could do to stop it.

The abyss was less than fifteen feet away. Without hesitation, Keri opened the unlocked door with her left hand as she undid her seat belt with her right. She grabbed the outer frame of the car and used it to propel herself out and away, even as she felt the front of the vehicle start to topple over the edge.

She landed hard on the turnout asphalt but only stayed there for a moment. Her momentum almost immediately pulled her backward toward the cliff and she found herself rolling quickly off the asphalt, onto a clump of weeds and dirt and then over a small hump of rock debris that slowed her briefly before she felt herself start to fall, with nothing beneath her.

Disoriented, she reached up and flailed desperately for anything to hold onto. Her hands clutched some wild plants before slipping and landing on a jagged rock. Her fingertips gripped it tight and managed to slow her downward motion for a second before the rock came loose from the dirt and she began to slide downward again.

She grasped at anything on the side of the cliff as she shoved her feet inward, hoping to lodge them against something solid. Her left toe stuck in a hole as her hands clutched at several more plants growing out of the side of the rock face. Her momentum stopped.

Keri took advantage of the moment. Ignoring the piles of dirt raining on her from above, which made seeing and breathing clearly nearly impossible, and pretending her entire body wasn't crying out in agony and fear, she looked down.

Her car was still tumbling down what looked to be about 1,200 more feet of near-sheer canyon. The drop-off directly below her was about 150 feet of empty space before a shelf of sharp rocks that would turn her into a pulpy mess if she landed in it.

She could already feel the plants she was holding onto start to strain at their roots and her tentative toe-hold beginning to give way. It was a good five feet back up to the lip of the cliff, but even if she could make it, what was the point? That was where the Black Widower was, likely approaching her position right now.

Glancing down to her right, Keri saw a small rock outcropping about the size of a square-ish bale of hay jutting out from the side of the cliff. It was at least a seven-foot drop and she might easily slip off it if she didn't get a good grip right away. But if she landed just right, she was pretty sure it would support her weight.

But to get to it, she had to jump to the right and that meant pushing off from her already tenuous position. Still, she had no choice. Her grip was failing, the plants were definitely giving way, and she could feel the dirt crumbling in the hole where her shoe was jammed.

Allowing herself one deep breath to regroup, Keri sucked in all the air she could without screaming in pain and then pushed off hard again with her left foot and her hands. As she plummeted across empty space, feeling the freezing canyon wind whip against her sweat-covered body, Keri kept her eyes focused on nothing but the outcropping, ignoring the hundreds of feet of nothingness that surrounded it.

She saw almost right away that she was going to make it far enough but that her landing would be especially hard. Unfortunately, she had no choice but to take the full brunt of the impact across her torso. If she curled up to protect herself, she worried that she might bounce right off and continue down to the rocks below.

So she spread herself out like an upside down U and allowed her body to collapse onto to the outcropping and absorb the force of the collision. As the rock knocked the wind out of her and she felt a surge of pain in her chest, Keri squeezed one side of the outcropping with her upper arms and elbows and the other side with her upper legs.

When she was sure the rock wasn't going to break free from the side of the cliff, she opened her eyes, pulled her knees up onto the outcropping, and slowly rolled over so that she was actually sitting on the small rock ledge, with her back against the cliff wall. For the moment at least, despite everything, she was alive.

"How's it going down there?" a disturbingly casual voice called out from above her.

Keri tried to look up but realized that at her angle, she could only see the top of the head of the person talking to her. The one good thing was that meant it was also likely hard for him to see, and therefore shoot, her.

"Peachy," she yelled back and almost immediately wished she hadn't. The adrenaline from the last thirty seconds, as she had gone from near-death to something approaching temporary safety, had started to fade. And as it did, shock waves of pain hit her.

Her chest burned as the words escaped her mouth, as if the simple pressure of air against her battered ribs and lungs was too much to take. The casual slacks she wore were ripped from thigh to shin and some of the pants material had embedded in her knees where she'd landed on the asphalt after jumping from the car. It was hard to tell where the bloody clothing ended and the shredded skin began.

She noticed that one of her shoes was missing. Underneath the layer of bloody dirt, she saw that her hands were completely raw and that she had lost several fingernails. And blood was dripping pretty generously onto her jacket from somewhere on the right side of her face.

"I'm really sorry about this, Detective," she heard the voice call from up above. She didn't even try to look up this time as her neck hurt when she arched it. "When I heard you were my next assignment, I was genuinely disappointed. And in my line of work, I almost never have an emotional reaction to an assignment."

Keri considered trying to come up with a line that might play into that emotion, to get him to reconsider. But she knew it was pointless. Feeling bad about the job didn't mean he wouldn't do it. Besides, she was too exhausted to say anything anyway.

"I've always been an admirer of your...gumption," he continued.

The voice sounded slightly different now. Despite the pain, Keri forced herself to look to up and almost wished she hadn't. She realized he sounded different because he was closer.

He had attached a rope to the rock above and had started to edge down the cliff side, about three feet from the top. He wasn't properly tied in and obviously had no intention of coming all the way down to her spot, another ten feet below. He was just trying to get a better angle from which to shoot her.

"Can't you just let me freeze to death?" she asked bitterly.

"That wouldn't be very professional," he replied, as she watched him wrap the rope around his left forearm several times while reaching into his waistband with his right hand for what she assumed was his gun.

His gun.

That's when Keri remembered that, although she'd left her primary weapon in her glove compartment when she'd gone into Cave's house, she still had her ankle pistol.

As quickly as she could, Keri leaned over, ignoring the shooting twinge in her midsection as she reached for her ankle. But when she pulled up what was left of her pant leg, the holster was gone. It must have gotten ripped off at some point during the whole car-jump cliff-fall thing.

She looked up at the Black Widower, who was smiling down at her as he pointed his gun at her. She could see his face clearly for the first time. With his dirty blond hair and his warm brown eyes, he was quite handsome.

"If you're looking for your ankle piece, I saw it up on the road here. I guess it came loose when you were tumbling toward the cliff. Nice try though. Like I said, gumptio—"

Before he could say anything else, Keri heard a pop and a thud. His body shuddered as a spray of blood exploded from the general area of his left shoulder. Then, ever so slowly, he careened backward and his feet slipped off the cliff side before he fell quickly and suddenly downward, straight toward Keri.

CHAPTER ELEVEN

There was nowhere for Keri to go and almost no time to react. Without even thinking about it and all in one motion, she pressed her back up against the cliff wall even harder than before and dropped her legs on either side of the outcropping, as if she was straddling a horse.

A moment later, the Black Widower thudded down on the rock, right where her knees had just been. The force of the collision bounced his body up a foot in the air before he toppled over the edge and into the void.

Keri waited for him to tumble down but he didn't. Instead, he dangled there in midair, only feet away from her, just slightly below the outcropping. It took her a second to realize that it was because the rope he'd wrapped around his left forearm was still attached. It had prevented him from falling to the canyon floor but it had also yanked his arm and shoulder into a grotesque, inhuman angle. In addition, the left shoulder was seeping blood from what was clearly a gunshot wound.

As he swung slowly away from her, he opened his eyes and a soft moan escaped his lips. His eyes were unfocused and he seemed disoriented, trying to get his bearings. His body softly bumped against the canyon wall and began to sway back in her direction.

As he got closer, Keri noticed that he was still somehow holding the gun. He didn't seem aware that it was in his hand. But if his head cleared, and he chose to, he would have a point-blank shot at her.

Rather than wait and hope, Keri forced her throbbing body forward so that she was lying flat on her stomach. When the Black Widower's momentum brought him within a foot of her, she reached out and grabbed for the gun.

That seemed to jostle him into a more coherent state of consciousness. His eyes cleared and bored in on her as he tried to rip the weapon free. But weakened by the fall, the damage from his twisted arm and the gunshot wound, he couldn't wrestle it free.

But he didn't need much strength to fire the gun and after a few seconds of wrangling, he seemed to register that his finger was on the trigger. Keri saw his eyes widen and knew what was about to happen. She heard the click of the safety coming off and yanked his arm down as he fired. The bullet slammed into the rock outcropping, sending a cloud of dust up into the air around them both.

Before he could fire a second shot, Keri jerked his hand toward her, slamming the gun into the rock. She felt it slip from his grasp and bounce off the hard surface. Even though she couldn't see it, she knew it was on its way to the bottom of the canyon.

She let go and the Black Widower swung away from her again in that slow arc that bent his left shoulder so far back she thought it might actually snap off. He winced but didn't cry out.

"Keri!" she heard a voice call out desperately from above. It was Ray.

She was about to respond when she saw the Black Widower reach for something with his right hand. As his body bumped against the cliff side again, he pushed off hard with both feet so that he would come back faster this time.

Keri saw him rip open the Velcro on an exterior pants pocket and pull out a six-inch hunting knife. As he flew through the air toward her, he tore off the sheath with his teeth, then raised the knife high above his head.

Keri realized that his momentum would lift him above the outcropping at the apex of his swing. He would actually be higher than her and able to jab the knife down at her as gravity forced him back to the ground. Her only chance was to somehow get upright again so she would be in a better position to defend herself.

So, with a speed she didn't know she was capable of under the circumstances, she did what was essentially a burpee on the canyon outcropping, pushing up to her knees, then leaping up and backward with such force that her head slammed into the canyon wall behind her.

Right as she felt that impact, she braced for another one as the Black Widower swung the knife at her. But in his weakened state and with them now at equal height, she was able to grab his wrist with both hands before he could get the point close to her body.

They struggled there for a moment, him trying to break free of her grasp, Keri attempting to twist his wrist to force the knife loose. She tried to brace her feet but they skidded slightly on the sandy, gravelly surface. For a second, she thought she might slip off the ledge entirely.

"Keri, are you down there?" Ray screamed. His voice had a tinge of desperation to it. She wanted to reply, to reassure him that she was safe. But the truth was, she wasn't safe. And she was too busy to talk.

Hearing the anguish in Ray's voice seemed to make the Black Widower happy. Keri saw a twisted grimace come over his face. His eyes gleamed with malice. Seeing that, Keri felt bubbles of venom rise in her throat, a fury she'd never experienced before. She was sick of playing defense with this bastard.

This ends now.

Before she knew what she was doing, she had dived forward and sunk her teeth deep into the soft underside of the Widower's right wrist. She heard his scream as she clamped down with all her might and ripped her head back. As she did, she felt sinewy tendons and cartilage and god knows what else come with her.

The Black Widower let go of the knife and she caught it in midair as it fell. As he swung slowly away from her, howling in agony, blood spewing from his ruined wrist, Keri spit out whatever it was she'd taken from him and called out to Ray.

"I'm down here. I'm okay...mostly."

"Thank God," he said. "I can't see you. What the hell is going on down there?"

"Just give me a minute to catch my breath, Ray."

With one hand holding the knife, she rested the other on the canyon wall for support. The rope eased slowly back toward her and she was able to reach out and grab it. The Black Widower, whose slumped frame was now a few feet below hers, looked up at her.

He was pressing his wrist against his chest to stem the bleeding but it wasn't doing much good. The blood coming from his shoulder wound was oozing even more profusely than before.

"Looks like my partner got you pretty good," Keri said, nodding at the gunshot.

"Flesh wound," he responded through gritted, bloody teeth.

"Yeah, I guess," she agreed, partly admiring his grim refusal to give an inch. "But you've got a lot of them—the gunshot, the wrist, the shoulder dislocated beyond comprehension."

"I've recovered from worse," he muttered.

Keri nodded. Her blind fury had faded. But it had been replaced with a cold sense of righteous vengeance. She grabbed the knife in her right hand and held the rope taut with the raw, swollen fingers of her left hand. Slowly, she began to cut through the rope.

"You're not recovering this time," she said softly.

"Don't you want to know who hired me?" he asked in what she knew was a desperate bid to bide time.

"I already know who hired you," she replied, her eyes focused only on the rope.

He opened his mouth and for a second it looked like he might try to convince her to stop. But then he stopped himself. He sighed deeply as if accepting his fate.

"I knew I shouldn't have accepted this assignment," he finally said, more to himself than to her.

"No," Keri agreed, "you really shouldn't have."

Then she gave the rope one last slice and it cut loose. The Black Widower never made a sound as he hurtled to the ground. A few seconds later, she heard a sickening wet crunch and knew that it was over. She had no desire to look down.

CHAPTER TWELVE

Ray was lowering the Black Widower's climbing harness down to Keri a couple of minutes later when her car exploded. Even a quarter mile above it, she could feel the hot gust of gasoline air on her skin.

Despite the shock of it, there was nothing for them to do but resume their efforts. Keri was still perched dangerously on the small rock outcropping. A major wind gust could send her flying down to join the broken body on the rocks below her. And with no cell service, Ray would have had to go down to the main road if he wanted to call for backup. They couldn't risk it.

So she strapped in and he pulled her slowly up until she was over the lip of the cliff. When she knew she was safe, Keri crawled over and sprawled out next to Ray, who had collapsed onto his back, teeming with sweat despite the morning cold. They lay there on the asphalt edge of the Tuna Canyon Road turnout until they felt the strength to stand.

Ray helped Keri into the passenger's seat of his car before shuffling over to the driver's side. He got in and simply sat there, too wiped out to start the car. After a good two minutes, he turned and got his first good look at her.

She saw his eyes grow wide as he took in her ripped clothes, torn up legs, raw hands, and dirty, blood-soaked face. She could still taste bits of flesh from the wrist of the man lying in the canyon below and could guess what her mouth must look like, stained with his blood.

"What the hell, Keri?" he finally asked.

"It was the Black Widower," she told him. "The assassin who killed the guy holding Evie, the guy who gave me that lead about the Vista without realizing it was me—Cave had him try to take me out."

"So I'm guessing your conversation with Cave didn't go as you hoped?" Ray said wryly.

"No, it did not. For a moment there, I thought it might. But then, not so much, as evidenced by the whole hit man thing. I can fill you in on all the details later. Right now, I just need a few gallons of water and a whole bottle of Advil."

"All right," Ray agreed. "Let's head down the hill to that diner. I think there was a convenience store attached to it. I need to get somewhere with a decent cell signal anyway so I can call this in."

"Actually, Ray, maybe you could hold off on calling it in. I had an idea I wanted to run by you."

Ray squinted suspiciously at her and she knew immediately that something in the tone of her voice had given her away. Her proposal was going to be trouble and Ray had picked up on it immediately. He knew her too well—as well as she knew him. And that's why she was pretty sure he was going to hate her idea.

*

As Keri had suspected, Ray hated her idea with a passion. But in the end, he agreed to go along with it. That was partly because he didn't have a better one. But she knew it was mostly because he didn't have the heart to fight her, not when he looked at her battered face and body and listened to her say that despite it all, she needed to push a little harder if it meant finding her little girl.

When they'd reached the convenience store at the corner of Tuna Canyon and the Pacific Coast Highway, Ray called for a cab. Then he'd gone into the store, gotten Keri two thirty-two-ounce water bottles, a bear claw, a bottle of Advil, and an extra large "Surf Malibu" sweatshirt with a hoodie.

He'd helped her take off her bloody jacket and put on the sweatshirt, even easing the hood over her head so that it completely obscured her face. When the taxi arrived, he helped her in and gave the driver his address and enough cash to cover the ride and a generous tip.

Keri went over the plan in her head repeatedly on the taxi ride back to his place. She wanted to make sure she had everything clear so she wouldn't forget. But staying focused on the plan also helped her ignore the pain that lapped up at her every second she allowed her mind to wander.

While Keri rode back to Ray's place in silence, he would call in the crash and attack. But his version of events would differ a bit from what actually happened. He would report that he'd seen a man in a black Lincoln Continental riding close behind Keri down the hill and ultimately force her off the road at the turnout.

He'd seen Keri's car go over the cliff, then the driver of the Lincoln get out with a gun and go to the edge of the cliff. He'd shot the driver, who fell into the canyon. When he looked over the side, he saw that Keri's car had exploded. He didn't see her body and assumed she must have been inside the vehicle when it exploded.

Ray had especially disliked this part of the plan but Keri had convinced him that it might actually be to their advantage for her to be "dead," or at least for everyone, especially Jackson Cave, to think she was.

For one thing, if everyone thought she had already died, people would stop trying to kill her. Keri especially liked that idea. Her body was one big, pulsating bruise and she needed at least a few hours to rest, if not really recover.

Also, if there really was a mole in their unit, as the Ghost had suggested, making the entire team think she'd died would prevent that mole from trying to determine what she was up to and leaking it to their connection. If she was dead, there was no reason to keep looking for intelligence to pass along.

In addition, if Cave thought she was dead, he might let his guard down. He wouldn't worry that she was coming after him and consider moving the Vista or cancelling it outright. She needed him to have the confidence to continue with the plan, to continue with the event that was supposed to lead to her daughter's death.

That was because, for the first time in a long time, Keri felt she had the upper hand. She was pretty sure she knew the identity of at least one person who would be attending the Vista tonight. And if she knew that, she could determine where it would be held, which meant she knew where Evie would be.

CHAPTER THIRTEEN

"Who's this guy again?" Mags asked, as she dabbed a cotton ball at the cut on Keri's right temple. "The name sounds familiar."

Keri was sitting in Ray's bathtub, soaking her entire body in warm water and Epsom salt, explaining the situation to her friend while trying to pretend the sting of the salt in her multiple open wounds didn't bother her, even though her eyes kept rimming involuntarily with tears.

Mags had come over to Ray's place about an hour earlier after getting a call on one of her burner cell phones from one he'd just bought. As per Keri's instructions, he'd filled her in on the basics and asked her to get to his apartment as quickly as possible, with just one stop for a pickup along the way.

Mags had done it all without question, making the unusual pickup and showing up at Ray's with all manner of first aid materials. Within minutes of her arrival, she was using tweezers to pick bits of gray slacks out of Keri's kneecaps as her friend caught her up.

"His name is Herb Wasson," Keri said. "He runs the Wasson Media Group."

"And what makes you so sure he's connected to the whole Vista thing?"

"It's just a hunch," Keri admitted, "but a really strong one. The first thing that made me suspicious was that I could sense Cave wasn't pleased that I saw Wasson. I don't think he wanted me to know he was there."

"That hardly seems like enough to go on, sweetie," Mags said gently, trying to curb her investigative journalist instincts but failing.

"On its own, that's true. But the name sounded familiar to me, and not just because he's some big mogul type. I let it go until Cave had his assassin try to send me off a cliff. As Ray was pulling me up afterward, I got to thinking—up to this point, nothing made Jackson Cave go to such desperate measures to stop me until today. In the past, he's tried to have me investigated by Internal Affairs and kicked off the force. Last night, he even tried to have me assaulted and, I assume, kidnapped. But it wasn't until today that something happened that made him decide it wasn't worth it to let me live. I think that 'something' was me seeing Wasson."

"What's so significant about him?" Mags asked, dabbing some balm on a particularly torn up portion of skin on Keri's left palm.

"He's a pedophile. Or at the very least, he travels in pedophile-friendly circles."

"What do you mean?" Mags asked.

"Do you remember about six years ago, there was a sex-trafficking ring that got busted out of Croatia? They were trading in all kinds of stuff, including underage prostitution. Some of the girls were as young as seven. Interpol broke it up, arrested over thirty traffickers and about three hundred clients."

"I remember," Mags said. "They believed the ring operated in something like eleven countries."

"Right," Keri said. "There was also talk that a number of the clients were high-profile Americans who went to these countries to get their kicks because they were so lax in enforcing sex crimes. Wasson was rumored to be among them. It was never proven. One newspaper was going to run a story mentioning his name but it was quashed when his lawyer threatened a lawsuit."

"How many guesses do I get as to the lawyer's name?" Mags asked bitterly.

"I think you'll only need one. There's other stuff too. Things I've heard but never been able to confirm. You hear so much about so many people in this town that it all starts to turn into noise after a while. You can't pursue everything, you know?"

"I know, darling," Mags soothed. "It's hard enough for you to catch the people you know are kidnapping children. Going after the ones who are rumored to be abusing them would be a second job altogether. Hold still, this might hurt a bit."

Before Keri could react, Mags tugged hard with the tweezers, pulling out a chunk of asphalt that had embedded deep in her upper shin. Blood began seeping from the open hole and Mags quickly pressed a bandage against it.

"Ouch," Keri muttered, almost as an afterthought.

"So," Mags said, pretending not to hear her, "assuming your hunch is right and this Wasson guy is going to be at the Vista tonight, what's your plan? I gather with your concerns about having a mole in your unit, you won't be asking for a police surveillance team."

"That, my dear Margaret, is why I had you make that pickup on your way over."

"The pimply-faced boy from the mall sitting out there in Ray's living room right now?"

"That pimply-faced boy has a lot more going for him than meets the eye," Keri said protectively. "Now, if you'll help me get out of this tub, dry off, get bandaged up, get dressed, and hobble out there. I'll make a proper introduction."

Twenty minutes later, Keri shuffled into the living room, clutching tightly to Mags's forearm for support. The pimply-faced kid sitting on the couch stood up to greet her.

He looked mostly as Keri remembered him, tall and skinny with a slightly hunched over back. But his skin, while still spotty, was less so than before. And both it and his hair had lost that greasy, shiny quality that came from total inactivity and being permanently indoors. She could tell he'd been at least trying to work out.

He tried to hide his shock at her appearance but his bulging eyes and paler than usual skin suggested she had made the right choice by not looking in the mirror before coming out to see him.

"How's it going, Keith?" she said, trying to smile. "Long time, no see."

"Oh my god, Detective Locke, what happened to you?" the young man asked. "I saw on the news the other day that you were released and recovering at home. It looks like you should be in intensive care."

"Actually, I think I look pretty good, considering I'm supposed to be dead."

"What?" he asked, clearly confused.

"Have a seat, Keith. I'll explain what's going on. And if you don't mind, I'll sit too because I don't think I can stand much longer without collapsing."

He did as she suggested and Mags helped her to the hard-backed rocking chair beside the couch and she eased herself into it.

"First things, first," she said. "I'm sure you two spoke on the way over here but let me make some formal introductions. Keith Fogerty, this is Margaret Merrywether—Mags to her friends. She works over at *Weekly L.A.* and she's one of my closest friends in the world."

Keri noticed Mags give her an almost imperceptible nod of thanks for not revealing what she did for the *Weekly*. She liked to keep her "Mary Brady" crusading columnist alter ego a secret and divulging it to random mall employees wouldn't help with that.

"Nice to meet you, ma'am," Keith said politely.

"Such manners," Mags replied, turning on the charm, Southern drawl in full effect. She didn't yet know who this kid was but Keri knew that based on her say-so, her friend was willing to give him the benefit of the doubt, despite her skepticism.

"And Mags, this is Keith Fogerty. As you already know from where you picked him up, he works security over at Fox Hills Mall in Culver City. You may recall I mentioned a security guard who got me a good bug detector? Well, this was him. But Keith was also instrumental in helping us find Sarah Caldwell last fall. I'm sure you remember her, the girl who was kidnapped and taken to that brothel south of Tijuana."

"I remember her very well," Mags said.

"Well, if it hadn't been for Keith's assistance early in the case, we never would have gotten our first lead. He's a real whiz with surveillance footage and technology in general and went above and beyond to help us out when we had hit a wall. I'm not sure we would gotten to Sarah in time if not for his help."

"That's very nice of you to say, Detective," Keith said, before turning his attention to Mags. "What Detective Locke isn't mentioning is that I told her I wanted to apply to the police academy. She helped me out, put me in touch with a former instructor who tutored me. She also sent me an online physical training regimen and offered suggestions for how to approach some of the application questions. Because of what she did, I was accepted and start next month."

"Congratulations, Keith," Mags said, properly impressed.

"Thank you," he said before turning back to Keri. "Now that we've met each other, can you please tell me what's going on? Because I have a feeling it's very bad."

Keri knew she couldn't stall any longer. She'd been hesitant to bring a twenty-three-year-old kid with no experience into such a volatile situation but she had no choice. So she told him everything: about her search for Evie, which he was generally familiar with; about her ongoing conflict with Jackson Cave, who had tried to have her killed this morning; about the Vista tonight, where Evie was to be sacrificed; about how she suspected a mole in her unit, which meant she couldn't go to them for help for fear of tipping off Cave; and finally about Herb Wasson, who she believed could lead her to her daughter.

Keith sat quietly while she talked, not interrupting once, occasionally looking overwhelmed but mostly seeming to be taking it all in, trying to process the details. That gave her hope.

When she finally finished, she looked at him and waited to hear what he thought. He was silent for a good ten seconds. When he did finally speak, his voice was quiet but firm.

"What do you need me to do?" he asked.

CHAPTER FOURTEEN

Keri awoke with a start.

It took a few seconds for her to get her bearings and remember where she was. Looking at the alarm clock beside Ray's bed, she saw that it was 5:17 p.m. She'd been asleep for just over four hours.

She lay there for a few minutes, allowing her body and brain to recalibrate to consciousness. The pain was already starting to worm itself back into her bones and muscles, despite the warmth of the bed covers.

Her head ached and her stomach felt raw and empty. She realized she hadn't eaten since Mags and Keith had left. And even then, it had only been chicken broth. She'd sipped little portions of the soup as they went over the plan one final time before Mags drove Keith back to the mall. It seemed so long ago.

Glancing at the mostly closed curtains, Keri saw that it was already dark out. Ray couldn't safely communicate with her under the circumstances but she suspected he'd be back soon, even with all the paperwork associated with processing the "death" of his partner, not to mention navigating the endless stream of cops who probably swarmed him upon learning the news.

The news. I should check out what the news is saying.

With great effort, Keri pushed off the comforter and rolled herself out of her prone position. Sitting upright, she eased herself into one of Ray's bathrobes and grabbed the headboard of his bed for support as she pulled herself upright and eased her way into the living room.

She made sure not to turn on any overhead lights. After all, Ray lived alone and she was supposedly dead. Anyone watching his place might get suspicious if they saw lights going on and off inside.

She turned the TV on low volume and sat down in the rocking chair, which she knew she could at least extricate herself from on her own. After she switched to a local station, it didn't take long for her story to run. In fact, it dominated every channel.

She watched for a few minutes, switching around to see if anyone had anything unexpected. But they all seemed to be sticking to the official story: Keri Locke, celebrated but controversial Missing Persons detective, who joined the force after tragically losing her own daughter to an abduction six years ago, was run off a Malibu mountain road by an unidentified assailant. She was believed to have died when her vehicle exploded after falling over a thousand feet to the canyon floor. Her partner, Raymond Sands, in another car further back, shot and killed the assailant but was unable to rescue Locke.

Keri turned off the TV and sat quietly in the semi-darkness.

If this plan doesn't work, I may as well be dead.

Her thoughts were interrupted by a key turning in the door lock. She turned to see Ray, who entered holding a bag from In-N-Out Burger.

"I figured you'd be famished," he said when he caught sight of her.

"My hero," she said, batting her eyes briefly before stopping because it actually hurt. "How'd it go?"

"About how you'd expect. I managed to get out of a lot of the bureaucratic stuff because Hillman 'knew we were close' and wanted to give me a day before I had to fill out all the forms. I did fill out a formal incident report but didn't actually sign or file it yet so I can't be officially charged with filing a false police report. A lot of people came by but I told them all I just needed some time alone and I'd talk to them tomorrow. No one pressed me. I figured that one way or another, I'll be coming clean then. How was your day, dear?"

Keri tried not to chuckle for fear of the pain.

"Mostly just trying to survive it. Moving has been hard. I just slept for a few hours, which I'm hoping helps. And Mags left me some Vicodin, which I plan to take before our big outing."

"Are you sure you're up for this?" Ray asked as he opened the bag and placed a double double with grilled onions on the table in front of her.

"No, but we don't really have a choice. We don't know who we can trust on the force and there's no one else I'd be willing to put in a situation like this."

"Are you sure you don't want to bring in Castillo?" Ray said. "You think she might be dirty?"

"I don't think she's dirty, Ray. In fact, she's helped me out of several jams off-book that make me almost positive that she's not the mole. But when it comes to my one chance to save Evie, 'almost positive' isn't good enough. I'm not taking any chances."

"Fair enough. What about your friend Uriel?" he asked.

Uriel Magrev was Keri's Krav Maga instructor. But before moving to LA he had spent six years in Shayetet 13, the Israeli Special Forces version of Navy SEALS.

"He'd be a nice addition," Keri acknowledged. "Unfortunately, he's currently visiting family in Tel Aviv."

"So it's just you and me, then."

"Don't forget our surveillance expert," Keri said as she nearly inhaled a bite of her burger. Something about eating regular food gave her a jolt of well-being that temporarily eased the soreness she felt everywhere.

"Yeah, you want to fill me in on his plan?" Ray asked before taking a bite of his own burger.

"I'll do my best. Keith lost me occasionally but I think I got the gist of it. Apparently there are these things called taggants. There are all kinds of variations and they get really technical. He used words like nanocrystals and quantum dots. My headache started getting worse as he talked."

"I actually feel one coming on now," Ray said.

"Anyway, smartass," Keri continued, sticking her tongue out. At least that didn't hurt. "This stuff is high-tech tracking technology, so small that it can be placed on the subject in the form of a dot or a liquid or digital dust and the person would never know. Depending on the substance, it can be placed on skin, clothing, even a vehicle."

"That sounds awesome," Ray said. "Why aren't we using it in the department?"

"According to Keith, for a long time, the military had a stranglehold on it. Drones could apparently use it to identify a particular enemy combatant inside a building from miles away. Now some corporations are using it to protect proprietary products and detect counterfeiting, stuff like that. But it doesn't come cheap. And the LAPD doesn't exactly have the resources to invest in this sort of thing right now. Plus there are the legal questions."

"I'll bet," Ray said. "So are you telling me that our local neighborhood mall security guy has access to this stuff? Because that's a little scary."

"No," Keri said. "But he's an enthusiast. And when I told him I needed to track Herb Wasson, that I needed to know where he was going tonight and that my daughter's life depended on not losing him, this is what he mentioned. Apparently he knows a guy who knows a guy."

"And how does he expect to secure this kind of stuff, even if this guy is willing to meet with him?"

"With the unlimited supply of money that Southern heiress and well-heeled divorcee Margaret Merrywether promised him."

"Wow."

"That's what I said," Keri agreed.

"So how do we know if he succeeded?" Ray asked.

"We'll know when we stop by the mall."

"What?" Ray asked, incredulous.

"Keith said he would leave us some secure communications equipment in the security office at the Fox Hills Mall."

"Keri, I have to tell you that when I woke up this morning, I did not think that I would be dealing with nanocrystals, mall security guards, and a girlfriend who had been declared dead but is currently munching on a double double burger."

"Yeah, well, that's not all, loverboy."

"What more could there possibly be?" he asked.

"If I'm going to be even mildly functional this evening, I'm going to need a little assistance. So be a dear and fetch your dead girlfriend a couple of Vicodin from the kitchen counter."

CHAPTER FIFTEEN

Keri forced herself to stay still even though every part of her wanted to run, to scream, to do anything other than remain quiet and motionless, as she had been for the last hour.

It was 10:22 p.m. and, despite everything, she still wasn't sure where the Vista was. She had followed all of the agreed-upon precautions and listened to all of Keith's suggestions. And yet here she was, still lying in the backseat of Ray's car, waiting for word on the location of Herb Wasson and the future of her daughter.

It had been like this for over four hours. After leaving Ray's apartment around 6:15 p.m., they'd driven to the Fox Hills Mall, where Ray picked up the fancy headsets Keith left them at the security office. Then they went to West Hollywood. Keri, who was supposed to be dead, had to lie down in the backseat the whole way so she wouldn't be seen.

After Ray had spent ten minutes weaving through traffic and was confident that he wasn't being followed, he handed Keri a headset and put on one himself. They turned them on and found Keith was already on the channel, ready and waiting with updates for them.

He had good news. He'd managed to buy a taggant and, after several failed attempts through intermediaries, even secure it to Herb Wasson himself. He'd apparently followed Wasson all afternoon, including to the Boulevard Lounge at the Beverly Wilshire Hotel, where the man had a meeting with some film director. Keith had applied it to Wasson himself when he "accidentally" bumped into him as the older man was leaving the restroom, rubbing it on his sweater and the back of his neck.

And while it was working as promised, sending out a signal that Keith could track on his laptop, the Hollywood Hills themselves were complicating matters. Every time the limo Wasson was currently a passenger in rounded a curve and a huge section of mountainous rock separated Wasson from Keith's surveillance equipment, he would temporarily lose the signal. It was slow going.

So now Keri lay in the back seat of Ray's car, which was parked in a strip mall at the base of Hollywood Hills near the corner of Sunset and Fairfax. She and Ray, who was seated in the driver's seat, listened as Keith gave them a running commentary of his slow-motion pursuit of Wasson's limousine, hoping it was headed to the Vista.

Then, at 10:30 exactly, the line went silent. Keri waited a minute before whispering to Ray.

"Did we lose the connection?"

"I don't think so," he replied without turning around. "I just think he's gone radio silent. Keith, are you still there?"

There was no response for another five minutes. Keri felt the ball in the pit of her stomach growing. She was worried Keith had been discovered and was about to suggest they go up the hill to look for him when his voice cut through the silence.

"I found it," he said. "I found the Vista!"

"What?" both Keri and Ray shouted at the same time.

"At least I think I did," Keith said, trying to rein in his enthusiasm without success. "That's why I was out of communication for a bit. I wanted to make sure. But Wasson's limo just entered through a gate onto a private estate. I could see at least two dozen other vehicles on the property, along with tons of security."

"Were they armed?" Ray asked.

"I didn't actually see any weapons but I wouldn't be surprised," Keith said. "I think they're trying to blend in. They were all wearing red blazers, like valets. But they don't look like valets, you know? Lots of buzz cuts and broad shoulders with purposeful expressions on their faces. All wearing earpieces. They could easily have guns under the jackets."

"Anything else?" Keri asked.

"Yeah, they were using mirrors on poles to check under the vehicles and checking both drivers and passengers as they arrived. This event is obviously not just your standard Hollywood orgy."

"Okay, great work, Keith," Keri said. "Send us the address and stay put. We're coming to you. We're going to figure out a way in on our way up there and get back to you."

She took off her headset and reached into her bag for a bottled water, half a bagel, and Mags's Vicodin.

"What are you doing?" Ray asked.

"It looks like we're about to get in gear and I'd like to be mostly pain-free for the festivities," she said as she tossed the pills in her mouth and swallowed.

"And the bagel?"

"Mags said the pain meds might upset my stomach and that I should eat something."

"That's your focus right now?" Ray asked incredulously.

"I don't want to be crawling through bushes with an upset stomach, Raymond."

"Fine," he replied, shaking his head. "So how do you propose we get into those bushes in the first place? It sounds like accessing that estate is going to be impossible."

"I have an idea for that," Keri assured him. "Let's head up the hill and I'll fill you in on the way. My other concern is what we're going to do about backup if we actually get in there and need help."

"*I* have a plan for that," Ray said, sounding pleased with himself as he pulled out of the parking lot and headed north on Fairfax toward Hollywood Boulevard. "Would you like to hear it?"

"Very much." She appreciated that he was trying to keep the tone light and tried to match him. Otherwise the magnitude of the situation threatened to overwhelm her.

"Now that we know the address of the Vista, once we're in position I'm going to call in the LA County Sheriff's Department. Since West Hollywood doesn't have their own police department, they contract out with the Sheriff. I'm going to reach out to their SWAT unit to—"

"But if you do that, Cave's mole might tip him off," Keri interrupted.

"May I please finish?" Ray said, pretending to be offended.

"Sorry," Keri muttered.

"I plan to call in a report of a meth lab five blocks over from the Vista address. I'll say that it looks like a deal is going down and that there are multiple armed men. The address shouldn't set off any alarms because it'll be a different street entirely."

"Okay. Sounds good so far."

"Thanks for the approval," Ray said snarkily as he turned left from Fairfax onto Hollywood. "When we're actually ready to make our move, I'll call in the correct report using my name and badge number. SWAT should be less than three minutes out. Easy."

"It's not a terrible plan," Keri admitted.

"Thanks for the vote of confidence. Care to share your master plan?"

"Sure. We're going to drive in right through the main gate."

CHAPTER SIXTEEN

Keri couldn't see Ray's face from the backseat but she could tell from his prolonged silence that he didn't love her idea.

She didn't see why he was so apprehensive. After all, pretty much the exact same plan had worked to get them into the guarded Mexican brothel they infiltrated to rescue Sarah Caldwell only months earlier.

Admittedly, the security then had been much more lax, those people didn't have any real concern about an intrusion, and Keri hadn't been borderline immobile and drugged up. But the general principle still held. At least that's what she told herself as she got back on the line to explain it to Keith.

He seemed more amenable to the plan but she wasn't sure if that was because it was a good one or because he was clueless when it came to this sort of thing. Either way, he was up for it.

The practical effect of that was that for the next several minutes, Ray sat parked on a side street, watching the traffic on Laurel Canyon Boulevard go north toward the Hollywood Hills. Keri, sitting upright for the first time in hours, watched the cars whiz by as well.

After what felt like an eternity, Keri saw a stretch limo pass them, dutifully following the speed limit while all the cars around it were speeding by.

"I think we may have a candidate," she said, pointing at the slow-moving vehicle.

"Got it," Ray said, pulling out onto Laurel Canyon and hitting the accelerator. It didn't take long to pass the limo. About a quarter mile up, he turned right onto Laurelmont Drive. If the limo was headed to the Vista, it would almost certainly turn here as well.

"Approaching you now," he said into his headset as he saw Keith pull into the middle of the road facing them and get out.

Ray swerved around him, driving up the road another fifty yards before doing a U-turn and looping back down the road. He pulled over to the side of the road behind a large SUV and got out immediately. Keri took longer to extricate herself from the car, as she'd been stuck in the backseat for so long and unable to move much at all.

"I think they're coming," both of them heard Keith say as they scurried down the side of the road, keeping hidden behind the cars parked along the street.

Sure enough, the stretch limo from below was coming to a stop in front of Keith's beat-up fifteen-year-old Nissan Maxima, unable to get past it on the narrow mountain road. The driver lowered his window.

"Move your car, kid," he said gruffly.

"I'd love to," Keith relied, putting on his most convincing, helpless millennial voice. "But I think I rode over a nail or something. I heard a pop and I'm worried about driving down the steep hills at night. Can you take a look?"

"Call the Auto Club. I have somewhere to be."

"I already did," Keith said in an impressively whiny tone. "They said they'd be at least a half hour. Can you at least help me push the car to the side of the road so I don't get hit while I wait?"

Keri heard the driver mutter a curse under his breath and knew they had him. She nodded to Ray and they both moved quickly into position. As she skulked past several more cars to get to the back of the limo, she heard the driver tell whoever was in the backseat that he'd be done in a minute. Then he got out and joined Keith at the back of the Maxima. He was a big guy, over six feet tall and African-American—perfect.

"I think if we just push it over there," Keith said, nodding at an open space between two cars, "that should do it."

"None of your tires look too bad, kid," the driver said, sounding slightly suspicious.

"I think the nail is holding in the air but I don't want to chance it, you know? I can see you're in a hurry, sir, and I appreciate your help, so let's just move the car and you can be on your way."

"Yeah, whatever," the driver agreed.

They pushed the Maxima to the side and Keith ran to the driver's seat to hit the brakes before it bumped into anything. Keri saw Ray wait until the limo driver neared the edge of the road, out of sight of any of his passengers, to step out from the shadows and jam his gun in the guy's ribs. Over the headset, she could hear him talking quietly.

"I need a ride to the party. Get me in without any fuss and you walk away easy. Give me trouble and you don't ever walk again, maybe don't breathe again. You got me?"

She saw the driver nod.

"We're going to walk back to the car. You'll drive. I'll be in the passenger's seat. Is your privacy glass up?'

The guy nodded.

"Good. Let's keep it that way. Are you the regular driver for this customer or is this a one-time thing?"

"I work for a service," the driver said. "I don't know the client. This is my first time driving him."

"Good. Let's go."

They reached the car and got in, Ray making sure to stay out of view of the rear passenger windows.

"What's your name, fella?" Ray asked. Keri could no longer see him but his voice sounded smooth as silk.

"Pete."

"Pete, tell your client you're sorry about the delay and we're about to get on our way."

Pete did as he was told.

"Now pop the trunk, Pete."

Pete popped it and Keri moved quickly from her hiding place, crawled into the trunk, and pulled the top down.

"I'm in," she whispered into her headset.

"Go ahead and drive, Pete," she heard Ray say.

As the car started up again, she heard Keith's voice over the headset comm.

"Good luck, you guys. I'll be down here if you need me."

"Thanks, Keith," Keri whispered as she shimmied herself further back into the bowels of the trunk.

She turned on her phone light briefly to look around and found an old floor mat, which she draped over herself. If she curled up into the fetal position, it almost completely covered her.

Something registered in the back of her brain and for a second she couldn't place it. Then she turned on her phone light again and realized what it was. The time was 11:02 p.m. Evie was supposed to be dead in less than an hour.

CHAPTER SEVENTEEN

Getting through the gate was easier than they expected. Pete had an extra chauffeur uniform in the front, which Ray changed into on the way up.

When Pete rolled down his window, the security staff didn't see anything unusual about two imposing African-American drivers. Maybe they were so used to their own clients having extra security that it didn't strike them as odd that other folks would too. And since the passenger was unaware of Ray's existence, he didn't say anything when he was asked to lower his window so they could confirm his identity. They never even checked the trunk.

After dropping off the client at the main entrance, Pete was instructed to drive around to the side where the other limos were waiting. He did so. Keri listened quietly as Ray explained how his evening would go.

"Pete, unfortunately, I'm going to have to knock you out. Then I'm going to tie you up and leave you in your car. My recommendation is that even if you wake up, you pretend to be unconscious. Don't try to be a hero and warn anyone, because you'd actually be warning the bad guys. I'm a cop and what's going on here is bad news. If your client is here, he's a bad guy too. Your best bet is to 'sleep' through the whole thing. That way, you have fewer questions to answer when it's all over. You understand?"

Pete didn't respond but Keri gathered he was nodding. A second later she heard a thud that suggested he'd been knocked out.

"I'm going to secure this guy," she heard Ray say. "Then I'm going to find out where I can take you where you'll be under the radar. There are a few people milling about and I want to get the lay of the land before popping the trunk. I'll let you out when I'm sure the coast is clear. You still okay back there?"

"Peachy keen. I think the Vicodin is starting to kick in."

"That is super news, Keri," he replied with mock enthusiasm. "I'm glad you're starting to feel a little better. I just hope you don't start feeling too good."

"Me too, actually."

Five minutes later, the trunk door popped and Ray appeared. He helped her out, threw a heavy cloak over her shoulders, and guided her through a side door and quickly down a hall and into a small bathroom. Keri could sense others in the area and kept her head down until he closed the door behind them.

"So I asked around," he said, making sure the door was locked, "and it turns out we've got some good news and some bad news."

"Okay," Keri replied hesitantly. "Why do I get the feeling that even the good news at an event like this is still pretty bad?"

"Because you are a very smart, intuitive lady. The good news is that this party is an 'Eyes Wide Shut' type situation. Everybody is wearing masks. I guess fancy folks don't want to be formally identified at a special occasion that involves child rape and murder."

"I'm waiting for the good news, Ray."

"The good news is that not only the guests wear masks. The wait staff do too. They don't seem to realize the extent of what's going on here. They know it's a sex party but they seem oblivious to the ages of the girls. A lot of them are actors and think this is a role-playing event, so they're just going with it. Since they're all disguised, you can be too. You should be able to get around without being identified."

"That is great, assuming I can get my hands on a mask and a uniform."

"That's the bad news. Getting a mask and uniform isn't a problem. In fact, I saw a bunch of them hanging up in the women's dressing room down the hall. But the uniforms are…revealing."

"What exactly are you saying?" Keri asked defensively.

"It's just that, while I enjoy spending long, uninterrupted stretches in the company of your uncovered body, it is currently torn all to shreds. People might notice. I mean, some of your injuries from this morning are still kind of oozing. I think if you go into the main party area in lingerie serving crudités, you're going to draw some unwanted attention."

Keri sighed deeply.

"Under normal circumstances," she said, "I would kick your ass. But you make a fair point. And since this medication is definitely kicking in and I'm starting to feel kind of warm all over, I'm going to let your impertinence go this one time. Maybe I'll just put on the outfit with a thin robe over it and then search the house. I'm assuming they'll be keeping Evie somewhere away from the main festivities. And that way, if someone finds me, I can just claim I got lost."

"Okay, Keri, but be careful," Ray replied. "You'll have to hide your gun in one robe pocket and the headset in the other. It'll look suspicious if someone sees you wandering around in what amounts to a bikini with a complicated piece of audio hardware on your head."

"Can I pipe in here?" Keith said over their comms. "Keri, you can actually remove the earpiece from the headset and still listen to what we're saying. It's so small no one will notice it. You won't be able to respond but at least Ray and I can keep you updated."

Keri and Ray exchanged looks and nodded.

"Good idea, Keith," Keri said. "You guys will just have to keep me looped in constantly."

"Will do," Keith assured her. "And as long as I'm keeping you looped in, I wanted to let you know, I have no idea who this house belongs to. I've been doing some web searching but everything comes back to a shell company. The true owner is well hidden."

"I wish I could say I'm shocked," Keri said. "But it makes sense. Anyone hosting something like this would want layers of paperwork hiding their involvement. But for the purposes of calling in reinforcements, the address is more important right now."

"Agreed," Ray said. "I'm going to go get you one of those uniforms now. Hang tight here."

After he left, Keri locked the door and removed the headset and gun, one of Ray's extras. Then she stripped naked and waited for him to return. Staring in the bathroom mirror, she saw what he was talking about.

While she was in pretty good shape these days and could look at her unclothed body without feeling too self-conscious, her body was riddled with bruises, scrapes, cuts, scabs, and bandages that were stained by seeping blood. The entire right side of her face, from her temple down to her lips, was scratched and purplish-blue. Despite being nude, she looked like she was prepping for a horror film more than a porn shoot.

The only good thing was that the meds Mags had given her had fully kicked in now. The intensity of the situation had cut into the warm feeling she'd felt earlier, so there was no high or especially good mood. But there wasn't a lot of pain either. She could feel the tenderness in her muscles and bones, hiding just below the surface. But for now at least, it was keeping a low profile, allowing her to function.

There was a soft knock on the door and Keri opened it. Ray reentered holding the uniform, a lightweight, cream-colored, silk robe, and a mask. She noticed him blushing slightly.

"Like what you see, big boy?' she asked playfully.

"Yeah," he said sheepishly. "I mean, you look like some sort of demon spawn who intends to drag me into the pit of hell. But you know, in a sexy way."

"What exactly is going on in there?" Keith asked over the headset.

"Mind your business, mall boy," Ray growled. "Way to ruin the mood."

"Sorry. I just thought this was supposed to be a serious situation."

Ray's face turned into a scowl as he opened his mouth to reply but Keri shook her head and leaned in to give him a peck on the lips.

"Can you hear me, Keith?" she asked. "I'm speaking into Ray's headset."

"I can hear you, Detective."

"You're right. This is a serious situation. We've got about forty-five minutes before my daughter is supposed to be ritually sacrificed. I can't think of any anything more serious. But it's a lot to process, you know? I'm trying to keep my head on straight so I don't completely lose it. Does that make sense, Keith?"

"Yes, Detective," he said.

"If I think about the consequences if we fail, I don't know that I'll be able to put one foot in front of the other, much less do what needs to be done to save my daughter. So Ray and I, we sometimes revert to a bit of gallows humor. It keeps us loose. It reminds us that even when things get grim, we can laugh. And it keeps me from completely losing my mind. You don't begrudge me that, do you?"

"No ma'am," he replied. "I guess I'm just nervous."

"That's okay. I am too. I just hide it better. But you're right. It's time to get our game faces on. So I'm going to get into this ridiculous outfit and mask."

"And I'm going to see if I can hunt up one of those red 'valet' jackets," Ray said. "If I can pass for one of the security guys, maybe I can get some info on where they might be holding Evie."

"What should I do?" Keith asked.

"You hold tight for now," Keri said. "Trust me. We'll be calling on you soon enough."

Keri finished getting dressed, then turned to face Ray.

"How do I look?" she asked.

He pushed a button on his headset, turning it off.

"I love you." he said, without a trace of snark.

He was staring at her deeply, almost as if he was trying to drink her in. Keri felt her heart open wide. She'd sensed how he felt but hearing the words out loud for the first time sent a shiver throughout her entire body.

"I love you too," she said back to him, her voice suddenly quavering.

He pulled her in gently and kissed her, careful to avoid the bruised side of her mouth, although she didn't really care at that moment. Then he wrapped her in his arms and hugged her for a good thirty seconds.

"I just wanted you to know that," he whispered in her ear, "no matter what happens out there."

"We'll have to continue this conversation afterward, because I have a few additional thoughts on the matter. Okay?"

"Okay," he agreed, stepping back.

"But for now, let's get to work, shall we?"

Ray nodded silently, then turned the headset back on.

"Keith, I'm heading out to find a security jacket. Keri will be close behind me. Keep us apprised of any developments. And remember, Keri will only be in audio mode from this point forward. Understood?"

"Got it," Keith said.

Ray gave one last half-smile before stepping outside. Keri waited sixty seconds, took a deep breath, and opened the door, walking out to face an uncertain future, armed only with a gun, her training, and a mother's undying love.

CHAPTER EIGHTEEN

Keri was initially nervous with each step she took, holding her breath as she rounded every corner with caution. She had even grabbed a tray filled with mushroom appetizers just in case she bumped into anyone. But after a while, she realized that with all the focus on the main party area of the house, no one really cared much what the staff was doing in the back part of the property.

But as she walked up a set of stairs into what appeared to be the residence section of the estate, Keri did notice a marked uptick in foot traffic and security. Every few minutes a man would walk down a hall into a bedroom, accompanied by a young girl. In each case, a man in a red sport coat would accompany them into the room. After what she assumed was a security sweep, he would step out, close the door, and assume a position guarding the room.

At one point, she realized she couldn't get any farther forward in the house without going down a hall with two guards stationed outside rooms about thirty feet from each other.

You're wearing a mask. The lighting is dark. They can't see your face or your bruises. Act casual. You belong here.

She inhaled deeply, gave a long, slow exhale, and stepped out into the hall. Giving her best uninterested sashay, she made her way toward the first guard, who eyed her warily but said nothing. As she approached the second man, he held up his hand for her to stop.

"What are you doing back here?" he demanded.

"Just serving food, man," she said, trying to sound bored and slightly annoyed. "My manager said to wander the bedroom halls occasionally to make sure no one felt left out back here. So I'm doing what I was told. Mushroom?"

"No," he responded gruffly. "But stick to the central event area from now on. No one back here is looking to eat."

"Okay. Sorry, dude."

She continued down the hall and made a left, in the direction of many loud voices and what she hoped was the "central event area." As she entered the next hallway, Keith's voice came on the comm. Keri had been so focused on her own task that she hadn't realized he hadn't spoken for a while.

"Listen up, guys. I've managed to hack into the CCTV for the house and from what I can tell, they're going to start some kind of presentation in less than a minute. There's a countdown clock and it has forty-two seconds left."

Keri felt a wave of panic rise in her gut. Was it midnight already? She glanced at her phone. 11:29.

"I'm almost in position in the main room," she heard Ray say. "It looks like everyone's starting to gather around the various monitors."

Keri picked up the pace, hoping to find her way to the main room before the presentation started. As she passed an open bedroom door, she glanced in and saw a flat-screen on the far wall. It looked to be showing the countdown as well.

She looked back down the hall in the direction she'd come from to see if the surly guard had followed her but she was alone. Quickly, she stepped into the bedroom and pulled the door closed. She looked around. The room was filled with several bouquets of flowers and multiple lit scented candles on the dresser. The bed sheet and comforter were turned back. But the room was empty.

Keri put the appetizer tray on the dresser and sat down on the end of the bed just as the countdown ended. The screen went black for several seconds. Then the word "Vista" appeared in bold, white letters. A deep authoritative male voice began to speak as pictures of the city appeared onscreen, dissolving into one another.

"For close to a decade, a discerning group of elites, dedicated to the pursuit of a new kind of pleasure, has met once a year for an event we call the Vista. What is the Vista? It is a new way of looking at things, of seeing beyond the everyday sameness of our daily choices, of looking into the distance, into the beyond, into a world where our erotic gratification, our sexual fulfillment, our carnal desires are treated with the respect—no, the reverence—they are truly due."

The iconic Los Angeles images were now replaced by snapshots of attractive naked women. Keri noticed that as the narrator spoke, the women seemed to get younger with each passing photograph.

"Each year, we convene to remind ourselves of what is possible for each of us if we just choose to take it for ourselves. The world is full of rules, of petty tyrannies, laid out by bureaucrats unworthy of the power they wield. But on this night, we are not bound by their rules, by their laws. On this night, we are the law. Life and death are in our hands, in your hands."

The screen went black again and then, to Keri's shock, her official LAPD photo filled the screen. She heard a small squeal of surprise escape her lips and glanced quickly at the door to make sure no one came in. The voice continued.

"As you all know, this year was very special, even before the events of this morning. The reward to the winner of our auction was always to be the offspring of this woman, a thorn in the side to all of us who appreciate pleasure without boundaries, a cancer on the freedom of free-thinking men. This is Detective Keri Locke, who made it her life's mission to interfere with the natural order of the world, to stop men of passion from satiating their cravings. She wished, in fact, to punish us for them. That will no longer be a concern."

Keri heard a rumble of cackling laughter from a room somewhere not too far away and knew the narrator had really wowed his audience with that one. She was glad the Vicodin was still flowing through her bloodstream. It helped numb her. Otherwise, she was pretty sure she'd either be throwing up or firing her gun at the television.

"But despite her absence, we can still cause her suffering, because her only daughter still lives. She was abducted six years ago, ripped from her mother's teat. But due to hard work and diligence, she has been found. And she is with us here tonight. She is our Blood Prize for the evening. And one of you has won the right to do what you will with her before cutting her throat and watching the life fade from her eyes. One of you has won the right to have purview over life and death and send this girl to meet her mother where they can rot together among the worms."

Despite the medication, despite the numbness, Keri felt herself gag involuntarily.

"Gentleman, meet this year's honored Arbiter."

Keri's photo disappeared, replaced by live video of man standing in a nondescript room. He was wearing a mask that covered most of his face but not the random tufts of hair atop his head. He had on a golden bathrobe which could not hide a mass of chest hair poking out above it. His double chin was glistening with sweat. It was Herb Wasson. He didn't speak, only smiled grotesquely, as if he couldn't hide the excitement of what was to come.

A second later, he was replaced by the word "Vista." The voice spoke once more.

"At the stroke of midnight, after our Arbiter has satisfied himself, we will congregate once more for the Blood Prize. Until then, please conclude any remaining delights and return to the Festivities Hall for the ceremony."

The screen went black.

Keri stood up, the ball of anxious fury rising from her abdomen to her chest and finally to her suddenly throbbing head. She started to pull out the headset to reattach it to her earpiece. But before it was even out of her robe pocket, Ray's voice was in her ear.

"I know you're probably bouncing off the walls, Keri, but we're going to solve this. Keith, I'm assuming that was Wasson in the video. Can you still track him using that taggant stuff?"

"Already on it, Detective Sands," Keith said. "I figured that might be him and I'm driving up closer to the house now to try to get in range. Once he entered the property, I stopped focusing on him. But I think I can relocate him. The problem is, pinpointing his location on my map doesn't tell me exactly where in the house he is. So I'm also pulling up specs for the estate, so I can try to pinpoint the actual floor and maybe even the room he's in."

How long is this going to take?" Ray asked.

"It might take me a few minutes. I have to get close enough to get a good trace on Wasson but not so close that I draw attention from the security guys. And pulling up an accurate floor plan for this place might take some work. My Internet connection is a little sketchy in these hills."

Keri finally got the headset attached.

"Can you hear me?"

"Yes," both men said at the same time.

"You have to move fast, Keith. I know it's a lot to ask. But that *was* Wasson. And I have a bad feeling about the 'do what you will' part of his time with Evie. They could be bringing her to him right now and I need to get there before he does anything to her. He doesn't just want to kill her. He wants to break her."

"I'm working on it, Detective," Keith insisted. "The good news is your headset works as a tracker too. So once I get accurate specs on the house, I'm hoping I can tell you exactly where you are in relation to Wasson and get you to him quicker."

"Where are you now, Keri?" Ray asked.

"I'm in an empty second-floor bedroom. It's in a corridor that can't be more than a hundred feet from the main party room. I could hear the crowd laughing clearly when the narrator guy joked about me being dead."

"Okay," Ray replied. "I think I know where you are generally. All of the johns and their girls have left the party area through the same exit so I suspect it leads to your neck of the woods. I'm going to try to work my way to you in a minute. But first I need to find a quiet, out of the way place to make a call."

"What call?" Keri asked.

"I think now would be a good time to alert County SWAT to that meth lab down the way, don't you?"

"Absolutely," Keri agreed as she stood up and grabbed the appetizer plate. "In the meantime, I'm not sure what to do here. I'm in this bedroom with a tray of cold mushroom appetizers and wearing a suspicious headset. If I run into a guard while searching the halls, it might be hard to explain away. But every second I'm stuck in here is a second wasted."

"Just stay put a little longer," Keith pleaded. "I've pulled over just down the road from the house. I see Wasson's taggant signature on the screen now. I promise I'll have a floor plan up soon and be able to tell you where he is."

Keri was about to sit back down on the bed when she saw the bedroom door handle start to turn.

"Change of plans," she whispered as the door began to open.

CHAPTER NINETEEN

For the briefest of seconds, Keri considered just flinging the tray at the head of whoever entered the room. But what if it was a john or some teen call girl and the security guy was behind them? She'd lose the element of surprise and a potential weapon. Better to use the disguise first and avoid a confrontation if possible.

"What does that mean?" she heard Keith say but ignored him.

The door opened wide and light streamed in, blocking her vision, which would have made throwing the tray accurately difficult anyway. A figure stepped into the light and she saw that it was indeed a security officer. His hand was on his hip where a weapon would be but he hadn't unholstered it yet.

"Hello?" she said warily, trying to sound as innocuous as possible.

"Who are you?" he demanded. "What are you doing in here?"

"I'm sorry. I'm part of the wait staff. I had to pee but the line for employees in the back was too long so I came looking for a bathroom up here. This bedroom door was open so I just came in real quick to take care of my business."

She saw his hand relax on his holster but not come off it. She could also see the earpiece cord dangling from his ear. All it would take was one word from him to call in others or alert his superiors.

"You shouldn't be in this area of the house, lady," he said, stepping inside and waving for her to pass by him into the hallway. "The instructions were very explicit about that."

"I know," she said apologetically as she moved past him. "It's just that when nature calls, everything else flies out the window, you know?"

He smiled in understanding, then gave the room a quick once-over to make sure everything was in order. She saw his smile fade slightly and, immediately realizing something was wrong, made her move.

"There's no bathroom in h—" he started to say.

But before he could complete the sentence she hit him in the right temple with the flat edge of the appetizer tray. Mushrooms flew against the wall. He stumbled back, slightly stunned but nothing more. Keri swung the tray back the other way, this time clocking him in the bridge of the nose just before he could get his hands up to block the blow.

With his arms now up and his torso exposed, Keri slammed into him as hard as she could, leading with an elbow to his solar plexus. As they both smashed into the bedroom wall, she heard a grunt as he exhaled and knew she'd knocked the wind out of him.

She didn't have long before he'd recover, just a matter of seconds, so she had no choice but to err on the side of decisiveness. She pulled out her gun and smashed the butt of it onto the top of the guy's skull. He moaned, disoriented but still conscious. His right hand was flailing, trying to grab at the "speak" button on his comm.

No choice.

She lifted the butt of the gun and came down hard again, only an inch away from where she'd landed the first blow. This time he slumped to the floor, out cold.

She wanted to roll over and lie down next to him, at least for a moment, so she could catch her breath. But she couldn't risk it. Instead, she forced herself to get up, hurried over to the bedroom door, closed and locked it.

"Can you guys hear me?" she asked as she returned to the guard and yanked his comm, earpiece and all, from his body.

"What happened?" Ray asked.

"I had an unexpected, unwanted visitor. But he's taken care of, at least for the time being," she said as she dragged his heavy body around behind the far side of the bed where it would be out of view.

"Are you okay?" Keith asked.

"Not too bad, all things considered. But I don't know how long we have before this guy's absence will be noticed. How often do they do check-ins, Ray?"

"Every fifteen minutes. Last one was four minutes ago, immediately after the video presentation."

"That doesn't give us long," Keri said as she used a pillowcase to tie the guard's hands together behind his back. "Once he fails to check in, I can't imagine they'll take more than sixty seconds to go into alert mode. These guys don't strike me as the casual type."

"Agreed," Ray said. "That means we've got about ten minutes, tops, before someone in authority decides there's been a breach. So I'm dispensing with the whole meth lab thing. I'm calling SWAT now to give them the address."

"Good," Keri said. "Just one thing before you do. I don't know what these guys' protocol is for a breach scenario but I'm guessing that it involves either moving or killing Evie. So midnight is out as our deadline. The new drop dead time to find Evie is…eleven forty-seven p.m. Got it?"

"Got it," Ray said. "I'm going quiet for a few to make that call now."

"You still there, Keith?" Keri asked as she stuffed one of the guard's socks into his mouth.

"I am."

"Okay, well, I've got this guard pretty well indisposed for the next ten minutes. So I'm hoping you've got a new assignment for me. How's that floor plan coming, buddy?"

"I've got it up now," Keith said. "Wasson's signal isn't moving, which means either something is wrong with the connection or the guy is already where he wants to be."

"I'm guessing the latter. They'd bring her to him, not the other way around. Where is he?"

"It looks like he's one floor up from you, in what seems to be some kind of massive third-floor bedroom."

"How do I access it?" Keri demanded.

"Well, I'm looking at your current location and you're actually not that far. The problem is that you'd have to go down two main hallways and up a set of stairs to get to the room. I'm guessing that there will be a fair bit of security along the way."

"Good guess, Keith," Keri said, trying to keep the exasperation out of her voice. "Any other routes that don't have me running into the guys in red jackets, alerting the entire security team to my presence and putting my daughter in even more mortal danger?"

"No pressure there. I do have one idea. But it will require that Vicodin to still be working pretty well."

"I'm listening," Keri said.

"If you go right at the end of the hallway your current room is in, there's a glass door opening onto a small balcony. That balcony is below the balcony for the third-floor bedroom. So theoretically you could climb up from the second to the third floor and get into the bedroom where Wasson is that way."

"Theoretically?"

"Well, it looks like a pretty big leap from floor to floor. The plans I'm looking at aren't that detailed but the jump looks to be at least...four feet high."

Keri looked at the time. 11:40.

I have seven minutes until all hell breaks loose.

"Let's do it. I'm going to try to pass for a waitress to get to that balcony, so I'm picking up my appetizer tray and putting away the headset. It's too suspicious when I'm walking the halls. I'll be in audio mode only. Keep me apprised of any developments on Wasson's movements and have Ray update me on security changes, got it?"

"You got it, Detective."

"Here goes nothing," Keri said.

She peeked out into the hall and, seeing no one, stepped out, making sure to lock the door behind her. She walked confidently in the direction Keith had instructed, made the right turn, and saw the balcony where it was supposed to be. There was no one in sight. Apparently everyone had followed the instructions to return to the Festivities Hall.

She reached the sliding glass door and pulled. It was locked. For half a second, she debated opening it. What if there was some kind of alarm?

If there is, I'm screwed anyway, so I may as well just go for it.

Keri unlocked the door and yanked it open. A frigid blast of air hit her with unexpected force. The wave of cold felt like an electric shock. Inside the warm house, she'd forgotten just how chilly it was outside.

But now, as goose bumps magically appeared over every inch of her exposed skin, it all came back to her. Standing there, in just lingerie and a thin robe in forty-something-degree weather, she felt her body start to shiver.

Keri stepped outside and yanked the door closed, hoping the cold air wouldn't waft down the hall and alert anyone to something unusual. She moved to the edge of the balcony and looked up. Keith was right—it was going to be a leap.

From the top of the second floor wall to the very bottom of the third floor was more like five feet than the four Keith had estimated. And the balcony wall wasn't really a wall. Rather, it was a railing comprised of a series of horizontal metal bars stacked on top of each other.

That was actually a positive. At least if she was able to jump high enough, she'd be able to grab onto the bottom bar and pull herself up rung by rung. That was, if she didn't miss the bottom bar completely and plummet to the ground below.

The main concern was that in order to grab the bottom rung of the third-floor railing when she jumped, she'd have to clear the base of the third-floor balcony, which was pretty thick. If she didn't get higher than that, there'd be nothing to grab on to.

Keri looked over the side of the balcony. It was too dark to tell the exact height. But the house was built into the back of a hill and she guessed it was at least forty feet to the ground—nothing survivable.

She put the tray down on the ground, kicked off her heels, and climbed up onto the top bar of the second-floor railing. She put her hands on the underside of the ceiling for balance and eased herself out over the empty expanse below.

She glanced at the clock one more time: 11:43 p.m. She bent her knees, steeling herself for the jump, when a voice suddenly cut into her earpiece. It was Ray.

"I'm back. Sorry for the delay. I put the call in to LA County SWAT. They're en route and should be here in six to eight minutes. But I have bad news. That may not be enough time. My call must have tipped someone on the inside here because they did an immediate security check-in. One guy isn't responding. They're sending a team to his tracker location now. So I'm guessing you have less than sixty seconds before they find him, order a general alert, and pull Evie out."

Keri clutched the ceiling tighter, suddenly afraid her legs would give out beneath her. For the briefest of seconds, she thought she might collapse under the pressure of the moment, as she had so many times before.

No. You will not crumble. You will be strong.

Her head cleared. Ray continued.

"Keri, I heard you say you're in audio mode only, so listen closely. I'm going to draw them to me down here, make them think the intruder is on the first floor, not the third. That should give you a little extra time—maybe even pull a few guards away. But it will be short-lived. So you need to move now."

Keri wanted to tell him not to do it, that it was a suicide mission. But like he said, she was in audio mode only, so she couldn't say anything. Besides, apart from the likelihood that it would kill him, it was good plan. It would draw them away from her.

But most of all, the decision was out of her control. She couldn't change it. And she had less than a minute before guards might burst into the room above her and take her daughter away or worse. She had no choice anymore.

So Keri jumped.

CHAPTER TWENTY

Her fingers found the bottom bar of the railing but she felt them start to slip almost immediately. Somehow, the index and middle finger of her right hand clung to the bar as she slammed her left palm down on the edge of the balcony, where the tile met the metal.

She pushed up hard, getting enough leverage and height to grip the railing with her entire right hand and hook her left arm between the first and second bars. She felt an odd twinge in her left shoulder as all her weight bore down on it at an extreme angle.

Ignoring the pain, she grabbed the highest bar she could with her right hand and hooked her elbow around it while she extricated her left shoulder from its position and flung it over the top railing. Using her remaining strength and the adrenaline coursing through her system, she pulled herself up the rest of the way until she felt her feet plant on the top of the balcony floor.

In Keri's ear, gunshots and yelling were audible, little of it coherent. She forced herself to push it out of her head and focus on what was in front of her.

From the balcony, she couldn't see past the heavy bedroom curtains. She climbed over the railing and grabbed the door handle, ready to shoot the glass if the thing was locked. It opened easily.

She stepped inside and was almost immediately overwhelmed by the strong scent of incense. The room was dark, with candles everywhere. Loud ambient music played over the sound system. It took her a second to get her bearings.

Then she saw him—a corpulent man on a huge bed. He was naked and his hairy back, with its endless folds of fat, was to Keri. He was thrusting down on someone who wasn't visible under his massive form.

Keri pulled out her gun and started toward him, trying not to let her fury overwhelm her focus. Suddenly a voice cut into her head. It was Keith.

"Keri, I can see you've reached the third floor. You need to move quick. I've patched into the security channel. They've found the guard you knocked out and they're sending guys for Evie now."

Almost on cue, the door to the bedroom opened and two men in red jackets rushed in, both holding weapons. Keri turned to face them. She felt surprisingly calm, considering the circumstances. Keith's voice, the sounds of music, gunfire, and shouting, the smell of the candles—they all faded into the background as she centered her attention on the men in red.

She shot the first one in the chest before he even had a chance to raise his gun. The second man was starting to aim at her but she pulled the trigger before he'd fully squared up in her direction and hit him in the right shoulder. The gun dropped from his useless hand as he fell to the ground. As she crossed the room to the door, she shot him a second time, this time in the chest as he writhed on the floor in pain. He lay still, no longer a threat.

Keri closed the door, locked it, and grabbed a chair, which she jammed under the doorknob. It wouldn't stop them for long. But she didn't need long.

She turned her attention back to the bed. Herb Wasson had been busy while she dealt with the guards. He was still on the bed, but now he was on his knees, facing Keri. He was holding a girl in front of him, clutching her close to his chest with his left arm wrapped around her. The girl's hands were cuffed behind her back. His right hand was holding a knife to her throat.

Keri refused to look at the girl's face. If it was Evie, she feared she'd lose her will, her focus. She needed to keep all of her attention on Wasson, staring into his beady, darting black eyes.

"Drop the knife," she said evenly, stepping slowly toward him.

"You're supposed to be dead!" he shrieked more than said.

"Maybe I'm a ghost, Wasson," Keri said, taking another step forward. "If you don't drop the knife right now, that's what you'll be."

"I paid good money to make the pig's kid squeal," he screamed, his voice rising crazily. "I paid good money!"

In his excitement, his hand moved and he nicked the girl slightly. Keri watched a trickle of blood dribble down her neck. She looked at Wasson and took a deep breath.

He opened his mouth, ready to shout again, when she fired.

The bullet hit him in the middle of the forehead and his eyes widened for a fraction of a second before the force of the shot sent him flying back onto the bed. The knife still rested in his clenched fist.

Keri allowed herself to really look at the girl closely for the first time. She was completely naked and had several pieces of duct tape tied to her mouth. Her hair was blonde, pulled back in an elaborate braid. Her face was heavily made up, although her tears had created long rivulets of mascara running down her cheeks.

Keri followed the wet, black lines back up to her eyes and stared into them. They were rimmed red around the edges from crying but in the center was the same familiar green she knew from both her memory and her dreams. They were the eyes of her daughter.

It was Evie.

Keri gasped, refusing to cry, reminding herself that they were far from out of the woods yet. She started to move toward her daughter when there was a rattle at the bedroom door. Then a banging sound as someone tried to slam into it.

Keri turned back to Evie and helped her off the bed.

"Stay behind me," she said.

A gunshot sounded and Keri saw that someone was firing at the door handle. She turned back to Evie.

"Actually, why don't you hide behind the side of the bed?' she instructed.

Evie nodded and crouched on her knees at the edge of the bed. As satisfied as she could be, Keri returned her attention to the door, which someone was trying to smash open. The chair was holding them back, but only temporarily.

Keri ran to the door and managed to get behind it right as someone smashed it open. The momentum sent the guy stumbling into the room and Keri had an easy shot, firing at his back, then immediately slamming her body against the door, making contact with the second guard entering the room.

As soon as she heard the second guard smash into the doorframe, she dove forward into the room and rolled over. She was just in time to see the guard, having regrouped, shoot into the door where she'd stood only a moment earlier. As he swiveled his head in her direction, realizing his error, she fired at him, nailing him in the neck.

He stumbled backward into the guard behind him, who was just pulling his trigger at that moment. Unfortunately for the man in front of him, who got in the way of the shot, the bullet lodged in his lower back. Before the third guard could get off a second attempt, Keri had dropped him with a chest shot.

She scrambled to her knees, looking for movement from any of them or any sign of other guards in the hall. She heard a groan to her right and glanced over. The first guard through the door, the one she'd gotten in the back, was still alive but seemed unable to move. He was coughing up blood. Just to be safe, she kicked away the gun lying inches from his fingertips.

Then she closed the door again, although with the lock blown off, it was a pretty useless gesture. Keri started to walk over to Evie again when Keith's voice came over her earpiece once more.

"Keri, if you can hear me, the guards are scattering. SWAT is breaching the estate and everyone is making a run for it. It's a madhouse. I hear the head of the security team telling his guys to pull out. So hopefully, you shouldn't encounter any more of them."

Keri started to fumble in the robe for her headset. She wanted to ask if Ray was okay, if he'd survived his diversion mission. But it was gone. Maybe it had fallen when she'd jumped balconies or when she was rolling around. Either way, it was nowhere to be found.

Evie poked her head up from behind the bed and Keri's attention immediately returned to her.

"It's going to be okay," she said, walking toward her. "All the bad guys are gone now."

But Evie, the duct tape still over her mouth, shook her head. It had been six years since Keri had seen her up close but she recognized the look of fear in her daughter's eyes. Something wasn't right.

"What is it?" she asked.

Evie jabbed her head slightly to the left, at the wall of the bedroom, as if to say "over there."

Apparently not *all* the bad guys were gone.

CHAPTER TWENTY ONE

Keri looked at the wall. As she did, something Keith had said a few minutes earlier popped into her head. Looking at the floor plans for the house, he'd described the third-floor bedroom as massive.

But this bedroom, while definitely spacious, was far from massive. In fact, when she'd been out on the balcony, she'd noticed that it seemed to extend far beyond where the wall currently stood.

"Behind the wall?" she mouthed silently to Evie.

Her daughter nodded. Keri desperately wanted to pull the tape off her mouth, to hear her child's voice. But she worried that focusing on anything other than the immediate threat at hand could put them both at risk, so she fought the urge.

Instead, she turned and looked at the wall, letting her eyes travel along its entire length, intent on finding anything out of the ordinary. It didn't take long to find the cameras.

She saw them at both corners of the wall, where they met the ceiling. They were tiny, circular, and painted to blend in but easily noticeable once one was aware of them. Keri glanced around and saw them at the other two corners of the room as well.

She stepped closer to the wall and tapped it softly. It felt like typical drywall. Glancing back at Evie, she saw her daughter nod at a section in front of them. Keri turned back around. The only usual item in that area was a long vertical painting framed to the wall. The bottom of it stood about two feet above the floor and it extended five feet up from that.

Keri walked over to it and stared at the ornate gold frame that jutted out from the wall. Without pausing to think, she grabbed the frame and pulled. There was a click and it opened out toward her, leaving a doorway-sized gap.

She stepped back and to the side, waiting for a gunshot or for someone to dive through the hole. No one did. Part of her considered just grabbing Evie and running downstairs, letting the SWAT team deal with whoever was in there.

But what if whoever was in there escaped and came back after her later? If this person was part of the plot to kill Evie, they had to be captured now. There might not be another chance.

Choosing to act rather than mull over the option, Keri dove through the hole, completing a roll and coming to a stop in a kneeling position. She surveyed the room, which appeared to be empty apart from a huge desk with a bank of monitors that showed the bedroom and the rest of the house.

She looked at the screens and saw the chaos on the floors below. There were dozens of people running along the expanse of green lawn in their tuxedos, trying to escape the main gate on foot even as police cars streamed through it. People were scurrying to their limos, which had been blocked in.

Multiple men in red blazers had their hands up or were being cuffed by uniformed officers. SWAT officers were slowly working their way through the house, hallway by hallway. But Keith had gone radio silent. And she didn't see Ray anywhere.

But she did see movement out of the corner of her eye and looked at one of the monitors that showed the bedroom she'd just come from. The angle showed both the bed and, in the background, the bathroom.

Someone had just pushed open what appeared to be a secret door behind a full-length bathroom mirror and was stepping out. It was a man with a baseball cap pulled low to cover his face.

Keri glanced into the corner of the room she was in and noticed something she'd missed before. There was a small gap in the far wall that exactly matched the spot where the mirror was in the bedroom. Someone had been hiding in the gap and waited until Keri had come in here to sneak over to the bedroom side, where Evie was waiting with her back to him.

Keri turned and dashed back toward the bedroom. As she leapt over the two-foot rise, something collided into her, slamming her into the back wall, She felt the gun fall from her hand as the breath escaped from her body.

As she started to slide down the wall, she saw the hand of the baseball-capped person reach for her weapon. She managed to thrust her right leg out to kick it away as she slumped to the ground. It slid under the bed.

The man in the cap looked at it for a second, then seemed to shrug and hurried over in the direction of the guard Keri had shot in the back, whose gun was still lying several feet away from him.

Keri, her breath still hard to come by, struggled to get to her feet. She'd never reach him in time. She could only hope this guy was a bad shot as she started toward him. But before she took her first step she saw that Evie had already started running in the same direction. Her hands were still cuffed behind her back so she did the only thing she could: she threw herself at the man in the cap, slamming into his back and sending them both careening past the gun.

Evie rolled several times before coming to a stop in front of the bedroom door. The man in the cap hit the far wall hard with his shoulder but didn't fall down. He gathered himself and turned around as Keri rumbled toward him. As he turned toward her, she saw that he'd lost his cap in the collision, and she could see his face clearly for the first time.

Looking back at her, with a twisted smile on his face and a malevolent gleam in his eye, was Jackson Cave.

CHAPTER TWENTY TWO

Keri barely had time to process who she was charging at before she slammed into him, knocking him up against the wall. Unfortunately, she also slammed the left shoulder she'd tweaked on the balcony, sending a sharp burst of pain down her left side. It was enough for him to wriggle free and dive for the gun.

But instead of grabbing it, he accidentally knocked it toward the open balcony door. It skimmed the hardwood floor of the bedroom and out onto the balcony tile, where it stopped, resting about a foot from the edge.

Cave got up and ran for it, with Keri right behind him. He had just stepped outside when she caught up to him and leapt onto his back, knocking him hard against the metal railing. She heard his body hit it with a brutal thud and felt her own body slam into his a moment later. They both sank to the ground in a heap.

Keri saw Cave reach desperately over in the direction of the gun. The back of his hand bumped the barrel and sent it skittering over the edge of the balcony. He didn't seem to realize what had happened and kept patting the tile.

Keri rolled off him and grabbed the sliding door handle to pull herself to her feet. Cave glanced down, saw that the gun was gone, and began to reach for the railing to yank himself up.

He had gotten up to mid-crouch when Keri barreled into him, this time with her right shoulder forward. She made solid contact and felt his ribs compress when they met the unforgiving railing behind him. As he started to slump, she raised her right knee to meet his face and connected cleanly with the bridge of his nose. He fell to the tile, face first, his arms and legs splayed out at his sides.

Keri bent over, resting her hands on her knees, desperately sucking in massive gulps of air. It took twenty seconds of this before she felt strong enough to speak.

"You hated me that much, Cave?" she spat, shaking her head in disbelief. "You wanted to watch in some private room while your pervert client murdered my daughter on TV?"

Cave tilted his head slightly and looked up at her from the ground.

"You ruined my life. Why shouldn't I ruin yours...Detective?" He said that last word with such disgust that Keri realized how much of an effort it must have been for him to hide the vitriol in all their prior conversations.

"I didn't ruin your life, Cave. I just wanted my daughter back. You're the one who traffics in sexual slavery, who sells little girls for money. You chose your path. And even this morning, I offered to walk away from all of it, if you returned her to me."

"You weren't serious," Cave hissed venomously, as he slowly pushed himself up onto all fours. "You were just trying to play me."

"Maybe I was. To be honest, I'm not even sure myself. But if Evie had shown up at my door, I'd have had a tough call to make. Instead, you tried to have me killed."

"I almost regretted that," Cave admitted, grabbing the railing and pulling himself back to his feet. "I wanted you to get to look into your daughter's lifeless eyes and know you'd failed her. Signing off on your execution meant I lost that. But look at us now, Detective. I guess I got a second chance."

"No chance, Cave. She's safe. And you're finished. Where you're going, you'll be the one bought and sold. I've got a friend who can make it happen."

"You mean your friendly neighborhood ghost, Thomas Anderson?" Cave asked mockingly, standing fully upright now, oblivious to the blood running freely from his nose. "I wouldn't count on him. He choked to death on his own tongue about an hour after you left him last night—a real shame."

Keri started to take a step toward him, the bile rising in her gut. But something in his expression made her stop. He continued.

"And as for Evie, do you really think she's safe now? Come on, after everything she's been through? No matter what happens to me, even if she never faces another nasty man for the rest of her life, she'll always have the memories; the nightmares. She'll always have that degraded face looking back at her in the mirror. She might be safe from the bad guys out there. But is she safe in here?" he asked, tapping his head. "I give her a year, tops."

Keri pretended not to notice the cold shiver that ran down her spine, ordered herself not to let this man bait her into giving him the easy way out. She was a cop, a detective with the LAPD, and she was going to bring in her collar.

"Jackson Cave, you are under arrest for the…you know what, it's too much to list. For now, you're just under arrest."

She stepped toward him, debating how physical she'd have to be without cuffs. But as she did, he lunged at her and she saw, almost too late, that he had a small switchblade that he must have snuck out while he was getting to his feet.

He had jumped at her with more energy than control and she was able to sidestep him at the last moment, swinging her right fist down on his forearm hard. She heard the knife clatter to the tile as she swung up with her right elbow, clocking him under the jaw and sending him careening backward.

Cave's back hit the top bar of the railing and his momentum sent him tumbling over backward. Keri managed to grab his left leg and slow him enough for him to grab the bottom bar of the railing before gravity ripped his leg from her grasp.

He clung to the bottom bar, trying to get a good grip on the cold, slick metal as his body swung out in an arc over empty space before careening back hard against the outer edge of the balcony. He was barely holding on. Keri reached over and extended her arm.

"Give me your hand, Jackson. I'll pull you up. Let me help you."

Cave looked up at her and for a moment he had the same expression as when she'd mentioned his brother, Coy—as if he was studying her, trying to determine whether to believe her sincerity or not. But it was gone in a flash and she knew what conclusion he'd drawn.

"Oh, Detective," he said, almost pityingly through gritted teeth, "you're the one who needs help. You think this ends with me? I'm just a spoke in the wheel. You have no idea how high this goes. Watch your back, Keri."

And then he let go. She didn't see him land but three seconds later she heard a stomach-turning crunch and then silence. She slumped to the tiled floor of the balcony, allowing herself a minute to recuperate before rolling over and looking for her daughter.

To her surprise, Evie had already stood up and walked across the bedroom to the balcony door. She was wrapped in a blanket from the bed. Keri saw that she was no longer handcuffed and realized she must have found the key. She had also pulled the duct tape off her mouth. Evie stood at the balcony door for what seemed like an eternity, just staring down at Keri.

Finally, she stepped outside and gingerly sat down beside her mother, tucking the blanket over her shoulders so that it covered both of them. Then, without speaking a word, Evie leaned over and rested her head on her mother's shoulder.

CHAPTER TWENTY THREE

The next few hours went by in a blur. Keri and Evie barely had a moment alone together before the SWAT team burst in. They didn't really try to talk anyway. Mostly they just held each other. Even as they were taken to the hospital in ambulances, had IVs put in their arms, and were wrapped in thermal blankets, they didn't let go of each other's hands.

Keri learned that Ray was alive. He'd already been transported to the same hospital as them with a grazing gunshot wound to the left forearm. He hadn't wanted to go but SWAT wasn't in a negotiating mood and basically forced him into the ambulance.

Apparently he had gotten the red jacket security team's attention by firing several rounds into the air above the Festival Hall crowd, then leading the guards on a chase to the pool house, where he'd locked himself inside a supply pantry and held off multiple attackers until the cavalry arrived. At some point in the excitement, he'd lost his headset, which explained his lack of communication.

Keith had lost communication because he'd been arrested. When the police found a random guy sitting in a parked car half a block from the estate with a headset and a laptop, they decided to take him into custody and sort it out later. He'd subsequently been released.

There was a brief lull after Keri and Evie had been triaged at the ER and determined not to have life-threatening injuries but before the doctors came in to do more thorough exams. Mother and daughter sat in mobile hospital beds next to each other, separated from the world by a thin, puke-green curtain. Neither of them spoke for a while.

"I knew you'd come for me," Evie finally said quietly.

"How did you know?"

"They took me, they hid me, and they used me for six years. But they couldn't keep the world out that whole time, Mom. I saw the news stories. The guy who took me actually showed me the press conference after he kidnapped me, the one where you were crying in the parking lot. He was laughing at you."

"I'm so sorry, sweetie," Keri said, trying to keep her voice from cracking.

"He thought it would break me," Evie continued, her voice surprisingly neutral. "But what he didn't get was that just seeing your face gave me comfort. Knowing that you cared so much...I held on to that for years when it seemed like there was no hope. And then..."

Her voice trailed off. Keri desperately wanted her to continue, but she didn't want to push too hard and shut her down. Anything her daughter volunteered was a blessing, considering the circumstances. But Evie regrouped and continued.

"And then I heard you became a cop. I saw some of the stories about you saving kids. And I knew that eventually you'd find me. I never had a doubt. Well, mostly."

Keri started to ask about the "mostly" but was interrupted by a phalanx of medical personnel who all swarmed into the room at the same time. They wanted to take Evie to a different room for a private examination but that was shut down by both mom and daughter immediately.

At some points during the exam, Keri could barely see Evie, there were so many people in the room. After a half hour, one doctor came over and whispered in Keri's ear that Evie had some internal vaginal bleeding and they needed to do a procedure immediately requiring general anesthesia.

She gave her consent, insisting that they share a room after the surgery was complete. While Keri waited for them to finish, the doctors caring for her provided the treatment she should have received after the cliff fall that morning.

It turned out that she had three cracked ribs from her leap onto the canyon rock outcropping. There were still tiny bits of asphalt and clothing embedded in her legs that she and Mags had missed in the bath cleanup session. The big chunk that had lodged in her shin had actually chipped off a small piece of her upper tibia, which helped explained the nonstop throbbing in that area.

A couple of her fingers were sprained and her left palm was so torn up that she might eventually need a skin graft. She required multiple stitches vertically along the right side of her face from her eye down to just below her nose. She had also mildly sprained her shoulder climbing the mansion balcony at the Vista and would need to wear a sling for a few days. She was a mess.

So when the doctors offered to give her a morphine drip while they dealt with much of that, she happily accepted. What she didn't expect was that she'd completely pass out while they were working.

When she woke up, light was streaming in through the hospital room window. Evie, fast asleep, was lying in the bed next to her. Ray, as he so often seemed to be, was sitting in an uncomfortable-looking chair beside her bed. He was asleep too and she saw a large bandage on his left forearm. Otherwise, he seemed uninjured.

He seemed to sense her eyes on him and stirred. After taking a moment to get his bearings, he whispered.

"What time is it?"

Keri glanced at the clock on the wall.

"Six fifty-six a.m."

"Good," he said. "That means you got about three hours of sleep. Better than nothing."

"And you? How much sleep did you get last night?"

"About…fifty-six minutes," he answered, smiling sheepishly.

"Raymond, you really should take better care of yourself."

He didn't respond to that, instead staring at Keri, then looking at over at Evie sleeping peacefully beside her.

"She looks so much like you," he said. It sounded like he might be about to add something else but he didn't. He just smiled.

"I can't believe I have her back," she whispered.

"It was a long time coming, Keri. I'm so happy for you."

"Thanks, Ray. You know, I wouldn't have been able to…without you, I couldn't…" She wasn't able to finish.

"Hey, don't get all soft on me yet, Thumbelina. There's still a long road ahead for both of you. This right here—lying in the hospital with tubes in your arms—it's the honeymoon."

"I know, Ray. I'm terrified of the road ahead. The damage that's been done to her, I don't know how to undo it."

"I hate to say it, but there's no undoing it. What happened, happened. It's not fair but those horrors will always be with her. Now it's about finding ways to deal with them, to move past them, to create something like a normal life."

"You're right," Keri agreed. "I guess the sooner I accept there's no easy solution, the better it is for both of us."

"I'm glad that's your attitude, partner," Ray said, sitting upright in his chair in a "down to business" way that made Keri nervous. "Because 'sooner' starts pretty much the second you walk out that door."

"What do you mean?"

"I mean that I gave the doctors and nurses strict instructions not to let anyone else in this room besides medical personnel. But you should know that there is an army of people out there champing at the bit."

Despite the pain, Keri used the button on her bedside remote control to force her hospital bed upright.

"What are you talking about? Who's out there?"

"For starters, Lieutenant Hillman, who'd very much like to know why someone I reported dead is in the hospital after conducting a rogue takedown of a sex slavery ring. The rest of the unit has a few questions too, as does LAPD police chief Beecher. The mayor is supposedly here too, along with a couple of city supervisors."

"Is that all?" Keri asked sarcastically.

"Actually no. The entire press corps is here. Not just local—national as well. They're setting up for a press conference. They've already had two of them overnight but the big one will be with you and…and Stephen."

"Excuse me?" Keri asked, trying to keep her voice down despite the anger she felt rising in her throat.

"Yeah," Ray said softly. "Your ex-husband has been out there doing interviews, saying how happy he is to have Evie back, how he always believed they'd be reunited one day."

"Are you kidding me? Every time I went to him for help, he told me I was crazy to keep looking for her. He said I needed to accept that she was dead. He resented me even bringing her up."

"I know, Keri. But that's not what he's saying for the cameras now. And he's been pretty aggressive about trying to get in here to see her. The only reason he hasn't is that I convinced the doctors not to let anyone else in while she's asleep, at least not until you were awake and could give consent. But once she wakes up, that won't fly. He *is* her father."

"Barely," Keri muttered.

Ray glared at her and nodded in the direction of Evie, who was beginning to wake up.

"I'm going to step outside so you can have some private time," he whispered. "But don't expect that to last long."

He blew Keri a kiss and closed the door just as Evie opened her eyes.

Ray was right. From the moment Keri opened the door to her hospital room, madness reigned. Almost immediately, she was accosted by her ex-husband, Stephen, who insisted on seeing Evie right away.

Despite his lack of interest in her whereabouts in recent years and her sense that his sudden return of paternal instincts was more opportunistic than genuine, she couldn't deny him. Evie was his daughter, after all. And before she'd been taken and everything had fallen apart, he'd been a good, loving, if slightly uninvolved father.

As he tore past her into the room and rushed over to Evie's bedside, Keri saw the rush of relief in his eyes at the realization that she really was alive. Maybe he'd insisted Keri was crazy to believe it all those years because allowing himself to share in that hope was just too painful. She could understand that desire. But she couldn't forgive it. Evie was their daughter and he should have kept fighting for her rather than just giving up.

Evie was still out of it and after about fifteen minutes she drifted off again. The nurses shooed everyone out so she could rest and Keri watched her through the door's window as she dealt with a succession of visitors.

First was Lieutenant Hillman, who looked torn between wanting to ream Keri out for faking her death and being involved in the infiltration of the Hollywood estate and just being happy she was alive and reunited with her daughter. Ultimately, he chose to focus on the latter, making only a passing mention of a major debrief down the line.

The rest of the team showed up to offer their well wishes too. Detectives Suarez, Edgerton, Patterson, and even Frank Brody, the generally surly vet just weeks from retirement, seemed truly happy for her. Only Officer Jamie Castillo was slightly reserved and Keri suspected she knew why.

Castillo almost certainly wondered why Keri let her think she was dead; why she didn't call her in to help break into the Hollywood estate and instead trusted some mall security kid who hadn't even entered the police academy yet.

Keri wanted to explain the truth—that there was a mole in the unit and though she was sure it wasn't Castillo, the only safe play was to keep everyone but Ray out of the loop for now. After all, with his dying words, Jackson Cave had warned her to watch her back and she intended to. That meant staying quiet until the mole was discovered, even if it left Jamie confused and angry.

The press conference was set for 8 a.m. Evie was sleeping comfortably in her room—heavily sedated on the recommendation of her doctors. Despite Stephen's suggestion that it might be cathartic for her to participate, Keri refused to let her anywhere near cameras or reporters.

Just before it started, Keri was pulled to the side by Reena Beecher, formerly the captain of her division and now chief of the entire LAPD. In her mid-fifties with deep worry lines and grayish-black hair tied up in a tight bun, Beecher was tall and slender, with angular features that reminded Keri of a hawk constantly in search of prey. She seemed about to say something when the mayor and several members of the Board of Supervisors walked up behind her.

"We ready to get this thing started, Chief?" he asked pleasantly. The mayor was tall and dark-haired and couldn't have been much older than Keri.

"Yes, Mayor Alvarez. Have you had the chance to meet Detective Locke yet?" Beecher asked.

"I haven't had the honor," the mayor said, shaking her hand. "I want to save some of my praise for the cameras but for now I'll just say thank you. I know you were trying to save your daughter. But in the process, you saved a lot of other young girls. Isn't that right, Carl?"

"Absolutely, Mr. Mayor," said an older, well-manicured man standing to Alvarez's right, who stepped forward at the mention of his name. "Carl Weatherford, County Supervisor for the Third District. Nice to meet you, Detective. The Vista estate was in my district. I don't know if you're aware, but each Supervisory District represents almost two million people. That's close to triple what a member of Congress represents. It's a huge, diverse community. And you've done an incredible service to our community by disrupting such an unsavory business."

"'Unsavory' strikes me as a pretty mild word for what was going on there," Keri said.

"Of course," Weatherford agreed. "I guess when something is that awful, I tend to hide behind euphemisms. But you're right. It doesn't begin to capture it."

An aide came over and indicated it was time to start.

"See you up there," the mayor said before heading to his seat, followed closely by Weatherford and the other supervisors who had managed to escape Keri's disdain.

She started to make her way to her seat when Chief Beecher grabbed her wrist and leaned in close.

"Detective Locke," she said quietly. "Remember to keep your cool up there. There will be a lot of grandstanding. There will be a lot of credit-taking. There will be a lot of blame-placing. But you need to keep your eye on the ball. You have your daughter back. The sex ring and the man who ran it have been exposed. But you are still on suspension and under investigation. Under the circumstances, the fact that you are an honest-to-goodness hero should get you enough brownie points to bury the mistakes you've made in the past. But only if you stay cool and let me help you. Do you think you can do that?"

"I can try."

"Trying won't be enough," Beecher said, looking at her sharply with her hard, birdlike eyes, the ones that had seen even more cruelty and violence than Keri's had. "It's going to be hardball up there and you're going to have to sit there and bite the bullet if you want to come out clean on the other side of this. Are you capable of that? Are you able to give bland, inoffensive answers to biting, accusatory press questions? Are you able to commend people you don't believe deserve it? Because in the past, that's hasn't been a sure thing."

"I didn't have my daughter back then, Chief Beecher," Keri told her. "So I was more about shooting bullets than biting them. But I have her now. And if saying the right thing or just keeping my mouth shut is what it will take to move past all this and get her started on a normal life, then that's what I'm prepared to do."

"Glad to hear it," Beecher said, offering a rare smile. "Let's do this thing."

For most of the press conference, keeping her promise to Chief Beecher wasn't too hard. The mayor was effusive in his praise of law enforcement generally and a mother's love and dedication in particular.

He promised to root out the corruption that was currently rocking the city and indicated that some of the community's biggest powerbrokers were among the clients of what the press was already dubbing "The Hollywood Child Brothel."

Supervisor Weatherford parroted the mayor's comments, with particular commendation for the LA County SWAT unit which had converged so quickly on the scene. Chief Beecher then got up and updated everyone on the status of the investigation before praising Keri, Ray, and a new recruit to the police academy named Keith Fogerty, who had assisted in the operation. She then surprised and angered the assembled reporters by saying that while Detective Locke would be making a brief statement, she would not be taking any questions at this time.

As Keri got to her feet with the assistance of Lieutenant Hillman, who was seated beside her, she saw someone else rise from across the platform. It was Stephen. As she approached the podium, he smiled and met her there, taking her hand. She felt a pit of uneasiness stir in her gut as he leaned in toward the microphone.

What the hell is he doing?

"Thank you all so much for coming," he said before she had a chance to open her mouth. "This is very hard because the truth is that losing Evie cost Keri and me so much. Not just our marriage but something deeper—our sense of optimism about the world. But one thing we never lost was our faith that our daughter would come back to us, right, Keri?"

She stood there, frozen, unable to speak. It wasn't true, not even a little bit. How many times had she gone to him, begging him to help her, to give her the money to help pay for a private investigator to follow up leads? And every time, he'd refused, acting as if the very request was an affront to the new life he'd created with his crappy actress wife and his bratty little new son. He'd lost faith a long time ago.

But what was she supposed to say? That it was all crap? What if Evie was watching from her room? Should Keri reveal that her own father was more interested in moving on with his picture-perfect life than finding the daughter he suspected was dead and feared would be a horrible complication if she was still alive?

Stephen was looking at her, the smile still plastered to his lips but his bluffing eyes filled with apprehension, wondering if she'd go so far as to call him out at the expense of their only daughter's love for her father. She wouldn't.

"There was always hope," she said quietly.

"That's right," he agreed, the relief obvious in his voice. "We always had hope. Sometimes Keri would come to me, after a brutal case, fearing the same fate might have befallen Evie. And I would tell her not to lose the drive that kept her searching, the sense of purpose that fueled her. And she'd return to the fight, stronger than before. We were no longer husband and wife. But in that way, we were still a team."

Keri felt the bile rise up in her throat. She wanted to retch so badly. But she forced the urge down, remembering what Chief Beecher had told her. Whatever grandstanding Stephen engaged in, whatever bullets she had to bite, whatever glad-handing and politicking was required to get her through this event and back to a normal life with her daughter, Keri would endure it.

Because she had endured far worse. And because this wasn't about her.

It was about Evie.

CHAPTER TWENTY FOUR

One thought stuck in Evie Locke's head, no matter how hard she tried to push it out.

Everything hurts.

It was the day after the big press conference—the one she'd slept through—and she was adjusting herself in the hospital bed, trying not to grimace as she sat upright. The pain from the surgery was still there but she didn't want to worry her mom. She had overheard a nurse saying that "the poor woman never goes to sleep until her daughter drifts off and even then it's fitful." Evie didn't want to make it worse.

She waited patiently as her mom gathered herself for what was clearly going to be an uncomfortable conversation. For half a second, she considered how weird it was that she automatically thought of the woman across from her as "Mom" now. The last time they'd really spoken she was calling her "Mommy" and yet she couldn't bring herself to think the word, much less say it.

Not that it really fit anyway. Her mom had aged a lot in the last six years. Maybe the image Evie had in her head all those years was a fantasy. But she didn't remember the flecks of gray hair or crow's feet or rough cheeks or red eyes.

Of course, her mom was almost thirty-six now instead of the thirty years old she'd been when Evie was taken. And she was recovering from the fight with the Cave lawyer guy (and, from what the nurses said, some kind of car crash and another fight).

But the age seemed to be deeper than that. Evie suspected it came from years of worrying about whether her daughter was alive or dead, what kind of abuse she was suffering. And it came from doing a job that made her mom constantly see other girls that reminded her of what might be happening to her own daughter. It was actually amazing that she didn't look worse.

She wondered what could have her mom so tongue-tied. They'd already discussed how she'd have to talk to detectives about everything that had happened to her the night of the Vista. She knew she was going to have to go to therapy. She knew she'd need a few more surgeries in the coming months to fix some damage that had been done to her "internally" over the years. She knew her mom and dad were divorced and that her dad had remarried some actress and had a little boy. What else was there?

"So honey," her mom began, "the doctors are letting you leave the hospital today. And I wanted to discuss the plan moving forward."

"Okay."

"Your father and I have talked and we've agreed that for the next little while, it might be better to have you homeschooled. That way, you can catch up to your grade level at your own pace. Plus we don't want to throw you back into a school environment right away. That could be pretty intense for anyone, especially…"

"Especially for a kid whose face has been plastered all over the news because she was going to be a ritual sacrifice at a Hollywood sex party. I get it, Mom—makes sense."

"Okay then," her mom said, "so far, so good. The other thing is living arrangements. For now, the plan is for you to live most of the time at my apartment in Playa del Rey. But you'll also spend some time at your dad's house in Brentwood so you can get acclimated there as well. Since school isn't an issue, we don't think it should cause too many complications. How does that sound?"

The truth was that leaving this hospital room terrified her. The truth was that the idea of school and multiple bedrooms was almost more than she could process. The truth was that she knew she wasn't wanted in one of those homes. But that was the wrong answer. So she gave the right one.

"Sounds like a plan," she said with as much enthusiasm as she could muster.

*

Her mom's apartment smelled like Chinese food. It made sense considering she lived right above a Chinese restaurant. The smell was pleasant but extremely strong and Evie figured she'd either learn to get used to it or grow to hate Chinese food pretty fast.

Her mom looked so apprehensive as she showed her around that making a joke about the smell didn't seem appropriate. It might not be taken as intended. So Evie pretended not to notice.

She got the apartment tour, which didn't take long, considering the place had a living room, a kitchen, a dining nook, a bathroom, and two bedrooms.

"It's cozy," she said appreciatively when asked what she thought.

That made her mom laugh. It was the first real laugh she'd heard from her since the rescue.

"What?" Evie asked.

"Nothing—that was just very diplomatic of you. You'd make a great real estate agent. Let me know if the sheets are okay for you. I wasn't sure what you'd like. Ponies and rainbows didn't seem right. But neither did Renoir watercolors."

"What's Renoir?" Evie asked.

"Oh, he was an artist."

"I guess that's the kind of thing I'll be learning in homeschooling. Can I ask you a question?"

"Of course," her mom said, although her tone sounded like she wasn't so sure.

"When did you get this apartment?"

"Last year."

"Why did you get an apartment with two bedrooms when you and Dad were divorced?"

"That's easy, sweetie. I was saving the second room for you."

*

That night, her mom invited over a couple of her friends and they had pizza and played board games. Evie thought she was a little worried about being alone in the apartment with her. There were so many people bustling around all the time at the hospital that there weren't a lot of quiet moments and she suspected her mom was worried about how to handle them. To be honest, Evie was too, so she welcomed the company.

Her mom's friend Mags was wild. She looked like this Amazon woman, super tall and gorgeous with blazing red hair and big boobs. But she had this really strong Southern accent that Evie was pretty sure she played up for effect. She acted all fancy like she was in *Gone with the Wind* or something but then she'd burp real loud and blame it on Evie's mom. It was pretty hilarious.

Evie actually already recognized her mom's friend Ray, even though she pretended not to. She remembered he used to sometimes ask her mom to consult on some cases back when she was a professor at LMU.

She also knew his voice from a conversation she overheard when he and her mom were talking in the hospital and thought she was still asleep after she had some surgery. He was telling her mom that her dad was telling everyone he'd always known Evie would come back. Her mom got so mad because she said that it wasn't true—that her dad thought she was crazy to keep looking for Evie and that he didn't even like for her mom to talk about her anymore. When Ray walked in and said hi, Evie realized it was the same person.

Her mom said he was her partner now, that they worked missing persons cases together. She didn't say it but Evie could tell they were more than just partners, more than close friends even. But even though it was obvious just from looking that they liked each other, her mom didn't say anything about it, so Evie didn't mention it either. She figured her mom had her reasons and she'd tell her when she was ready.

*

When Keri woke up to the screaming that night, it was 2:04 a.m. She had grabbed her gun, cocked it, and pointed it at the bedroom door before she realized it was coming from Evie's room.

She dashed over and turned on the light. Her daughter was sitting bolt upright in the bed, clutching her pillow to her chest, sweat pouring down her face. Keri put the gun on the hall bookshelf before Evie could see it and hurried over to the bed.

She sat down and pulled her daughter close. Evie dropped the pillow and wrapped her arms around her mom instead. For several minutes, neither of them spoke.

"Do you want to talk about it?" Keri eventually asked quietly.

Evie shook her head.

"That's okay. You have your first therapy session tomorrow. If you want to talk about it then, you can. For now, just rest, all right?"

"Will you stay with me?" Evie asked plaintively, her voice partly muffled as her face was burrowed in Keri's T-shirt.

"Of course, sweetie. Let me just turn down the lights a bit."

"But not off!" Evie insisted.

"Not off," Keri agreed, "just lower."

She turned on the reading light before turning off the overhead one.

"I'll be right back," she promised.

She returned the gun to her bedroom, reminding herself that she didn't need it with all the exterior cameras Ray had set up outside the apartment, along with the roving patrol car that had been assigned to monitor the area 24/7. Neither of them considered Jackson Cave's claim that the conspiracy didn't end with him to be an idle threat.

She grabbed a washcloth from the bathroom, wet it, and got back into bed beside Evie. She dabbed her daughter's forehead, mopping up the beads of sweat that clung to her brow.

After a few minutes, Evie's breathing slowed and she curled up beside Keri, who was lying on her back. She wrapped her arms around her mother's waist and drifted off, whimpering occasionally. When she did, Keri would coo softly or hum a lullaby until she settled. This lasted all night.

CHAPTER TWENTY FIVE

Keri sat in the waiting room of Evie's therapist's office, trying to keep her eyes open. After initially meeting the doctor together, Keri had left them to finish the session without her. Evie had been inside for about twenty minutes and the quiet solitude and bland wallpaper of the room was making staying awake a challenge.

Suddenly an image of Evie, sweaty and scared in her bed, popped into Keri's half-conscious brain and her eyes popped open. Tingling with adrenaline as if it had just happened, she knew she wouldn't be able to catnap. She decided to take advantage of the free time and took out her phone.

Rita Skraeling picked up on the second ring. Rita ran the South Bay Shared Home, a residential facility in Redondo Beach that served as transitional housing for girls who were trying to get out of the world of underage prostitution.

That's where Keri had taken Susan Granger, the girl who had tipped her off that Evie was to be the Blood Prize at the Vista. Keri had found Susan hooking on a street corner in Venice last year and rescued her from her pimp.

Since then, Susan had made remarkable progress. Under Rita's mentorship, she'd resumed school, done intensive therapy and, inspired to become a detective like Keri, even started a Nancy Drew book club. If anyone could offer "on the ground" advice on how to help teenage girls find their way back from the horrors of forced prostitution, Rita was that person.

"I was wondering when you'd call," Rita's raspy, cigarette-tinged voice said without a formal greeting. "Save dozens of girls from sexual slavery and you think you're too big for your britches, do you?"

"Sorry, Rita," Keri said, laughing despite herself. "I've been a little busy lately."

"That's okay, Detective. I figured you'd call when you had the time. But I can't say our friend Susan will be as forgiving. She's been bouncing off the walls waiting to hear from you. I think she's also expecting some kind of civilian commendation from Chief Beecher for that tip about the Vista."

"Will you let her know how grateful I am and tell her I'll call when I can? I just have my hands full right now."

"I already have and I will again," Rita assured her. "I can tell from your voice that something's eating at you. Why don't you tell me what's going on?"

"It's Evie," Keri admitted. "I'm just not sure how to treat her. With all those other girls, I had some distance. I had some perspective. But this is my baby. I breastfed her. I put her hair in pigtails. And now I have to take her for reconstructive surgery on her uterus. I feel like I'm suffering whiplash every other second."

"Detective... Keri, I'm going to give you some advice. It may not always work. But I think it's a good general rule. You ready for it?"

"I am," Keri said.

"Evie was eight when she was taken. The girl you have now is still your daughter, but she's a different person with different experiences. She's not eight anymore. She's what, thirteen now?"

"Fourteen next month," Keri noted.

"Exactly. Even if she hadn't been through all these horrors, this would be a difficult time—raising a teenage girl as a single mother. But you've got it ten times worse. Still, you have to treat her as the person she is, not the little girl she was."

"What do you mean?"

"I mean, she's Evelyn Locke, an almost-fourteen-year-old young person. Your baby is gone. Your pigtailed princess doesn't exist anymore. Those monsters snuffed her out. Don't get me wrong. She still needs you desperately. She may still revert to being a little girl at times. But don't baby her. You have to accept who she is now so she can start to accept it too. The sooner she sees that you are willing to move forward rather than dwell on the past, the sooner she'll start to do it too."

"Rita, can I ask you something?"

"One more question," Rita said, "but then I have to start charging you."

"How is it that you can dispense such pearls of wisdom but you can't seem to quit your Newport addiction?"

"That's the true mystery, isn't it?"

*

The main word Evie would have used to describe her first visit to her dad's house was "awkward." Her mom stuck around for the first five minutes, doing her best to be polite.

It was almost funny to see her standing in the foyer of his fancy house, wearing her bulky sweatshirt to cover the bandages on her ribs, limping around in the walking boot meant to protect her chipped shinbone, with the wrap on her left hand to protect the reconstructed skin on her palm and the angry set of nine stitches running down the right side of her face.

Her mom seemed very out of place amid all the art and expensive furniture. And even though she was obviously reluctant to leave Evie alone, she knew she had to. Besides, she had to go to a funeral for some FBI agent who had died in a bomb blast while investigating a case with her last week.

Of course, once she left, Evie was the one who felt out of place. Her dad introduced her to his wife, Shalene, who invited her into the kitchen for a snack. She said their three-year-old son, Sammy, was napping, but would be up soon.

Her dad was a talent agent at a major agency and Shalene was one of his clients. She was an actress who had a recurring role on a sitcom called *All Aboard*. Evie had watched about a half dozen episodes out of curiosity. It was like a half-hour version of *The Love Boat*. Shalene showed up every other episode or so as the assistant cruise director who was always screwing up and causing headaches for her boss. Evie thought the show was awful and Shalene was terrible on it, mostly there to act dumb and wear really tight clothes. She was great at that at least.

Both of them tried to be nice to her but there was nothing to talk about. It's not like they could ask her about school or how her week had been. Shalene brought up a few singers and movies but realized after a bit that Evie hadn't really had many chances to keep up with pop culture in the last few years.

It was almost a relief when Sammy woke up. He was blond, super-cute, and pretty clearly a spoiled brat. When Shalene introduced Evie as his half-sister, he threw his fruit cup at her and then threw a tantrum. Her dad apologized repeatedly but Evie was just happy for the attention to be on someone else.

When her mom picked her up two hours later, she had a searing pain in her stomach. Her mom took her to urgent care and that's when Evie learned what an ulcer was.

*

137

The next day, Mags and Evie were sitting in the mall food court waiting for her mom to get back from the bathroom when she decided to ask what was really going on with her mom and Ray.

To her credit, Mags didn't get flustered or anything. She just took a sip of her iced tea and in that fantastic drawl, asked Evie a question.

"What do *you* think is going on, darling?"

"I think they're into each other for sure, definitely having sex, maybe dating. But they don't want anyone to know because they're partners and that's against the rules or something."

Mags nodded in a way that didn't confirm anything other than that she had heard what was said.

"How would you feel if any of that was the case, Evelyn?"

Evie noticed that in the last few days, Mom, Ray, and Mags had started calling her Evelyn instead of Evie. No one had asked her permission. But she kind of liked it so she didn't stop them or say anything.

"I think I'd be cool with it. Dad has his bimbo wife. I don't see why Mom can't get a little action too."

A look flickered across Mags's face that made Evelyn wonder if she'd said something wrong. But it was gone in a flash.

"Do you think that's what your mother is after with Raymond—a little action?"

Evelyn shrugged. Mags seemed to be debating how to proceed. Then she glanced up and saw Evelyn's mom heading back in their direction.

"Look, darling, it's not my place to say, as much as I would dearly love to. But I think you might want to talk about this with your mom. I think she wants to protect your feelings. And it seems you care about her happiness. Maybe it would be best if you were both straight with each other. But maybe once I've said my goodbyes."

*

That night, as they were looking through old photo albums from when Evelyn was a toddler, she brought it up.

"I know about Ray, Mom," Evelyn said out of the blue.

"What do you know?" her mom asked, deliberately not looking up from the photo she was staring at.

"I know you're more than just partners."

"That's true," she said, finally looking up at Evelyn. "How do you feel about that?"

"I'm cool with it. I like him. He's nice but not 'fake' nice. I like that he looks scary until you get to know him a bit."

"Yeah, I like that about him too," she said.

"Is he your boyfriend?" Evelyn asked.

"It's a little complicated. But yeah, I guess he kind of is."

"Weird," Evelyn said.

"What's weird?"

"It's just weird to say 'my mom has a boyfriend.'"

"You have no idea."

*

Keri was ready for the screaming that night.

It usually started around two or three in the morning. If she put Evelyn to sleep and went back to her own room it would resume again momentarily. The only way to prevent it completely was to stay in bed with her the rest of the night.

For whatever reason, on this night Evelyn just couldn't get back to sleep again.

"What are you thinking about?" Keri asked.

"Can I tell you something, Mom?' she asked. "Promise you won't get mad?"

"You can tell me anything, sweetie."

"I hate sleeping," she said. "Every time I do, the nightmares come back."

"Do you want to talk about them? It might help."

"There are so many. Most of them blend together. After a few years, I learned to block a lot of what happened out, to just make myself go numb. But a few stick out."

"Like what, sweetie?"

"I still sometimes have nightmares of the day I was taken in the park, of that man running off with me and you chasing us, trying to catch up."

"I still have nightmares about that too," Keri admitted quietly.

"And sometimes I flash back to a few months ago, when I saw you for a second as that old guy shoved me in the van in the middle of the night. Do you remember that?"

139

"I do," Keri said, remembering the night she'd come so close to saving Evelyn, before having her ripped away once again.

"For a second I thought I was safe—that you would rescue me—and then he smashed his van into your car and sped away. And I thought you were dead."

"I'm so sorry about that, sweetie."

"It's not your fault," Evelyn said. "I was just worried for you. It took a long time to find out you hadn't died. That was rough. But it wasn't the worst."

"What was the worst, sweetie? You can tell me."

After a few seconds, Evelyn decided to.

"There was one man. I guess he considered me a favorite because he kept coming back. No matter where I got moved, no matter who I was living with, he'd always show up every few months."

"Could you identify him?" Keri asked before she could stop herself, realizing too late that this wasn't an interrogation, it was a confession. But Evelyn didn't seem to care. She continued, staring off at some distant spot on the far wall.

"No. He always wore a mask. I don't think he wanted me to know who he was. But he was old. I could tell from the wrinkles at the edge of the mask on his face and because of…his body. And I think he was rich. He always wore fancy suits and had on strong cologne. But that wasn't what stuck with me."

"What then?"

"He would bring this needle with him and inject something into me. It would make it so I couldn't move. I would be awake. My eyes were open. I could…feel things. I just couldn't move my body at all. And while he did things to me, he would hold up his phone in front of my face so I couldn't look away and show me videos—videos of you. From the press conference after I was taken. From interviews you did after saving a kid. He always had something. And while he did what he wanted to me, he'd whisper things about how you didn't love me, how you were never coming for me, how you'd moved on to other kids, how this was the closest I'd ever get you. I could feel the tears streaming down my face and he'd giggle at it. He'd say you didn't want some crybaby for a daughter."

"I'm so sorry," Keri said, overwhelmed at the emotional abuse her daughter had suffered on top of the all the physical brutality she'd endured.

"I thought I had gotten over it. But I guess what that lawyer, Cave, said on the balcony that night opened it all up again."

"What Cave said?" Keri asked.

"About me always having to look back at my degraded face in the mirror for the rest of my life…"

She stopped talking and looked Keri in the eyes.

"That's why I can't sleep."

*

Evelyn's third visit to her dad's was the worst.

He was late getting home because of a work meeting so she was stuck hanging out with Shalene and Sammy. The little boy, whom Evelyn had never seen be pleasant, was screaming about not getting a third rice cereal bar when she arrived.

Shalene handed him off to the nanny and tried to make small talk but her heart clearly wasn't in it. Part of Evelyn felt a little bad for her. She was married to a workaholic, had a horror of a child (although that was partly her own fault), and now had to contend with a damaged stepdaughter who had shown up out of nowhere. Even so, Evelyn could feel the chill coming off her from across the room.

When her father arrived home, he announced that the two of them would be seeing the latest movie from one of his clients, whom he described as the "hot new young hunk of the moment." Evelyn agreed to go, happy for the excuse not to talk.

The actor was indeed cute, although it turned out he was more like the seventh person in the credits than the star. And the movie, about a group of FBI trainees who take on a sea monster that rises out of the ocean for some confusing reason, was a loud waste of time.

When it was over, they went for ice cream and Evelyn could tell right away that her dad had something unpleasant he was preparing to say. She kept her mouth shut, enjoying him squirm a little bit.

"So, Evie," he said. "I have some exciting news I want to share with you."

"It's Evelyn now," she reminded him.

"Right. Anyway, Shalene and I have decided that we're going to pursue getting primary custody of you."

"What?" she demanded, feeling a ball of panic form in her chest. "Have you talked to Mom about this?"

"Not yet. I wanted to let you know first."

"Why are you doing this?" she asked incredulously.

"Isn't it obvious? Your mother does her best, Evie. But her circumstances aren't the greatest. She lives in that place over a diner."

"It's a restaurant."

"Whatever. It's not the best environment for you, with people coming and going at all hours. And her job doesn't have the most stable hours. Sometimes she's working all night on a case. Is she just going to leave you in that apartment by yourself?"

"Dad, not every detail has to be worked out this second. I've been back less than a week."

"I understand that, Evie. But I want to establish the right patterns up front, the right lifestyle, and I just don't think she provides it. Her living situation isn't...appropriate."

"Are you talking about Ray?"

"Yes, Evie," he replied. "I don't want you exposed to them...shacking up."

"Are you kidding me, Dad? I've been raped hundreds of times in the last year alone, thousands since I was taken. I'm being treated for multiple sexually transmitted diseases. The doctors aren't sure I'll ever have kids because my insides are so torn up. I've been beaten and drugged and used as a human sex doll. I've seen girls murdered in front of me for saying the wrong thing to the wrong guy. And you think me seeing Mom cuddling with her boyfriend is bad role modeling?"

"Jesus, Evie," he said, looking around nervously at the now silent ice cream shop. "That's not what I..."

"No, just stop," she said, holding up her hand. "It's not like you really want me anyway. I know you gave up on me a long time ago. I know you thought I was dead. I know part of you hoped I was dead because it was easier than dealing with the mess that is the real me. I know having me back is an inconvenience to your perfect little life with your ice queen wife and your spoiled little prince of a son. You don't want me. You just don't want to look bad by not going through the motions."

"That's not true, Evie!"

"I told you, it's Evelyn! Just take me home."

She didn't speak to him on the ride back to Playa del Rey. Nor did she say goodbye when he dropped her off on the street in front of the apartment. She got out and slammed the door without looking back, taking the stairs two at a time.

Keri returned from the hospital just as the sun was setting around 5 p.m. The doctors had taken off the walking boot, giving her permission to put her full weight on her leg, as long as she didn't overdo it.

She saw the text from Stephen saying he'd dropped Evelyn off at the apartment around 3:30 that afternoon. Apparently, the visit hadn't gone very well and he wanted to talk. She didn't feel up to it at the moment and decided to wait until after she'd had a chance to hear Evelyn's version of events.

She knew something was off the second she unlocked the door and stepped inside. All the lights were off but she could hear the water running in the bathroom. She pulled out her personal gun and edged into the living room. Nothing seemed out of place.

Slowly and quietly, she moved past Evelyn's empty room. The bathroom door was slightly ajar and she could see what looked like the flicker of candlelight emanating from inside. She took the safety off the gun and shoved the door open a bit with her toe.

Multiple candles were lit, sitting on the shelf above the sink. Evelyn's clothes from that day were lying on the floor, soaked. Then Keri noticed that the entire bathroom floor was covered in a thin layer of water. She pushed the door open all the way.

Evelyn was lying in the tub with her eyes closed, her arms resting on the sides. The water in the tub, more red than clear, was spilling out onto the floor. Blood was dripping down her daughter's fingertips from deep cuts in both wrists. A kitchen knife rested on the tile below.

"No!" Keri heard herself scream as she dropped the gun and rushed to her baby's side. She grabbed a towel and wrapped it tightly around Evelyn's right wrist as she looked for any sign of life.

"Evie!" she screamed. "Evie, wake up!"

She grabbed a second towel and wrapped it around her daughter's left wrist before lifting her naked body out of the tub and laying her on the bathroom floor. She took out her phone, dialed 911, put it on speaker, and placed it on the edge of the sink before kneeling down and listening for breath sounds. Hearing none, she began CPR.

The phone rang and after about four minutes of a recorded voice telling her to continue to hold, a voice came on the line.

"Nine-one-one emergency. What are you reporting?"

"This is Detective Keri Locke, LAPD. I need an ambulance at the 400 block of Culver Boulevard in Playa del Rey. My daughter has attempted suicide. She slit her wrists and has lost a lot of blood. She's unconscious. I'm performing CPR but she's not responding."

"All right, Detective, Stay calm. An ambulance will be there very soon."

"Get it here now, God dammit!"

CHAPTER TWENTY SIX

THREE MONTHS LATER

Keri stood at the front door for a long time before she finally knocked. She forced a smile onto her face even though she found it hard to remember how to form one. Her stomach twisted up in a knot despite her best efforts.

Breathe. Remember to breathe, Keri.

After a few seconds, a familiar raspy voice on the other side of the door shouted "Hello," calming her a little even before she saw the accompanying face.

Rita Skraeling undid the multiple locks and pulled the door open. It dwarfed her tiny, wizened frame, and the bright April sun cast an unflattering spotlight on her wrinkled, spotted skin. She adjusted her tight bun of gray hair and stared at Keri through her thick glasses.

"How's it going, pretty lady?" she wheezed.

"You tell me," Keri replied. "Is she ready?"

"Are any of us ever truly ready?"

"Okay, Yoda," Keri said, rolling her eyes. "Is she ready to get in the car, I mean?"

"I think they're just finishing up Book Club. Want to come in?"

"Yes, please," Keri said, trying not to sound too anxious as Rita closed the door behind her. "How'd it go last night?"

"Not too bad, I think. They spent most of the evening chattering away in Susan and Darla's room. I mostly left them be."

"Did she seem, you know, pretty well adjusted?"

"All things considered, I'd say so," Rita said as they walked down the hall.

"All things considered," Keri repeated, considering the weight of those words.

"Well, you have to keep some perspective, Keri. Three months ago, your daughter tried to kill herself. To be where she is now is pretty impressive."

"You don't think I'm rushing her?"

"Personally, I think waiting any longer would be coddling her. After getting out of the ICU, she spent how long in the psychiatric hospital?"

"A month."

"Where she got intense therapy," Rita noted. "And how many days did you visit her there?"

"Every day."

"And after they gave her authorization to leave, you decided to ease her transition back into the world by having her stay here with us for a while. How long was that again?"

"Another month," Keri reminded her.

"That's right," Rita said. "I thought that was a pretty good idea, by the way. Getting to talk to other girls who went through what she did offered a whole different kind of therapy from what she got at the hospital. Plus, she got to eat lots of s'mores. Who doesn't love s'mores? How often did you visit her here by the way?"

"Every day?"

"Oh yes, now I remember," Rita said wryly. "I couldn't get you out of here. So after we finally sent you two on your way, you took her home. And things have gone okay there, with the homeschooling with the tutor and the tour of the school she'll be going to and play dates with the neighbor girl?"

"I don't think they call them play dates when they're fourteen," Keri said. "But I take your point. Things have gone pretty well. Fewer nightmares, medication seems to be working. It was kind of a bummer to celebrate her birthday in a psychiatric hospital. Still, the therapist says she's making progress."

Rita stopped walking just before turning the corner of the hallway.

"And you're concerned that you're rushing her?" she asked skeptically.

"You have to admit, it's a lot in a pretty short amount of time. And then she asks to spend her last Saturday night before starting school back here. I didn't know if she was maybe backsliding."

Rita smiled. Keri was surprised at the warmth of it. Very occasionally this woman who seemed so hard and tough let her guard down. It felt as rare as an eclipse and it usually meant something significant.

"First," Rita said, "it *is* a lot. But Evelyn's been through far more than this. She's tough. She can take it. Second, maybe she is a little nervous about starting school tomorrow. But I consider it healthy that she decided to seek out her support system when she started feeling that way. These girls are part of that support system now."

They rounded the corner and Keri saw four girls seated in the sun room that served as the library. Susan Granger was leading them in a discussion of their most recent Nancy Drew book club entry.

Keri was amazed at how healthy and self-assured the girl looked, nothing like the teenage prostitute she'd found on the street last year. She was wearing sweats, with her blonde hair tied back in a loose ponytail. Her face, free of heavy makeup and fear, appeared almost serene.

Evelyn sat in a beanbag chair by the window, her head down in concentration, studying a page and nodding in agreement at something Susan was saying. She seemed to sense eyes on her and looked up.

"Mom," she exclaimed happily, her face breaking into a smile. She dropped her book on the floor and leapt up, rushed over, and wrapped her arms around Keri.

"Nice sleepover?"

"It was really great," she said. "Have you ever heard of 'Mad Libs'?"

"I have. Wow, that's borderline educational. I'm impressed."

"Not so much," Susan said, walking over, "especially when you use 'fart' as your noun every time. Hi, Detective Locke."

"Hi, Susan," Keri said, pulling her in for a hug. Then assuming a mock angry tone, she added, "I hope you didn't teach my daughter that word."

"Me? Never."

"No, you, never. Well, I hate to cut book club short but Evelyn and I have to do some last-minute clothes shopping before the big day tomorrow."

"Oh yeah," Susan said. "Don't you start back as a detective tomorrow too?"

"I do. I feel like it's the first day back at school for me as well."

"So they cleared you in that investigation and everything?" Susan asked.

"My goodness, Susan Granger, I didn't know you had time to read the metro section of the *Times* in addition to all your book club selections. The situation is a little complicated but the short version is that my suspension is lifted for now and I'm allowed to go after the bad guys again."

"They better look out!" Susan said.

"Yes," Rita agreed. "I think they'd better."

She saw them to the door and gave them both hugs as they left.

"Bye, Ev!" Susan called to Evelyn from down the hall, using the nickname she'd enthusiastically embraced.

"Bye, Suze!" Evelyn called back, waving.

Keri smiled involuntarily at the nicknames and kept the grin plastered on her face even after she saw her daughter's waving hand and caught a fleeting glimpse of the ugly red scar that ran horizontally along the inside of her wrist.

CHAPTER TWENTY SEVEN

Despite everything, Keri was nervous. On the surface, there was no reason to be. Everything had gone well that morning. She had gone into Evelyn's room to get her up for school and found her already awake, dressed and reading.

School didn't start until 8 a.m. but that's when Keri's shift started so she'd arranged to drop Evelyn at a neighbor's house at 7:45. Keri knew this kind of arrangement wasn't unusual for working parents. But this one was a little out of the ordinary.

The family she had dropped Evelyn with was the Raineys. What made the circumstances different was that their then twelve-year-old daughter, Jessica, had been abducted by a religious fanatic who planned to kill her. Keri had managed to find and save her just in time. That all happened only days before Keri rescued Evelyn.

It just so happened that Jessica and Evelyn were the same age, would be attending the same school, and lived half a mile from each other. Tim and Carolyn Rainey had insisted on having Keri and Evelyn over for dinner a few times in recent months. The girls had bonded, partly over ridiculous TV shows and partly, Keri suspected, because they had both experienced horrors few other kids their age could even imagine. So the Raineys had no problem taking Evelyn to school.

With carpooling resolved, Keri had to admit that there must be another reason she was sitting anxiously in her car in the LAPD West Los Angeles Pacific Division parking lot. The truth was it was probably multiple reasons.

One had nothing to do with work and she tried to push it out of her head. Despite the fact that it was an argument with him that had precipitated Evelyn's suicide attempt, Stephen was still pursuing primary custody. He'd hired a big-time law firm that was already drowning Keri in paperwork. She had yet to hire a lawyer.

The other issues that had her insides churning were at least work-related. First and foremost, she wasn't sure just how safe her job really was. She had hinted at it to Susan but her employment as a member of the LAPD was still not secure.

Her original suspension was a result of her killing Brian "the Collector" Wickwire," the man who had abducted Evelyn. If she were to be drugged with truth serum, Keri might admit that, in a fit of rage, she had choked Wickwire to death, even as he was already at death's door due to a massive head wound suffered when they both fell ten feet onto concrete during a fight.

But there was no way to prove it. Besides, the only person who seemed interested in doing so up until recently was Jackson Cave, who wanted to keep Keri off the force so she couldn't interfere with his business. So he'd used his police contacts to get her investigated by Internal Affairs.

And yet, with Cave now dead and the Chief of Police intent on closing the investigation, it was somehow still ongoing, if mostly dormant right now. That meant there was someone else out there with enough power to keep it alive despite the wishes of the most powerful cop in the city and despite Keri's legendary status as the Saver of Lost Children, including her own daughter.

Beyond that unpleasantness, there was also the fact that somewhere in that police station, in her very *unit*, was a mole, someone who was passing information to the very people who had been hiding Evelyn all those years. And even though she had her daughter back now, it still meant she didn't know who she could trust when things got bad. That made her very nervous.

A knock on her window snapped her back to reality. She looked up to see Ray standing by the door. She opened it.

"I've been standing here for a good five minutes watching your mouth contort itself all different ways," he said. "Are you having some kind of seizure?"

"Is that the kind of comment I should expect from a supportive boyfriend?" Keri demanded, trying to sound put out.

"I thought that around here I was just a supportive partner," he replied, assuming a mock secretive tone.

"Are we even partners anymore?" she asked.

It was a reasonable question. When Keri had gone on leave after Evelyn's suicide attempt, Ray was temporarily partnered up with Frank Brody, who had been about to retire.

Brody, a slovenly excuse for a human being and perhaps the laziest detective Keri had ever encountered, generally seemed more interested in finding the right condiments for his hot dog lunches than finding witnesses for his cases. But she had to admit that he had stepped up when she went on leave, postponing his retirement so that Ray could re-team with Keri upon her return, rather than be forced to get a new, long-term partner. Now that she was back, this was to be his last week on the job.

"I think Frank will be happy to make way for you," Ray said. "I've replaced you as his least favorite work colleague."

"Well, I guess I better get in there and see if I can regain the title," Keri said, closing her car door and walking toward the station with a purposeful stride that didn't reflect how she felt inside.

When she stepped through the doors, she was met with a surprise. The whole station team was crowded into the lobby and began applauding her.

"What the...?" she said, looking at Ray.

"Sorry," he replied, shrugging. "They made me keep it a secret."

"What is this for?" she asked, when the clapping had died down.

"It's for never quitting," shouted Detective Manny Suarez. "No matter how many times you got knocked down."

"And for getting the bad guys," Lieutenant Hillman added. "You know how many cases we closed because of that Vista bust? Thirty-two. That made our whole year in January."

"Now we can really rest on our laurels," Frank Brody said.

"So, nothing different for you then, Brody," Keri jabbed.

Everyone laughed and with the glory of the moment punctured, folks began to shuffle out of the lobby and back to work.

"Fun's over," Hillman shouted over the crowd, making it official. "I need Missing Persons in Conference A for a status meeting."

Keri followed Ray into the conference room and took a seat as the rest of the team assembled. The unit wasn't big but they were close-knit and, until the Ghost's warning about a mole, Keri had felt comfortable trusting her safety to almost any of them.

They were led by Lieutenant Cole Hillman, a gruff, graying, paunchy man in his early fifties with deep worry lines and a penchant for short sleeves with loose shirt-tails. Sitting casually to his right was Brody, who made up for his boss's harried demeanor with an unconcerned and worry-free disposition that almost shouted "I'm retiring in a week."

On the other side of Lieutenant Hillman sat Detective Manny Suarez, whose sleepy eyes and forty-something stubble masked a keen intellect and tough, relentless investigative skills. And despite his diminutive size at barely five foot five, he was a pit bull. Keri had seen him take down men a foot taller and a hundred pounds heavier than him using little more than elbows, knees, and fury.

Beside him sat Kevin Edgerton, the unit's resident tech genius. He was the one who typically used his unparalleled computer skills to uncover the connections the rest of them couldn't immediately see. Tall and lanky, he looked like he rarely brushed his brown hair. He had just turned thirty and in recent months, Hillman had been pushing him to do more field work in the hopes of making his street instincts as sharp as his online ones.

To his left was Garrett "Grunt Work" Patterson. In his mid-thirties, Patterson was slender and bookish and wore wire-rimmed glasses. He was even more reticent to go in the field than Edgerton. But unlike with Edgerton, Hillman seemed to have accepted that Patterson had reached his peak.

The guy was a solid tech man but his real gift was his willingness to spend countless hours devouring the driest, most mind-numbing data for patterns than might be useful. Property records, financial reports, even cell phone numbers made him giddy in a way that Keri found borderline disconcerting. She didn't love how he sometimes seemed to forget that they were dealing with crimes and not just statistical thought experiments. Empathy wasn't really his strong suit.

Finally, there was Jamie Castillo, sitting one seat over, next to Ray. She wasn't quite staring daggers at Keri. But she didn't have a warm, welcoming smile on her face either. She was still clearly pissed that she hadn't been looped in when Keri had faked her death after the Black Widower sent her car over that Malibu cliff.

Keri had badly wanted to tell her the truth back then and still ached to now. She was almost certain that there was no way Officer Jamila Cassandra Castillo, who said she joined the police force because she was inspired by Keri, was the mole. But when it came to Evelyn's safety and finding out who had put it at risk, almost certain wasn't enough. So she held her tongue.

"Okay, everyone," Hillman began. "It's nice to have the whole gang back together, even if it's only for a little while.

Brody, since this is your last week, we're switching you out to avoid leaving you with any pending cases at the end of the week. You'll team with Castillo on any cases that look like quick hits."

"After thirty-five years of service, this is how you reward me?" Brody whined. "By pairing me with some rookie female who doesn't have her detective's badge yet?"

"Believe me, Brody," Castillo said, "the feeling's mutual. The thought of spending the next week in a car with you, your sauerkraut hot dogs, and your uncontrollable gas is enough to make me want to walk a beat again."

"Okay, I get it," Hillman said, cutting her off. "You two are doing a great job of throwing us off the scent of your secret affair. Now shut up so I can get through this. Patterson, as usual you'll hold down the fort here with me at HQ. Suarez and Edgerton, keep looking into that string of missing homeless vets downtown. What are we up to now?"

"Four in the last month, Lieutenant," Suarez said. "All of them have gone missing in the same six-block radius."

"Keep me posted," Hillman said before turning to Keri and Ray. "And now for what everyone's been waiting for, the reunion to end all reunions. The partnership that gets my gastric juices all unsettled, it's Sands and Locke together again."

The rest of the unit gave a smattering of sarcastic applause. Ray, though sitting, pretended to bow. Keri gave everyone the finger.

"Looks like that sprained finger is all healed up," Suarez said, smiling.

"Be careful, Suarez," Keri said. "Everything's healed—ribs, leg, shoulder. So I'm in prime hobbit ass-kicking shape."

"Luckily," Hillman interrupted, "since you're in such good shape now, I have something to help you hit the ground running. I got a call about a half hour ago from a local university about a sorority girl gone missing. Her name is Tara Justin. There was some kind of pledge prank last night so they don't think it's serious and she may have just gotten lost. But they called it in just to be safe. Seems like an easy case to get your feet wet again, Locke. You up for it?"

"Sure," she said, standing up. "Let's do it. Where are we headed?"

"That's the one wrinkle," Hillman said. Keri could tell from his tone that it was more than just a wrinkle.

"What is it?" she asked.

"The university is LMU."

Keri stared at him, trying to keep her expression neutral. Loyola Marymount University was the school she used to teach at, where she'd worked as a professor when Evelyn had been abducted, when it had all first gone wrong.

CHAPTER TWENTY EIGHT

Keri let Ray drive, in part so she could think, in part because her fingers and toes had felt numb since they left the station. Hillman had offered to give the case to Brody and Castillo if she wasn't up for it but she had simply shaken her head and walked out of the conference room toward the car.

Now, as they approached the school's main entrance, she wondered if she should have taken him up on the offer. Keri hadn't been on the LMU campus since she'd "resigned" her position five years ago. Technically, it was voluntary. But the parents of the student she'd slept with, who thought he was in love with her and dropped out of school, had threatened to sue the school unless something was done.

It was the final blow to her slow-motion professional car crash, which began when Evelyn was taken. It got worse when she and Stephen became emotional strangers afterward, exacerbated by her heavy drinking and decision to seek sexual solace in the arms of other random men. When Stephen left her and she started showing up at class drunk, it was only a matter of time. The sad little affair with a needy student was only the nail in the coffin of her career and, for a while it seemed, her life.

This would be the first time she'd been on campus since security escorted her and her one banker's box off school grounds all those years ago. As they turned left off Lincoln Boulevard onto LMU Drive, Keri tried to ignore the dull feeling of nausea that tickled her gut.

She had to admit that the place still looked as gorgeous as she remembered. Resting on a series of hills in Westchester, the campus had a view of the entire city and overlooked the Pacific Ocean, which was only about two miles away. The school's strong Jesuit tradition was visually contrasted by the casual, beachy vibe of the place.

Ray checked in at the guard gate and parked at University Hall, the administration building, which was a long office complex monstrosity set down the hills and off from the main campus. They passed through the maze of hallways, Keri leading the way to their destination by memory. As they got closer, Ray leaned over.

"You good?" he asked.

Keri nodded and he left it at that. When they arrived in the Dean's office, his secretary looked up and her eyes grew wide. Keri remembered her and could tell it was mutual.

"How may I help you?" the woman asked.

"We're here to see Dean Weymouth," Ray said, taking the initiative. "I'm Detective Raymond Sands. This is my partner, Detective Keri Locke. I believe our lieutenant called ahead."

"Ah, yes," the secretary said, trying to act as if everything was normal. "I'll let him know you're here. Just give me a moment, please."

She stepped into the office behind her and Keri and Ray exchanged a familiar look.

It's game time.

The secretary returned after a few seconds and ushered them in. Keri had only been in this office once before, the day she'd met with Weymouth, the university's lawyer, the parents of the boy she she'd slept with, their lawyer, and her official faculty rep.

"Thank you for coming," Dean Weymouth said, standing up to greet them. "Please sit down."

In his early sixties, lean and bearded, Weymouth was much as Keri remembered him. He even wore the same three-piece-style suit that she always thought a bit much for an academic environment. His broad smile was so convincing that no one without prior knowledge could have guessed his shared history with Keri based on his demeanor.

"Thanks for seeing us, Dean," Ray said. "If you don't mind, we'll stand. In a situation like this, every second is crucial and we'd like to get started right away if we could."

"Of course, and I'll help in any way I can. But do you really think it's as time-sensitive as all that? I mean, officially, yes, this girl is missing. But as I believe you were made aware, this was part of a sorority event—unsanctioned, mind you—that often results in students temporarily falling off the radar. My understanding is that the only reason you were called was due to a hyper-vigilant sorority sister."

"Better too vigilant than not vigilant enough," Keri said, speaking for the first time. "I'm sure you'd agree, Dean."

"Most assuredly, I would. I didn't mean to suggest otherwise. And may I say what a pleasure it is to see you again under such... dissimilar circumstances to our last meeting, Profess...um, Detect...what should I call you these days?"

"Detective Locke is fine, thanks. The PhD is on ice for the time being."

"No doubt. So what I can I do for you?"

"Why don't we walk to save time?" Keri suggested, turning on her heel and leaving the office as she continued. "We're going to want to meet with all the girls in the sorority as soon as we leave you. I understand that this may just be a pledge hazing ritual that went a little sideways. But until we've got Tara Justin securely back on campus, we need to treat this like any other case."

Keri led the way back down the hall toward the elevator. Ray followed, with Dean Weymouth rushing to keep up. He motioned for his secretary to follow and she jumped up from her desk, grabbing a pen and notepad to scribble furious notes.

"We'll need all her student and academic records as well," Ray added.

"Is that really necessary?" Weymouth asked, breathing heavily as he tried to catch up.

"Probably not," Ray admitted. "But since we're cops we tend to stick to the whole 'too vigilant' thing. Better safe than sorry."

"We'll also need contact information for her family," Keri said. "Do you know where she's from?"

"I only glanced at her student record," Weymouth admitted. "It appears she's local but much of the other information was nonspecific, frustratingly so."

"That's odd, don't you think?" Keri noted. "I thought these kids had to give you everything short of DNA analysis to get in."

"That might be an overstatement, Detective Locke. But I will admit that it is unusual to have such an imprecise student record."

"Send everything to this guy," Ray said, handing him Garrett Patterson's number. "He'll figure out what's going on there."

"As to the sorority," Weymouth said, handing the number over to his secretary as they reached the elevator, "they don't have an official house. None of the LMU fraternities or sororities does. But they do have a rented house where many of the girls live. It serves as an informal house of sorts. I've arranged for their Greek Advisor to be there when you meet with the students. We have a strict policy about protecting those in our charge from anything untoward."

The elevator door opened. Keri and Ray stepped inside and turned to face the Dean, who had a self-righteous half-smile on his face. His unspoken callback to Keri's "untoward" behavior of the past hung in the air.

She knew something like this was coming at some point—a subtle dig at her disreputable history at the school. And though she she'd been dreading it, Keri found that now that it was out there, it didn't have the sting she'd anticipated.

For whatever reason, maybe years of dealing with the horrors of missing children and the human scum who harm them, a jab from an overdressed academic didn't have the impact she had expected. Still, Keri Locke wasn't the type to let it pass. She opened her mouth to respond but Ray beat her to it.

"We'll take that under advisement, Dean Weymouth," he said in a tone as cold as ice. "We respect your policy, of course. As I'm sure you'll respect that we have the right to fully interrogate anyone over the age of eighteen as we see fit. That might be in the presence of an advisor. It might not. It might be in groups. It might be solo. It might be on campus. It might be down at the station. After all, we at the LAPD have a strict policy of upholding justice, no matter what. You dig?"

The elevator doors closed before Weymouth could pick his jaw up off the floor.

CHAPTER TWENTY NINE

It took less than a half hour of interviews with the sorority sisters for Keri and Ray to come to two conclusions. First, no one was entirely sure what had happened to Tara Justin last night. Second, no one seemed to be as concerned as they should be.

After talking to multiple sisters and pledges, all with the Greek Advisor sitting unobtrusively in the corner of the room, they were able to at least nail down the basic situation and timeline.

Last night had been the final evening of a weekend-long pledge initiation. It culminated with all the pledges, in this case seven girls, being driven, blindfolded, to a semi-remote mountain road in Malibu, where they would be dropped off individually around 10 p.m. at night. They had to find their way back to the sorority house by 6 a.m. this morning. The sisters called the event The Expedition.

According to the sisters, it wasn't as challenging as it sounded. All the pledges were dropped off within a half mile of each other. And while their surroundings seemed remote at first, they were actually only about three miles from a popular campground and the heavily traveled Pacific Coast Highway.

They were allowed to keep their wallets and phones, which didn't get cell signals where they were dropped off, but did once they got lower down the mountain. Most girls joined up with some or all of their pledge class with an hour or so.

They were allowed to get back to campus however they liked, whether via bus, Uber, cab, or even calling a friend to get them. They were not, however, allowed to hitchhike. Typically, girls made it back by 3 or 4 a.m. No one had ever missed the 6 a.m. cutoff until today.

None of the other six pledges reported ever running into Tara at any point on their walk down the mountain. But since they arrived back at campus in two separate groups of two and four and basically crashed right away, neither group realized she wasn't among them.

It turned out that the sister who had called 911 was the one who'd dropped Tara off in the first place. Her name was Jan Henley and she was a senior. She'd just happened to drop by the house this morning on her way to her job at the student center to see how things had gone.

She wasn't able to determine for sure that no one could recall Tara coming back until around 7:30 a.m. because most sisters were sleeping in after staying up much of the night partying while waiting for the pledges to return. Due to the extended Easter holiday, there were no classes today or tomorrow (the reason the pledge initiation was planned for tonight). As a result, reaching everyone was a challenge.

Eventually, when it became clear she wasn't back, people called her cell, her dorm phone, and her roommate, all without success. That's when Jan, against her sisters' wishes, called the police.

"I need you to show us where you dropped Tara off," Keri told her.

"Now?" Jan asked. "I'm already on break from work to talk to you. They won't be happy if I just bail."

"Yes, now," Keri said, trying not to sound annoyed at the girl's myopia, "It's after ten a.m. That means's Tara's been missing for over twelve hours. As to your job, we'll smooth it over. You're helping with a police investigation, Jan. No one's going to give you a hard time. And I need the number for Tara's roommate too."

On the way to Malibu, Keri called Edgerton to have him trace the GPS on Tara's phone. He said the battery was dead but the GPS was active and still in the general area that Jan claimed to have dropped her off.

"Do you have a photo of Tara?" she asked Jan, who nodded and scrolled through her phone until she found one. "Send it to me."

When it arrived, Keri studied the image. Tara was an extremely attractive but unpretentious-looking brunette. She appeared to be a typical eighteen-year-old college freshman, with her hair pulled back in a practical ponytail, her smile warm but slightly guarded. Keri thought there was something familiar about her large brown eyes, as if they'd perhaps met before, but she couldn't quite place it.

Frustrated, she shook off the feeling and called Tara's roommate, a girl named Alice Oberon. She got voicemail and left a message making it clear that she needed a return call urgently. But she hadn't heard anything by the time she lost cell service as they started into the mountains an hour later.

Keri tried to ignore the shiver of anxiety that rippled up her spine as they drove past the road that led up to Jackson Cave's place and the canyon where she'd almost died three months earlier. She saw Ray glance at her out of the corner of his eye but he said nothing.

Jan had them turn right at Mulholland Highway, just past the Leo Carrillo Campground. They drove up the mountain road about three miles before she pointed to a small turnout off to the left. Ray pulled over and they got out.

The turnout abutted a small wooded area with a bench and a covered trash can. They wandered around for a while but didn't see anything unusual.

"When did you take off her blindfold?" Ray asked.

"Once I parked," Jan answered.

"And did you tell her anything?" he asked. "Give her any hints?"

"Yeah, I said 'everybody likes going down.'"

"Really?" Keri asked incredulously.

"It was the only hint we were allowed to give," Jan said, sounding embarrassed. "I didn't come up with it. The guys in our partner fraternity thought it was funny."

"They sound like real charmers," Keri said, feeling a mix of disgust and something else she couldn't quite put her finger on.

Jan looked like she wanted to reply but bit her tongue at the last second. Before Keri could call her on it, Ray jumped in.

"What do you want to do now?" he asked Keri, choosing to steer clear of discussion of sexual politics.

"I'm going to walk back down the road," Keri said, "follow the path Tara would have likely taken last night. Why don't you and Jan go down to the campground? If she made it there, maybe someone saw her. I'll meet you there."

Ray nodded and they headed out. Keri walked over to the bench and sat down for a moment, trying to push all the frustrations and anxieties out of her mind. Tara Justin needed her full focus and attention. She closed her eyes, took several long deep breaths, then slowly stood up and looked around.

Nothing was different but she felt somehow calmer and more alert. She began to walk down the hill, keeping to the edge of the road as she imagined Tara would have. After about a quarter of a mile, she came to another small turnout with a wooded area next to it. This one was slightly more elaborate, with a picnic table and both a trash and a recycling bin.

She walked over and glanced around but didn't see anything out of the ordinary. She was about to move back out to the road when she noticed the sunlight reflecting off a surface near a bush about twenty yards deeper into the forest.

She walked over and looked down. It was partially covered by leaves but easily identifiable as a cell phone. Keri put on her evidence gloves and picked it up. The thing was beat up pretty bad. She couldn't tell if it had been intentionally smashed or just hit the ground wrong, but the screen was shattered and there were bits of plastic hanging loose.

She bagged it and continued down the hill. By the time she reached the campground thirty minutes later, she hadn't found anything else noteworthy besides a blister on her pinkie toe from all the steep walking.

As she wandered into the main campground area, she saw some kind of commotion and picked up the pace despite the discomfort in her foot. Ray had a shirtless man with a backward baseball cap in cuffs sitting in the backseat of his car. Another guy and two women, apparently his friends, were speaking loudly and getting uncomfortably close to Ray, who was trying to talk them down. They all wore swimsuits and seemed to be in varying stages of drunkenness.

Jan, standing behind Ray, was pointing at the man with the cuffs on, and sounded borderline hysterical. Keri unclipped the holster of her gun but otherwise stayed cool as she approached.

"What's going on here?" she asked.

Jan turned to her and she could see the girl was crying.

"That girl," she yelled, pointing at one of the women, "is wearing Tara's headband! And that guy in cuffs had her wallet!"

CHAPTER THIRTY

The woman in the headband, who had aggressively bleached blonde hair, gritted her teeth and her face twisted up. Suddenly she was shouting too, leaning in across Ray so that her nose was inches from Jan's.

"Bitch, don't accuse me!"

"What did you do to my friend?" Jan shouted back, not giving an inch.

"Don't get up in my woman's face like that!" yelled the cuffed guy, trying to stand up.

"Everybody calm down," Ray said as he put his left hand on the man's shoulder, firmly shoving him back down. With his right forearm, he eased the headband woman back a foot, creating some much needed personal space for everyone. Keri followed his lead and grabbed Jan's forearm, pulling her back behind her.

"Don't *you* put your hands on my woman!" the cuffed guy shouted at Ray from his neutralized position.

Keri's patience was already running low after the long walk down the mountain and she didn't much like the way the guy said "you" to Ray. So she decided it was time to stretch some of the cop muscles that had atrophied over the last few months.

"You," she said, pointing at the guy in cuffs, "shut your mouth now. That is, unless you want to spend the next twenty-four hours in county lockup in your swimming trunks and nothing else. You'll be *very* popular, I promise."

His "woman" started to respond but Keri wheeled in her direction and shut her down with a withering glare before focusing her words on her.

"You will stop getting in my partner's personal space and you will stop eyeballing that girl behind me. I have a pair of cuffs too and I'm itching to use them. So take five steps back, along with your friends there, and don't say another word until you're spoken to. The first one of you who opens your mouth gets a free trip to downtown LA. And I don't think that's what you had in mind for this little vacation."

The woman's mouth twitched in silent agitation but she did what Keri instructed, as did her friends. Keri looked at Ray, who leaned over and spoke quietly in her ear.

"Wallet definitely belongs to Tara Justin—has her ID and everything. The guy says he found it on the ground last night. Can't speak to the headband but Jan there seems pretty sure of herself. Hard to imagine that it just fell to the ground too."

"What are you thinking?" Keri asked.

"I've already called for backup. One way or another, this guy's going down for something. But we need to interrogate him back at the station. I genuinely don't know whether he found the wallet, stole it, or worse."

"What about the headband?" Keri asked.

"Things got out of hand before I could ask any questions about it."

"Mind if I take a go at her?"

"Go for it," Ray said. "But maybe find somewhere a little more private?"

"Okay, you got things under control here?"

"I'm going to try not to be insulted by that question."

"Sorry, partner," Keri said and gave him a quick pat on the butt to reinforce her remorse.

"You're forgiven," he muttered, trying not to smile.

"Jan, you go hang out in the park ranger's office until we get you," Keri said, before turning to the bleach-haired woman in the headband. "And you're with me, Blondie. We need to chat."

She led the woman to the picnic table of an unoccupied campsite about fifty feet away and motioned for her to sit down.

"Okay, Blondie, what's your real name?" she asked.

"Marla."

"Marla, I'm going to be straight with you. I'm looking for a missing teenage girl. She was in this area last night. Her friend thinks you're wearing her headband. I'm inclined to believe her. Despite that, unless you were somehow involved in this girl's disappearance, your best bet is to come clean and tell me what you know. If you had something to do with her going missing, by all means, lie. But if you didn't, lying to me now will get you in more trouble than telling the truth. I'm willing to cut you some slack for any minor legal transgressions. But this is a one-time offer. So think before you speak."

Marla was quiet for several seconds, seemingly fighting an internal battle between her sense of pride and her good judgment. The latter finally won out.

"Listen, the girl was crazy," she finally said, her words coming out in a rush. "We were coming back from the beach and ran into her. At first I thought she was heading out there because she was wearing a bikini. But then I realized they were her underclothes. She was walking around in her bra and panties!"

"Did she say anything?" Keri asked, choosing to accept Marla's version of events for the time being, no matter how skeptically she viewed them.

"She sounded real out of it, like she was high on something. But nothing good, I think. Her eyes were all red like she'd been crying. I didn't get that at first. I really did say I liked her headband. She just took it off and gave it to me, said she didn't need it anymore."

"And the wallet?" Keri pressed.

Marla looked at her with equal parts suspicion and hope.

"You promise nothing bad will happen to Nicky if I tell you?"

"I can't promise that, Marla. All I can tell you is that it will be worse for both of you if something happened to this girl, you weren't involved, and you still keep quiet."

"I'm gonna trust you here," she said reluctantly. "She had the wallet in a little backpack, one of those girly ones. She was just dragging it around. After she handed me the headband, Nicky joked and said could he have something? She just kind of looked at him with a blank stare. So he kind of pried the backpack out of her hand. She didn't fight him or nothing. After a couple of seconds, she just sort of wandered off. The wallet was in the backpack. Nicky kept it and tossed the pack in the trash."

"Where did she go?" Keri asked, forcing herself to ignore her general sense of revulsion. "Which direction?"

"Just off toward Carrillo Beach, maybe more north. I wasn't really watching. We wanted to get back to camp and drink some more."

"Did she say anything else?"

"She muttered something about hooking up with her old buddy, Herbie or Hurley, something like that. I'm not totally sure about that. Like I said, she was really out of it."

Keri led Marla back to the main group, where she found that the Sheriff's Department had arrived and Nicky had been transferred to one of their vehicles. Ray was on the phone with someone.

165

"You said it would be better if I was straight with you," Marla pleaded upon seeing the scene.

"I'll see what I can do," Keri said, walking over to Ray and waiting for him to finish his call. He hung up.

"That was Hillman," he said. "He wants us to bring this guy in and formally interrogate him, on video. He doesn't want to risk undermining a conviction with, as he put it, 'some half-assed question and answer session in a campground.'"

"We can do that," Keri said. "But I'm not confident it's going to get us anywhere. Talking to the girlfriend, I'm not convinced they did anything more than take minimal advantage of a girl who was already compromised somehow."

"What do you mean?"

"According to Marla over there, Tara was already half naked and half out of her head when they ran into her coming back from the beach."

"And you believe her?" Ray asked incredulously.

"She admitted that Nicky strong-armed the wallet from Tara, who didn't even seem to notice. I just don't think she'd have copped to any of it if they were behind something worse."

"Well, Hillman's going to need more convincing," Ray replied skeptically. "I hope you brought your A game today."

*

Ultimately, Keri decided that Nicky wasn't worth her A game. Back at the station, Hillman wanted to formally question Nicholas "Nicky" Carpenter about the disappearance of Tara Justin himself. Keri didn't think he was the guy. But on her first day back, getting into a battle of wills with her lieutenant on behalf of some scumbag who had at least taken the missing girl's wallet didn't feel like a priority. Marla would feel ill-served but Keri didn't really care. If the worst he'd done was take her wallet, he'd be okay.

Besides, she had other priorities. Tara's roommate had gotten back to her and was coming in to talk. While Keri waited for her to arrive, she walked over to Garrett Patterson's desk to see if he'd uncovered anything unusual in Tara's student records. He had.

"It looks like Tara Justin didn't exist until about two years ago," he said.

"That's kind of big news," Keri said. "Who was she before that?"

"Not sure just yet," he answered. "I was originally spending most of my time going through her grades, current bills, that sort of thing. I only just started looking through her admission documents a couple of minutes ago when I noticed that the financials were a little fuzzy."

"Maybe she fudged something to get financial aid or could it be she's not here legally?" Keri suggested.

"Definitely not the first," he said. "She's paying full tuition. Not sure yet on the second. Give me a few minutes and I may have something for you."

An officer tapped Keri on the shoulder.

"There's an Alice Oberon here to see you," he said, pointing to a petite, black-haired girl standing meekly in the corner of the bullpen.

"Thanks," Keri said, waving the girl over before muttering quietly to Patterson, "Let me know what you find, Grunt Work. But not in front of her."

He nodded and clicked on a different window as Alice approached.

"Hi, Alice," Keri said. "I'm Detective Keri Locke. Thanks for coming in. Why don't we find somewhere a little quieter to talk."

Alice nodded and Keri led her back to an interrogation room. She left the door open to subtly let the girl know she was free to move about as she wished.

"You hungry?" Keri asked, looking at the clock. It was almost 12:30.

Evelyn will be finishing up lunchtime right about now. Where did that come from? Get that out of your head! Stay focused on the case.

"No thanks. I'm not hungry," Alice said, oblivious to Keri's internal back-and-forth.

"Okay," Keri said, settling into a chair at the table and motioning for Alice to do the same. "So you know that Tara has been missing since last night, right? What can you tell us?"

"I actually didn't know until I got a message from Jan Henley in her sorority this morning. I knew she was doing The Expedition last night and I just figured she crashed at the house when she got back this morning. It never occurred to me that anything was wrong until I got the call."

"First thing before we dive in—did Tara ever mention anyone named Herbie or Hurley to you, a buddy of hers?"

"No," Alice said. "I never heard her say either of those names."

"Do *you* know anyone with those names?"

"No, I don't think so."

"Okay. What can you tell me about her experience in her sorority? Has it been positive? Did she have any concerns?"

"Not more than anyone else," Alice said. "I mean, there was a lot of, I wouldn't quite call it hazing, but emotional and physical manipulation. That's why I quit."

"You were a pledge too?" Keri asked, surprised that no one had mentioned this until now.

"Yeah, we joined together. But I just got sick of all the stuff where they broke us down."

"Like what?" Keri asked.

"I'm not supposed to say."

"Unless it was illegal, that's not my concern," Keri assured her. "I'm not trying to get you or the sorority in trouble, Alice. I'm just trying to get a picture of the world Tara inhabited when she went missing, to get into her headspace."

Alice was quiet for a second. But when she finally spoke it was as if she'd been waiting to say her piece for a long time.

"There was just a lot of body image stuff. All the clichés you've ever imagined. Stripping down and having forty girls circle your 'problem areas' with different colored markers. But they went the extra mile for us. They took photos and kept a poster board for each of us so we could constantly reference it and 'improve' ourselves."

"That sounds pretty awful," Keri conceded.

"Yeah, and we had a 'service' requirement that seemed to consist of everything from doing upperclassmen's homework to the occasional waxing session. It just got old and I couldn't see the benefits outweighing the hassles. So I quit."

"Did Tara feel the same way?" Keri asked.

"It didn't bother her as much. She said she'd been through similar stuff in high school. In fact, she was weirdly psyched for The Expedition because she knew it would be in Malibu somewhere. She said she used to love to go hiking with her family there when she was younger."

"Wait," Keri pushed. "So she was cool with all of the stuff you described?"

"No. She didn't love some of the activities with the partner fraternity. She thought some of the guys were a little aggressive, like they acted entitled and grabby because of the official partner connection, you know? But as far as the hazing routine, she mostly let that stuff slide off her back. First off, her body is pretty much perfect so there wasn't a lot to circle. But in general, she just had a casual attitude to the whole thing. Like I mentioned, she told me she went to some fancy high school where the popular clique had the same routine. So nothing here shocked her. Plus, she said if this was how these girls felt important, so be it. She once told me that she almost felt sorry for them because it all seemed so desperate."

"So if she had such pity for these girls, why did she even want to join the sorority? Why did she want them as friends at all?"

Alice looked at her like she'd just asked the dumbest question in the world.

"Because she earned them," she said.

"I don't understand what that means, Alice."

"I mean, because for the first time in her life, she could trust that these girls wanted to be friends with her just because of her and not the rest of it."

"What 'rest of it'?"

"Are you serious, Detective? Don't you know who Tara is?"

Keri shook her head.

"Enlighten me."

"Tara's real name is Tara Jonas. Her dad is Roan Jonas."

"The actor?" Keri asked.

"Yes, Detective, the biggest movie star in the world."

CHAPTER THIRTY ONE

It seemed like the activity level in the station intensified tenfold the minute Alice revealed Tara's true identity. Keri asked her to stay put and was just walking out to the bullpen when Patterson accosted her to tell her what she'd just learned herself.

She pulled Hillman out of his interrogation of Nicky and filled him in. Within minutes, he'd organized a Unit meeting in the conference room. Keri sent Alice home with thanks and specific instructions not to share anything about Tara's actual name with anyone.

"I guess we should cut Nicky loose," Ray said wryly as everyone quickly assembled around the conference table.

"He's still going down for taking the wallet," Hillman insisted. "And frankly, I don't want any loose lips out on the streets. I'm actually shocked that this hasn't gotten out to the press yet."

"Whoever set up her new name did a solid job," Patterson said. "It took some real digging to figure it out. And unless someone was really interested, there wouldn't be reason to dig. I think it will stay quiet a while longer unless someone talks. I don't know how her roommate managed to figure it out."

"She didn't, Garrett," Keri said. "Tara told her. Alice said that after living in the same room together for months, they got close and Tara confided in her. Alice thinks she's the only one at school who knows the truth."

"Why use a fake name in the first place?" Suarez asked.

"I asked Alice that as I was walking her out," Keri said. "She said that Tara was just sick of being viewed as Roan Jonas's daughter. She considered college a chance at a fresh start, an opportunity to create her own identity, independent of his. Apparently, she'd been planning the whole thing out since her junior year of high school—getting the paperwork in order, carefully curating her social media presence, that kind of thing."

"I wonder how her dad felt about his daughter disassociating herself from his name," Castillo said. "Wasn't he hurt?"

"Alice says they were estranged. Tara wouldn't tell her much about it other than that they used to be close and weren't anymore. He supposedly signed off on the name change and paid for college but that was the extent of their interaction in recent years."

Hillman stood up and addressed them all.

"Despite whatever measures this girl took to protect her identity, we have to consider the possibility that it didn't work, that someone found out who she was and this might be a ransom situation."

"What about Nicky and Marla finding her wandering around in her underwear?" Ray asked.

"Don't know," Hillman said. "Could be she was kidnapped, drugged, and escaped. Could be she got high, told the wrong person about her past, and got abducted. Could be she never ambled through that campground half naked at all. Edgerton's checking the place's security cameras on that as we speak, isn't that right, Edgerton?"

"Well, not right as we speak, Lieutenant," Edgerton said.

"Don't get sassy, Kevin," Hillman said. "Whatever the case, we need to proceed based on worst-case scenarios. So Edgerton, you get back to checking that footage. Patterson, you check her social media accounts. I want to know if anyone hacked them to find out who she really was. Brody and Castillo, you go back to LMU and check out the girl's dorm room. See if you can turn up anything suspicious. Sands and Locke, I'm having someone call to see if Roan Jonas is in town. If he is, I want you to go talk to him. Maybe he's already gotten a ransom demand. If not, we need to let him know his daughter is missing."

"Yes sir," Keri said. "Maybe we should also have boat and helicopter teams search the area. If she really was drugged, it's possible she stumbled into the ocean or the woods. We should at least check out the possibility."

"Good idea," Hillman said. "Can you honcho that, Suarez?"

"On it, Lieutenant," Manny said, heading off to his desk.

"All right, everyone," Hillman said. "Let's keep it close to the vest on this one. Once the media gets wind of this case, investigating is going to get a hell of a lot harder."

"I'm going to grab something to eat from the kitchen real quick," Ray said to Keri as the rest of the team scattered in different directions. "Want to head out after that?"

Before she could reply, Hillman interrupted.

"She'll meet you, Sands. I need to talk a minute with Locke," he said, then turned his attention to her. "Let's go in my office."

Keri followed him across the bullpen, looking back at Ray, who simply shrugged in confusion. She stepped inside Hillman's office and he closed the door behind her, gesturing for her to sit in the metal chair across from his desk as he sat himself.

"Bad news," he said without easing into it. "Internal Affairs is back in your business."

"What? I've been on the job again for five hours!"

"I know, Locke. But I got an email a few hours ago saying that your case, which was technically open but pretty much gathering dust, has been reactivated."

"What does that mean exactly?" Keri asked.

"In your day-to-day life? Not much. You've already met with them. Nothing has changed. There's no reason to re-interview you. I don't really know what else there is for them to do at this point other than issue a formal recommendation."

"I thought Chief Beecher shut this thing down," Keri said.

"I did too. The man you killed abducted your daughter. The guy pushing for you to be ousted turned out to run a sexual slavery ring. It's not like your enemies were pillars of the community. I thought it was pretty much open and shut. But apparently someone else with real juice wants to pry this thing back open. If I had to guess, someone wants you off the force permanently."

"Any guesses as to whom?" Keri asked, watching him closely. Part of her wanted to take Hillman into her confidence. Despite being such a hard-ass, he'd always had her back. It was hard to imagine that he was the mole who'd been working against her interests all these years.

"Locke, if I was able to suss out that kind of thing, you would be calling me Chief right now instead of Lieutenant. But what I do know is that you should tread lightly for the next little while. Handle your cases. Do your job. Don't rock the boat."

"When do I ever rock the boat?" Keri asked with a smirk, deciding to keep the mole particulars to herself for now.

"You're a human hurricane, Detective. And I'm about to send you off to talk to a movie star worth a couple billion dollars. Don't make me regret it."

"Of course not, Lieutenant," she said pleasantly as she got up and headed for the door, knowing that her ability to keep her word depended mostly on how that fancy movie star answered her questions.

Ray was already waiting for her in the idling car when she got outside. She hopped in the passenger's seat and he tore off before she'd even shut the door.

"What was that about?" he asked.

"IA reopened my case," Keri said. "I don't want think about it right now. Where are we headed?"

"Brentwood," Ray answered, letting the IA thing go without another word. "Turns out Jonas is between movies right now. He's at his house prepping for some kind of fund-raiser he's hosting this weekend. His people are expecting us but they think we're investigating a possible threat against him. We can tell him the truth when we get there."

"Probably smart," Keri said. "What's the fund-raiser for?"

"I think it's for the governor, some kind of reelection thing. Remember Jonas has gotten pretty political in the last few years."

"Oh yeah," Keri said. "He's not making as many movies anymore, right? I don't really keep up the way I should."

"For a detective working in Los Angeles, you are pretty dense when it comes to Hollywood. Shall I school you?"

"Oh, please, Professor," Keri said, batting her eyes sarcastically.

"My pleasure. You might remember that Roan Jonas started his career as an action star with the *Thermal Fury* series."

"How many of those were there again?" Keri asked.

"There have been six but he only did the first three. He got out before they started sucking. Then he segued into action comedy with that lawyer flick, *Buck the Barrister*. After that, he did the romantic comedy thing with *My Stars*. That's when people started to take him seriously."

"People take him seriously?" Keri asked mockingly.

"They do when your movie makes three hundred million dollars. That allowed him to do that big war movie, *Last Man in Baghdad*."

"That got him the Oscar?"

"The first one," Ray corrected. "The second one was for the Calvin Coolidge biopic."

"What was that called again?"

"*Coolidge*."

"Very clever," Keri said. "And after that?"

"That's the last thing he did," Ray said. "It came out two years ago. He's supposed to start directing his first movie later this year but that's all hush-hush."

"Raymond Sands, I've never been exposed to this side of you. Do you secretly watch *Access Hollywood* when I'm not around?"

"I'm just not totally immune to pop culture. I'm hoping now that you have your life back, you might make room for a bit of that silliness from time to time yourself."

"We'll see," Keri said. "For now, though, let's stay focused on the less starry elements of this guy's life. Any reason someone might want to abduct his daughter? Anyone he might have pissed off? Any skeletons in his closet?"

"Not that I know of," Ray admitted. "But there's someone else you know who might have a better bead on that kind of impropriety."

"I think you may be right," Keri agreed, dialing Mags's number as they shot up the 405 freeway toward Brentwood.

"How's it going, darling?" Mags purred.

"Hey, Mags," Keri said, putting her on speaker. "I'm here with Ray and I need some information. What do you know about Roan Jonas? Any dirt that might make him vulnerable? Anybody he's pissed off that might want retribution?"

"And how are you?" Mags replied as if she hadn't heard a word of it. "I hope Evelyn's first day back at school is going well. Sounds like you're keeping yourself busy at work. I'm fine, thank so much for asking."

"I'm sorry, Mags," Keri said, forcing down the frustration she felt. "You're right. I shouldn't just jump in like that. Ev's good. I'm good. I hope you're well too."

"Oh my, I think I can actually hear you chewing at your lip, trying to control yourself and not yell at me. Points for effort, Keri. I will now consent to answer your question."

"Thank you," Keri said, amazed at both her friend's understanding and her patience.

"Roan Jonas is looking to run for office at some point. The fund-raiser he's hosting on Saturday for Governor Macklin isn't really about his reelection, it's about Jonas's future. If Macklin gets reelected, he'll almost certainly run for president two years after that. And Jonas has his eyes on swooping into the Governor's Mansion if that should happen. It's why he's switched to directing. That title has more of an adult sheen than 'actor.' It's why he's on the board of several nonprofits. It's why he will be announcing the creation of his political action committee next month."

"So is it possible someone who might not want him to run would target him in some way?" Keri asked.

"I suppose anything is possible," Mags conceded. "But truthfully, his political ambitions aren't that well known in most circles. And his politics are nothing that would surprise folks. He's a conventional, run-of-the-mill, moderately left of center Democrat; kind of bland on that front, if you ask me."

"Is there any front on which he's not so bland?" Keri asked, leaving the question hanging in the air.

"Ah well, now we're into the realm of rumor and innuendo, which I cannot definitively confirm."

"Come on, Mags. I'm working with a ticking clock here."

"Very well," Mags sighed, pretending as if she was about to share what she knew reluctantly. "He's a dog, Keri. Or at least he was. He had a reputation as a notorious womanizer. He's married with a couple of kids, I think. But it was well known that he had multiple affairs on sets and elsewhere."

"You said *was*?" Keri noted.

"My understanding is that he cleaned up his act a couple of years ago, likely in anticipation of his forthcoming political aspirations. Whatever the reason, I haven't heard anything on that front in some time."

"Anything else?"

"Yes, he's positively dreamy in *My Stars*. You should really check it out if you haven't already."

"Thank you, Margaret."

"You're welcome, Keri. And you should know that, generally speaking, when you call up a reporter and ask these kinds of questions, it's wise to go off the record first. Next time I won't give you a pass."

"Noted."

"Goodbye, darling. Goodbye, Raymond."

"Later, Red," Ray said.

Keri hung up and looked at Ray.

"What do you think?" he asked.

"I think our basket of suspects just got a lot bigger," she said.

CHAPTER THIRTY TWO

As they drove past the security gate and up the Jonas property to the house, Keri couldn't help but notice how cleverly the size of the place was hidden. Because of all the foliage, nothing was visible from the street. Even overhead helicopter shots would be misleading, as much of the house was covered under a canopy of tall trees.

But the house was gigantic. As Ray and Keri got out of the car, an assistant was already walking toward them, wearing a headset and holding a clipboard. A short, sinewy twenty-something guy wearing wire-rimmed glasses, he introduced himself as Jeremy.

"Roan is in his office working on location prep," he said. "I can take you back there now."

"I thought he'd be preparing for the governor's fund-raiser," Keri mused as they were led through the front door into a long hallway.

"Oh, that's all set to go," Jeremy said casually, "at least on his end. All that's left now is buttoning up catering, valet, security, that kind of thing. He leaves that to the professionals."

Jeremy moved at a shockingly brisk pace and it was hard for Keri to keep up. She barely had time to take in any of the noteworthy features of the house, although she was pretty sure some of the art on the walls was museum-worthy.

"So he's prepping for the movie he's directing?" Ray asked, unable to help himself.

"Yes, it starts shooting next month in Estonia," Jeremy answered as if it wasn't any kind of secret at all. "He's just trying to nail down a few tricky location approvals."

They came to a small sitting room outside what was clearly Jonas's office.

"Just give me a moment to let him know you're here," Jeremy said, "Can I get you anything, by the way? Coffee, tea, water?"

"We're good," Ray and Keri said in unison.

Thirty seconds later they were ushered into Roan Jonas's office, a gorgeous, thickly carpeted room comprised mostly of

176

dark wood and windows. Jonas stepped forward to greet them and Keri realized why Tara's large, inviting eyes had seemed so familiar in the photo she'd seen. They were exactly the same as her famous father's.

"Nice to meet you," he said warmly, shaking their hands. "I'm Roan. Please sit down."

"Thank you," Ray said as they both sat in the plush seats across from his massive mahogany desk. Keri settled in as Jonas returned to his seat. Despite all her mockery earlier, she had to admit the man was stunning, even in jeans and a casual buttoned-down shirt.

He looked to be in his mid-forties, about six foot two and maybe 190 pounds. His black hair was dotted with bits of gray that he seemed self-deprecatingly uninterested in hiding. He had the start of wrinkles that crinkled charmingly when he smiled broadly, which seemed to be often. But more than his physical handsomeness, he exuded a vibe of effortless self-assurance that was confident without slipping into arrogance.

"Maybe you can fill me in on what this is all about," Jonas said as he sat down. "The police liaison was a little cryptic on the phone. She just said it was related to a credible threat made against me."

Ray and Keri looked at each other, debating who should go first. Keri started to open her mouth when her partner dived in. She actually preferred that, partly so she could observe Jonas more closely. But partly, she hated to admit, because she didn't want to be the one to give him the bad news.

"We'd like to keep this conversation confidential, Mr. Jonas," he said, glancing in Jeremy's direction.

"Of course. Give us a few minutes, would you, Jeremy?"

If Jeremy felt put out, he didn't show it. He stepped outside, closing the door without a word.

"I'm afraid the threat we're dealing with isn't about you," Ray said. "Your daughter Tara is missing, Mr. Jonas."

"What?" he asked, as if he hadn't heard the words correctly.

"Your daughter was participating in a sorority initiation event last night," Ray said slowly and clearly. "She was dropped off on a mountain road in Malibu around ten p.m. and hasn't been seen in over fifteen hours."

"Have you tried calling her cell phone?" Jonas asked, his words sounding calm but his eyes indicating he was having trouble processing what had been said.

"We found her phone just off the road," Keri said. "We have teams looking for her right now throughout the area. And we know this is a lot to take in, Mr. Jonas. We're sorry to throw this at you so suddenly. But we didn't realize until very recently that Tara was even your daughter. So we hadn't considered the possibility of an abduction somehow related…to you."

"Me?"

"We have to consider that someone might be using Tara to get to you. Has anyone reached out to you recently, asking for money or making any other kind of demands?"

"No. Nothing. Nobody has…." He looked up at Keri. "Are you sure it was Tara? Maybe there was a mistake and it was a different girl?"

"We're sure, Mr. Jonas," she said. "I'm sorry. I know this is overwhelming. But we need a few things from you. I want you to get out a pen and piece of paper and write these down. I've found that writing things down helps."

"Okay," Jonas said absentmindedly as he grabbed a pen and a notepad. He looked up at her again, waiting for instructions.

"Once we're done," she said, "I want you to write down a list of everyone in your personal and professional life who might have a vendetta against you for any reason. You may not have received a ransom call yet. But it's still possible that you will. We need to be prepared for that. We're going to have a team bug your phones in case. Okay?"

"Yes," he said. She saw him write down the words "enemies list" and "bug phones." At least he was functioning on that level. She continued.

"All right. I realize this may be painful. But I need you to explain to me why Tara changed her name and kept her family identity hidden from people at college."

Jonas sighed deeply. He seemed to find some semblance of his old self for a moment.

"She said it was because she wanted to be her own person, apart from my fame, and this was the only way she could do it. But that wasn't the real reason."

"What was the real reason?" Keri asked softly.

Jonas lowered his head, unable to make eye contact.

"It was me," he said, his voice cracking slightly. "She said she was ashamed of me. When she was sixteen, she saw me with…someone other than her mom. She walked in on us. She had heard stories before then. But she could always ignore them, as my wife had for years. But after that day, she couldn't ignore

178

them. She wouldn't speak to me for three months and when she did, it was to hand me paperwork changing her name. She said she couldn't bear to share the same last name as me, that it stained her."

"So you signed it?" Keri asked.

"I did. She said she needed to know we didn't share that connection anymore, even though she didn't start officially using the name 'Justin' until she left for college."

"Things didn't improve then?" Ray asked.

"Not really. After that, she spoke to me occasionally, perfunctorily. My wife demanded to know what happened but neither of us would say. I think she knew anyway. She just wouldn't admit it. Tara's younger brother was mostly oblivious, thank god. But it tore the rest of us up. Eventually she said she was going to LMU. We said we'd pay and agreed to do it through some Delaware-based LLC she set up so my name wouldn't be involved. It was very impressive actually, how organized she was."

"When's the last time you saw her?" Ray asked.

"She was here in February for her little brother's birthday. She was thinking of coming back this weekend for Easter but couldn't make it because of some sorority event. I guess this was that."

They peppered him with a few more questions, none of which revealed anything new. Eventually he asked a question of his own.

"Should I hire an investigator?"

"I wouldn't do that at this point, Mr. Jonas," Ray said. "Right now, you've got the resources of the LAPD at your disposal. A private investigator would likely only get in the way. And truthfully, the quieter we can keep this for the time being, the better for Tara. Once word gets out that a movie star's daughter is missing, there will be a media frenzy. That whole area will be crawling with rubberneckers. I wouldn't tell anyone you don't absolutely have to."

"Is that how you handled it, Detective Locke?" Jonas asked Keri, indicating for the first time that he knew who she was. The look in his eyes suggested he was hoping she could provide him some kind of reassurance. Unfortunately, years of personal and professional experience had taught her that offering hope, justified or not, was usually a mistake.

"I wasn't famous, Mr. Jonas," she said evenly. "So our situations aren't really comparable. In any case, I think my partner's advice is the best way to go at this point."

"You'll let me know if that changes?" he said.

"Of course," Keri promised him, standing up. "We're going to have a couple of local units come up and stay with you if that's all right—one in the house and one outside."

"Okay. Can I ask one more question?"

"Absolutely," Ray said.

"You said she was dropped off in Malibu. Where exactly?"

"On Mulholland Drive," Ray said, "just up from the Carrillo Beach Campground."

"Oh," Jonas replied, clearly disappointed.

"Tara's roommate said your family used to hike in Malibu a lot," Keri noted. "Is that close to where you usually went?"

"No, not really. I mean, we've been there. But we spent more time in the Santa Monica Mountains National Recreational Area. That's miles away from the campground. We once hiked the entire Backbone Trail—sixty-seven miles—in a long weekend..." He trailed off, remembering.

"That must have been fun," Ray said gently, trying to bring him back to the present.

"It was. I remember her favorite spot was Sandstone Peak—highest spot in the Santa Monica Mountains, she used to say. She loved it because she could sit up there on a clear day and see from the Channel Islands in the Pacific all the way to the snow-covered San Bernardino Mountains. I loved it too. I always assumed she'd eventually forgive me and we'd get to do it again someday."

Keri wanted to tell him that maybe he would. But again, experience suggested that wasn't a good idea. As often as not, all a parent was left with were memories and regrets. They left Roan Jonas alone in his study and silently followed Jeremy, who led them back to their car.

When they got in, Ray checked a message he'd missed when they were in Jonas's office.

"That was Hillman. He said the Coast Guard boats haven't turned up anything in the water for miles near the campground. Copters have been searching the wilderness for miles around and haven't come across anything. They'll keep looking for another hour or so but then they have stop before it gets dark. And the campground cameras were no help. None of them were pointed in the area where Marla and Nicky say they ran into

Tara. Hillman thinks we'll have more success putting resources into a possible ransom call."

"What do you think?" Keri asked.

"I think if someone was holding her ransom, Jonas would have gotten a call already."

"He didn't seem like a guy who had gotten that call," Keri said.

"True," Ray agreed. "But he is an Oscar-winning actor. If he believed his daughter's life depended on deceiving the cops, maybe he decided to deliver the performance of a lifetime."

CHAPTER THIRTY THREE

Keri and Ray ambled along the sidewalk, licking their ice cream cones, with Evelyn ten paces ahead of them. Now over three months free of captivity, her daughter still had the capacity for wonder at the smallest things.

She would stop at a business and window shop with such intensity that it was borderline scary. She'd stare at a law office or a barber shop with the same focus as she would a toy store.

Keri found it adorable while trying not to think too much about why Evelyn found everything so fascinating. Despite that, watching her made Keri forget the ugliness and uncertainty of the day. Hillman had told her there was nothing more for her to do tonight and she'd decided to believe him. She hadn't thought about work more than fleetingly since she'd picked Evelyn up.

Apparently her first day at school had gone well. Nobody had made fun of her, at least not to her face. People had been nice, but not so nice that it made things awkward. Jess had been really great, introducing her around and referencing the two of them as the "survivor twins." Apparently she was a minor celebrity.

"I wanted to show you something," Ray said to Keri when he was sure Evelyn was out of earshot, handing over several unopened envelopes. They were all addressed to her "care of Raymond Sands" at his address."

"What are these?" she asked as she started to rip them open. Within seconds, she realized they were brochures for the Criminology departments at UCLA, USC, and several other local universities.

"I remember you talking about the old days when you used to teach and I thought it was something you might want to reconsider again at some point."

"I was just reminiscing, Ray—not trying to hint at anything. Are you trying to get rid of me, partner?" she asked, nudging him playfully in the ribs.

"Not in a million years," he said. "I just know that you're concerned about the custody issue and how being a cop fits into that and, well, I just wanted you to know I'm cool with whatever you need to do. This is just my way of saying I've got your back."

"That's very sweet and forward-thinking of you, Detective Sands. You know, you could have my back on a more regular basis if we reworked our living arrangement a bit."

"That's something else I was hoping to discuss with you once you resolved the whole custody thing."

"It would seem we have a lot of issues to discuss, Gigantor," Keri said, standing up on her tiptoes to kiss him, getting mint chocolate chip all over his lips.

"It would seem so, Dory," he agreed, kissing her back. "So are you ready to tell her yet? Or do you want to stall a little bit longer?"

Keri glanced over at her daughter and sighed, knowing that their pleasant evening reverie was about to end.

*

Evelyn pretended to look through the window at the computers in the accounting office, pretended not to notice them kissing. Not because she was embarrassed by it; she was long past that. But because every time they saw her watching, they stopped. And she liked for them to kiss. She could see it made her mom happy, which she deserved, especially considering the last few months.

She still wasn't positive what made her do it, cut her wrists that night, three months ago. Part of it was the argument with her dad for sure. He had been awful—the way he'd talked about taking her away from her mom.

But it was something more than that, something she was still trying to work out. The way he'd tried to just take over her life like that, when she finally thought she had some say over it, reminded her of the cruel men that had passed her around the previous six years.

Obviously it wasn't the same. But it *felt* the same. And it had taken her to a dark place that she'd only just barely been keeping at bay. The empty, helpless, shameful feeling that she'd known all those years crept back inside of her and threatened to consume her. And for a moment, she thought that if she could make the world go away, at least then that awful feeling would go away.

It was complicated and confusing and she still didn't totally understand it. But Evelyn felt pretty good after today. With her mom and Ray and Mags and Jessica and Susan and Rita and her therapist, whose name was Joan but who let her call her JoJo, she felt like she had a team on her side, ready to fight for her when the going got rough.

"Ev," her mom said, calling her over. "I'm glad you had such a good day today, sweetie. I'm hoping tomorrow is good too, even though it might be a bit more…challenging."

"What do you mean?" Evelyn asked, feeling a little pit of anxiety pop into her stomach right near where the ulcer the doctor had diagnosed used to be.

"The court says your father is entitled to a visit with you. I didn't tell you until now because I've been fighting it, trying to prevent it from happening. I've actually gotten it postponed twice. But the court finally said you're required to see him tomorrow."

"Tomorrow?"

"Yes. I'm sorry. It's going to be supervised by someone appointed by the court. They'll drive you there and be in the house the whole time. And Mags has agreed to pick you up since she lives so close. It won't be so bad."

"Not as bad as last time, you mean?" Evelyn said icily, letting the statement hang in the air.

"Swee…" her mom started to say but Evelyn turned her back on her and stomped off ahead, throwing what was left of her ice cream cone at the wall of a nearby building.

In the window, she saw her mom start to come after her before Ray put a hand on her shoulder and quietly said, "Give her a minute."

Yeah. Give me a minute. Don't I deserve a minute to deal with you sending me back into that house of walking vampires?

She stormed ahead for another minute before she got tired and decided to sit on a bench. Looking back, she saw her mom and Ray slowly making their way over to her. A van that had been leisurely moving down the road stopped near her and the driver looked in her general direction, squinting. Suddenly she heard footsteps and looked up.

Her mom was sprinting toward her, moving faster than she'd seen since…that day when she was taken, being carried through the park, her mom fading into the distance despite chasing after her.

A second later, her mom was in front of the van, a gun pointed at the driver.

"Hands up!" she yelled.

"What the...?" the man said, raising his hands, his face a mix of shock and terror.

"Who are you?" her mom demanded. "What are you doing trolling down this street?"

Ray caught up and leaned in close to her.

"Lower your weapon, Keri," he said. "Look at the sign on the van."

Evelyn looked at the sign herself. It read "Delivery Dude."

"Answer my question," her mom demanded of the guy, her voice still hard, her gun still pointed at him.

"I'm making a delivery," the guy said. "I'm supposed to drop off some insulin but I can't tell if the number on this address is a three or an eight. I was just trying to tell which place looked more like a residence, lady."

"So you stop right in front of some teenage girl?"

"I didn't even notice her," he said. "I was looking at the numbers, I swear."

"Keri," Ray muttered under his breath, "can you please holster your weapon and take a walk with your daughter, who looks like she's about to pee herself. I'm going to try to defuse this situation. I'll meet you back at the apartment."

Evelyn's mom put her gun back in its holster and motioned to Evelyn.

"Let's go," she said firmly and started in the direction of home. Evelyn got up and joined her without speaking.

Behind her, she could hear Ray talking to the delivery guy in a friendly voice.

"We've had a rash of molestations in the neighborhood and everyone's on edge. You just happened to be at the wrong place at..."

Neither Evelyn nor her mother spoke the rest of the way home.

CHAPTER THIRTY FOUR

The morning was uncomfortably quiet. Ray had left early to get a head start on the case. Keri planned to meet up with him at the station after dropping Evelyn off at the Raineys'. She reminded her that the custodial appointee would be picking her up directly from the school office but otherwise didn't mention anything about the visit to Stephen's house. Neither did Evelyn. They each said a perfunctory "I love you" before her daughter slammed the door.

I guess having a pissed-off, surly teenage daughter is a kind of progress.

Pushing the thought out of her head, Keri tried to focus on the day ahead. She knew no advances had been made in the Tara Justin aka Jonas case or she'd have been contacted. Roan Jonas now had taps on all his phones and every form of online communication. If someone reached out, they'd know. That is, assuming someone hadn't already done so.

Realizing there was little she could do on that front at the moment, Keri mentally reviewed her conversations with Tara's friends from the day before for leads she might have left unresolved. She retraced the Alice conversation in her head but nothing jumped out at her.

Then she did the same with Jan. As she went over what the girl had said, she vaguely recalled how one comment she'd made on the mountain road had struck her as odd. But she'd somehow gotten distracted at the time and lost the thread before she could nail down what it was.

But now, with a day's distance, she remembered what she'd found peculiar. She dialed Jan's cell, got voicemail, and left a message instructing her to call back right away. She considered going straight to the campus but decided it was better to hold off. Besides, she needed to check in at the station and see the status of the investigation.

She arrived just as Hillman called the unit's all-hands meeting to order. Unfortunately, he didn't have much new to share. The taps on Jonas's phones and devices were in place but had revealed nothing so far. Coast Guard and Search and Rescue were resuming their hunts again this morning. Amazingly, nothing had leaked to the press yet about the daughter of the biggest movie star in the world going missing. That was the gist of it.

Keri noticed Jamie Castillo giving her occasional sidelong glances throughout the brief meeting and wondered what new affront she'd committed to offend the officer. She got that Jamie was pissed for being left out of the loop when Keri and Ray decided to fake her death, but it had been three months now.

How long does this girl hold a grudge?

When the meeting broke up, Castillo walked over to her.

"Can I talk to you privately for a minute?" she asked.

"If this is about me not confiding in you before the Vista raid, can we deal with that some other time? I have a lead I want to follow up on."

"It's not about that," Jamie whispered, looking around furtively as she spoke. "It's important."

"Okay," Keri said. She followed Jamie out of the room. Ray caught her eye as she went and raised his eyebrows questioningly. She just shrugged in return.

Castillo led her out the back door to the small covered patio that served as the smoking area for the division. It happened to be situated next to the station's large, noisy air conditioning unit. Jamie stood as close to the A/C as possible and waited. When Keri was standing less than two feet away, she finally leaned in and began to speak.

"You know IA reopened your case, right?" she asked so quietly that Keri had to put her ear almost to Jamie's lips to hear her. She nodded yes in response.

"Well, I was talking to one of my informants last night, a guy who specializes in getting drugs to powerful people who don't want to risk exposure. He operated on the edge of the world Jackson Cave dominated, brushed up against some of those people, never really interacted much, never really wanted to. You know what I mean?"

Keri felt a familiar tightness in her chest, the one that always emerged whenever she got a sense that a tidbit related to Evelyn's case was forthcoming.

"I know what you mean," she replied as calmly as she could.

"Well, this guy says he's been hearing that a big-time local politician was in deep with Cave. He'd smooth the waters for him in exchange for money, girls, drugs—you name it. Apparently this politician guy was worried he'd be exposed when Cave was. Yet somehow he slipped through. But now that you're back on active duty, he's worried you're going to start digging to see who Cave was working with. So he's using all his clout to get you dismissed for good. That's why the IA case was suddenly reopened yesterday when you started working again."

"Does your guy have any guesses as to who this politician is?" Keri asked.

"No. I pushed hard and he genuinely didn't seem to know. He said he cut himself off from everyone in that world after the Vista bust so everything he hears now is third or fourth hand. But it makes sense, right?"

Keri looked hard at Jamie. The younger officer was staring back at her with nothing but concern in her eyes. Keri had never really suspected her of being the mole. And if she was, bringing up the fact that someone powerful was still after Keri was an odd move. It risked exposing herself.

Beyond that, Jamie had put her own life on the line more than once to save Keri's. And she'd once told her she'd joined LAPD after being inspired by seeing Keri find a missing little boy in her neighborhood when no other cop took his disappearance seriously.

It's time to make a choice. Trust this person or not. Decide, Keri.

"Jamie, I need to tell you something—something I probably should have told you a long time ago."

"What?"

"There's a mole in our unit."

Castillo stepped back as if she'd been zapped with electricity. After taking a moment to regroup, she leaned in again, her eyes wider than Keri had ever seen them.

She proceeded to tell Castillo everything, from the prison visit to the Ghost where he warned about a mole, to the decision after the cliff crash to fake her death so the mole wouldn't have anything to pass along to their contact. When she was done, Jamie took a few seconds to process it all, then asked a question.

"What do we do now?"

"I have an idea but you're not going to like it," Keri said.

"What's new? Just spill it."

"Can you look through the personnel records of everyone on the team? See if anyone has a personal connection to any local politicians? It would probably be from early in their career, before they ever joined West LA Division, much less the Missing Persons Unit."

"What about financials?" Castillo asked.

"No. They're harder to access and would draw more suspicion. Your search might get flagged somehow. A personnel search is innocuous. It could be for any reason. If something pops, let me or Ray know. But no one else, okay?"

"Okay. And Keri?"

"Yeah?" Keri said apprehensively.

"I get why you did this, why you kept me in the dark. But you could have trusted me."

"I should have. But I was in a pretty intense place. I hope you can understand. And maybe forgive me one day."

"Already done," Jamie replied, smiling, "although you've got the next round when this is all over."

"That seems fair."

They returned inside. Jamie went to her desk. Keri was headed for hers when she noticed she had a message on her cell. She must have missed it because the air conditioning unit was so loud. It was from Jan, returning her call.

She grabbed Ray and they stepped into the conference room and closed the door, where she dialed Jan's number. Just before hitting "send" she looked up at him and spoke.

"I told Castillo everything. She's on board."

For a second, Ray looked surprised. Then his face broke into a wide grin and he nodded.

"About time," he said and left it at that.

The phone rang twice before Jan picked up. Keri asked her question before the girl could even say hello.

"Jan, it's Detective Locke. You said the guys in your partner fraternity came up with the idea to tell the girls that 'everybody likes going down' as a way to let them know to walk downhill when they got to the drop-off spot, right?"

"I'm sorry, Detective," Jan said, obviously thrown off by the question. "I know that wasn't very sisterly. I feel bad about it, all right?"

"That's not my point," Keri said. "If the guys knew to tell them to walk downhill, then they knew where the pledges were being dropped off, correct?"

"Yeah, I guess."

"If this was some secret sorority ritual, why did the guys know about it?"

"Come on, Detective," Jan said defensively. "It was a secret but it was an open secret. We're not the CIA. Sisters talk to their boyfriends."

"So how many guys in the frat know?" Keri asked.

"I don't know. You'd have to talk to them."

"Then that's exactly what I'll do."

CHAPTER THIRTY FIVE

It felt like an eternity to Keri. But it was really only an hour later that she and Ray stood in the kitchen of the fraternity's unofficial house, about to address the entire membership. Dean Weymouth had been surprisingly accommodating when Keri had called and said what she needed.

In fact, his lack of combativeness made her suspect he'd learned Tara Justin's true identity and was desperate for the girl to be found before the case broke into a tabloid story that consumed the entire university. He promised that emergency texts would be sent to every fraternity member instructing them to be at the house for an urgent 10 a.m. meeting.

They were just about to walk out into the main meeting room to address the guys when a trim, muscular man in his late twenties wearing a sports coat and jeans stepped into the kitchen. Before he even opened his mouth, Keri knew she wouldn't like him.

"Hello, Detectives," he said, extending his hand. "I'm Gerry Brockenbock, an assistant professor in the Political Science Department. I'm the boys' Greek Advisor. It's my job to serve as a mentor and liaison for the fraternity whenever they interact with the larger community. A couple of the guys let me know about this impromptu meeting and it seemed like the kind of event that fit my job description. What are we doing today?"

He had been doing fine up until that last line. Keri could tell Ray felt the same way because she saw his back stiffen at the same moment she felt her own spine get hard. She could sense he wanted to speak first and was fine letting him. But when she glanced over at him, he nodded at her, as if to say, "He's all yours."

"Well, Gerry," she replied, using the tone she saved for abusive bosses, unprincipled landlords, and other self-important jerks with a little power and a lot of attitude, "we'll be asking the boys a few questions about a missing girl. You'll be sitting in the corner, observing quietly, not interfering."

"Detective Locke, is it?" Gerry replied, full of an unexpected arrogance. "So great to see you in person. I'm aware of your exploits, of course. Oh dear, I mean your exploits on the force, of course. I had not yet joined the university when you were making your name for your...exploits here. Those I only know through oral tradition."

He let the comment hang in the air, wondering if Keri would respond. She didn't, only giving a tight smile, letting him continue, and seeing how far he'd dig. Ray, standing beside her, seemed to sense she had a plan and stayed quiet too.

"No matter," Brockenbock continued when greeted with silence. "I will of course offer any assistance I can. But as a proud alumnus of this fraternity and the sworn Greek Advisor to these young men, I will serve as their advocate in this matter and not as just some potted plant sitting in the corner."

Keri remembered this kind of guy from her academic life— the pompous young academic who sometimes fancied himself a campus Adonis. With all the fawning co-eds and the late-night chats about Ayn Rand over scotch in the faculty bar, it was easy for men like this to lose sight of the outside world. But even in her darkest days as a professor, she'd eaten chumps like Brockenbock for lunch. And after years as a cop on top of that, she was licking her chops.

"Gerry," she said, a sweet smile on her face. "Thanks for letting us know where you're coming from. Now let me tell you where I'm coming from. I've got a missing teenage girl. She's been gone for about thirty-six hours now. That's my priority. I don't give a rat's ass about your sworn advocacy. Every guy in that room is eighteen or older. That means they are adults and subject to interrogation. You don't have a say in it. Hell, their parents don't have a say in it."

"This is a private university—"

"Shut up, Gerry." Keri said curtly. "This isn't the Russian Embassy. You don't have diplomatic immunity. We're in Los Angeles, California, and I'm a detective with the LAPD—end of story. So unless you are an attorney—their attorney—you don't have much say in how this goes. And another thing, Gerry; just between you and me, I don't love your tone. Your belligerence makes me wonder if you're the kind of fella who ignores traffic laws and parking instructions. I'm wondering if I need to assign a car to keep a regular eye on you to make sure you're not a menace on the roads. So many potential motor vehicle violations out there, you know, Gerry?"

Gerry stared at her, clearly seething, but said nothing. Still smiling, she moved on.

"So we're going to go in that room, Gerry. My partner and I are going to conduct our investigation as we see fit. And you're going to keep your sworn advocate mouth shut unless you want to have your sworn advocate ass tossed in jail for interfering with an investigation. And if you doubt that I'll do it, why don't you just do a check of my...exploits?"

Gerry stayed quiet. Next to her, Keri could hear Ray trying hard to do the same. He turned his head and coughed to cover the chuckles.

*

Unfortunately, the actual meeting with the fraternity didn't turn up much. Brockenbock gave a brief statement asking them all to be cooperative before Keri provided the broad strokes on Tara's situation and asked if anyone knew anything. No one raised a hand.

After that, they broke the guys up into smaller groups and questioned them, looking for anyone acting out of the ordinary. But it was impossible to gauge who was feeling guilty and who was just nervous at being questioned by a cop. Ultimately, they handed out some business cards, wrote their phone numbers on a whiteboard, and left.

"That was a mistake," Keri said as they returned to the car. "If we were going to interrogate them, we should have done it formally and individually down at the station."

"You want to drag sixty college kids down to West LA division?" Ray asked. "We don't have the manpower to question them all even if we knew what we were looking for."

"Maybe not," Keri agreed, "but this was useless. Even if someone knew something, this wasn't the environment where they would be forthcoming. I feel like we wasted an opportunity here. There's a connection we're missing."

They were halfway back to the station when she got a text.

"Check this out," she said. "It's from one of the brothers—a guy named Logan Mattis. He's asking to meet us at the bowling alley coffee shop at Lincoln and Manchester in ten minutes."

"Maybe we didn't waste our time after all," Ray said hopefully.

Keri and Ray had each already downed a cup of coffee and were on their second when Logan Mattis arrived. Tall and tanned with a tangled mess of sun-stained blond hair that suggested he was a regular surfer, he strolled in trying to look casual but was obviously nervous. He sat down across from them in the booth.

"I'm sorry I couldn't say anything back at the house," he said sheepishly. "But there's supposed to be a code among brothers, you know? I didn't know how far the other guys thought it extended so I didn't want to say anything in front of them."

"We understand," Keri said. "We'll take information any way we can get it, Logan. What do you know?"

"I'm not sure that it's anything so I almost didn't want to bring it up. But I figured, if it's nothing, you guys will be able to figure that out pretty quick and he won't get into any major trouble."

"You've got to give us more specifics than this, Logan," Ray said, having difficulty hiding his exasperation.

"It's just that no matter what, I'm ratting out a guy drinking and driving. Would you bust him for that?"

"Maybe we should," Keri told him. "But if this is from two nights ago and he wasn't arrested then, there's not much we can do about it now. If that's the extent of what this guy did wrong, then you shouldn't worry about telling us what you know."

"Okay. On the night of the Expedition, one of the guys was really drunk and he started talking about how he was going to follow the sorority's pledges to the drop-off point on Mulholland, then pick them up and drive them further up the road so that it would be more challenging, to mess with them a bit. He said the whole thing was too easy, not like the stuff we have to do."

"Did he do what he said?" Keri asked.

"That's the thing, I don't know. He was talking about it, especially how Tara seemed too cocky, like she wasn't even worried about the Expedition at all. The next thing I knew, he was gone. No one else really seemed to notice. He might have just gone home. He might have gone to his girlfriend's. But I guess he could have gone up there and done what he was talking about."

"It sounds like you're leaning that way, Logan," Ray said. "Any particular reason?"

"It's just that the next morning, I saw his car. It was parked at a crazy angle across two spots and it looked like it had been dinged a few times. If he'd gone to his apartment or his girlfriend's, both of those are walking distance. So that made me think he drove somewhere and that he was probably really wasted on the way back."

"What's this guy's name, Logan?" Keri asked quietly.

"Taylor Hunt. He's a senior. He's our Rush Chairman."

"Pretty powerful guy on campus, I'm guessing?" she asked.

Logan nodded.

"You have no idea," he said and she could hear the anxiety in his voice. It had taken a lot for him to come forward when he could have just kept his mouth shut.

"Oh, I have a pretty good idea, actually," she said. "Thanks for telling us, Logan. And we'll do our best to keep you out of this."

"Thank you. I don't want any trouble. It's just Tara seems like a really sweet girl. I don't want anything bad to happen to her."

"You're doing the right thing, Logan," Keri assured him. "Just one more question. Who is Taylor's girlfriend? We'll want to talk to her in case he uses her as an alibi."

"It's this girl named Jan, Jan Henley. She's Tara's sorority big sister. That's how Taylor noticed her in the first place."

CHAPTER THIRTY SIX

Keri, charged up with adrenaline, wanted to turn right back around to campus and confront Taylor Hunt. But Ray convinced her they should at least check in with Hillman before taking that step. Reluctantly, she agreed.

"It's a good thing you came back," Hillman said after they filled him in. "We got a call from Roan Jonas a few minutes ago. He's anxious and wants an in-person update. I was going to send Brody and Castillo but he's insisting on you guys. To be honest, I was hesitant to send Brody anyway. Who knows what inappropriate thing he'd say?"

"I feel for him, Lieutenant," Keri said. "But we can't drop a possible lead to go babysit a worried parent, even a movie star. It's not a constructive use of our time."

"Making sure this guy plays ball and doesn't go to the press is far from babysitting, Locke," Hillman said, an edge in his voice. "It could be what keeps this case from turning into a circus."

"I can go," Ray interjected, obviously not wanting things to escalate. "Maybe he'll remember something relevant he didn't think of yesterday. Keri, why don't you go talk to Hunt on your own? I have a feeling it might be more effective anyway."

"How so?" she asked.

"He sounds like a rich, entitled little jackass. If he sees some big, intimidating, one-eyed black cop, he'll probably just clam up. But if it's some petite, harmless-looking, MILF lady officer talking to him, maybe he'll drop his guard a bit."

"Worth a shot," Hillman said, shrugging. "Just please don't go from harmless to assault without justification, Locke. It's your second day back, after all."

"I'll be a delicate flower," Keri said, batting her eyes flamboyantly.

"That would be a first," Hillman grunted.

*

It wasn't hard to find Taylor Hunt. Keri had Patterson track his cell signal, which led to a sports bar just off campus on Lincoln Boulevard called Tower Pizza. While she was at it, she had him do a little more searching to determine some of Hunt's recent activity.

Keri found Hunt seated in a booth with three other guys. He looked vaguely familiar from a group interview back at the fraternity house, although she didn't remember him actually saying anything at the time. Blandly handsome, with light brown hair and an easy smile that college girls likely found winning, his whole bearing exuded an air of privilege.

She was surprised at how raucous the guys were in the middle of a school day until she remembered the university was closed for the holiday. Thinking that might work to her advantage, she undid one more button than usual on her shirt, exposing an extra bit of cleavage. Then she tucked the shirt into her pants so the material pressed tight against her chest. Finally, she undid her ponytail, fished a rarely used tube of lipstick out of her purse, and applied it before walking over.

"Hi, Taylor," she said warmly, leaning in close and bending over. "Can I talk to you for a minute?"

He looked up at her, first noticing her chest through fuzzy eyes before blinking a few times when he got to her face. It took a couple of seconds for him to register where he recognized her from.

"I know you. You're the detective lady from this morning."

"That's right. How's it going?"

"Good. You look different from before. Better."

"I guess this light just suits me. You got a minute? Can we talk in private? Or do you find older women intimidating?"

One of his buddies elbowed him in the ribs and started hooting mockingly. That was all it took for him to hop up and follow her over to a corner table, his beer still in hand.

The waiter came over and Keri ordered a beer she knew she wouldn't drink but figured would set Taylor at ease.

"So Tara's your girlfriend's little sorority sister?" she said, diving right in.

"Yup," Taylor said.

"So does that make you her big brother?" Keri asked, her tone flirtatious.

"I don't know about that. I mean, I guess I kind of look out for her a little, but nothing official."

"Is that why you went out to Malibu after Jan dropped her off, to make sure she was doing okay on the Expedition?"

"What?" Taylor asked, looking unsettled for the first time. "I didn't…"

"It's okay, Taylor. I already know you were out there. We can track cell phone records and the GPS in your car shows that you were there. I just assumed that it was so you could make sure the girls were all okay and that no one was messing with them. Is that right?"

"Uh, sure. I mean, that's what I *was* going to do. But when I got out there, I couldn't find the girls. I guess they had already gotten rides back. So it was kind of a wasted trip."

"That is a real bummer, Taylor," Keri said, putting her hand on top of his sympathetically, before letting it slide over his fingers and back onto the table again. "You know what though? It would really help if you could show me where you were when you checked on the girls. We're creating a map of Tara's last known location and knowing where she *wasn't* can sometimes be as helpful as knowing where she was. You think you could help me out with that?"

"You mean, like now?" he asked uncertainly.

"Sure. No time like the present. Maybe we can even get some seafood and beer on the way back. Besides, it's not like you have school today, right? What do you say? Care to help a lady out?"

*

About forty-five minutes later, as they passed El Matador State Beach, Keri noticed that Taylor's buzz seemed to be wearing off slightly. He wasn't as chatty and his mood had turned slightly sour.

She glanced at her watch. It was just after 3 p.m. That meant the court-designated custodial appointee was driving Evelyn to Stephen's house at this very moment. Fighting the strong urge to text her daughter that she loved her, Keri instead focused her attention on the increasingly uncomfortable college student in the passenger seat.

"So would you say you and Tara were friends?" she asked.

"Friendly, I guess. I wouldn't say friends. I mean, she was a freshman and I'm a senior. It's not like we hung out."

"She didn't look like a freshman though, right?"

"What do you mean?" Taylor asked suspiciously.

"I'm just saying, for a girl her age, she looked very…mature. Is that fair to say?"

"I didn't really notice," Taylor said far too defensively.

"Good call, my man," Keri said approvingly. "I'll bet Jan would have been pissed if she thought you were taking an interest in her little sister. The real question is—did Tara ever take an interest in you?"

"What?"

"Like, she did ever give you a side-eye glance when Jan wasn't looking? I mean, you are the Rush Chairman of your fraternity, right? That's a big deal. And you're pretty easy to look at. Are you telling me she never tried to get with you? Not even once?"

"I mean, sure, she gave me looks sometimes," he said, as if he hated to have the tidbit dragged out of him.

"I'll bet. Any chance she told you to visit her after Jan dropped her off so you two could spend a little quality time together? I mean, no prying eyes up there, right?"

Taylor looked over at her, as if he was deciding if she was messing with him. After a long pause, he spoke.

"We might have hooked up."

"Oh yeah?" Keri said, keeping her suddenly pounding heart under control by focusing on her own voice. "That's kind of hot. How did it go down?"

"You won't tell Jan, right?" he asked.

"No, of course not. Like I said, we just want to map her last known location, that kind of thing. Besides, I always like a good 'sex in the woods' story. I'm divorced myself so I can use the fantasy material, you know? Call me Keri, by the way."

She felt borderline sick to her stomach saying this stuff, but every time she did, it seemed to throw the kid off, make his suspicions dissipate, turn his attention to her chest. That was a fair trade-off.

She saw the sign for the Leo Carrillo Campground and knew the turnoff was imminent. She needed him to start spilling soon.

"All right," he said, seeming to decide there was no harm. "After the sisters took the girls, I decided to follow them up. My first plan was to put a few of them in the car and drive them further up the mountain, to make it a bit harder. They're such wusses."

"Right," Keri said, egging him on as she turned off the Pacific Coast Highway onto Mulholland Highway. "You've been through much worse, I'm sure."

"Exactly. So by the time I get up there, the only girl I could find was Tara. I was gonna do the whole trick but then at the last minute I started to feel bad and offered to give her a ride back down instead so she could avoid the long walk."

"That was cool of you."

"I know. So we're hanging out in the car, kind of talking, and one thing leads to another. Next thing you know, we're doing it."

"Whoa," Keri said, hoping she wasn't laying it on too thick.

"Yeah, it was pretty awesome. Anyway, like I said, afterward I offered to take her back down the mountain. I even said I'd drive her all the way back to campus if she kept it quiet."

"So she wouldn't even have to finish the challenge?"

"Right," Taylor said. "I probably went too far with that one. In fact, she said no to all of it. She actually had me drop her off back where I'd picked her up. She said she wanted to finish the challenge for real, which I really admired."

"She sounds like one heck of a girl, Taylor."

"Yeah, I guess."

"Well, we're heading up there now. So just keep your eyes peeled and you can point out the spot where you dropped her off. That will really help us out with our investigation, okay?"

"Okay," he agreed.

The car got quiet as they made their way up the winding road. Keri stole a glance at her phone and saw that she no longer had any reception.

CHAPTER THIRTY SEVEN

Evelyn sat curled up on the bathroom floor, her back pressed against the locked door, her body heaving in near silent sobs. It had taken less than an hour for everything to fall apart.

She really had tried. The court appointee, a mousy woman in her thirties named Carla, had picked her up from school and tried to make small talk on the way to her dad's house. She explained that the visit would last about two hours and that she would be in the room the whole time.

That sounded great but it turned out to be only technically true. After they got in the house and settled in the living room, Carla took out her phone and put in her earbuds. Shalene and Sammy hung around for about ten minutes before he had to go down for his nap, which seemed pretty convenient to Evelyn.

Her dad was pleasant for about a half hour after that—asking how school was, what her friends were like—and completely avoiding the topic of her trying to kill herself after her last visit. But around the forty-minute mark, he started talking, ever so casually, about a really great private school in the area.

Then he mentioned that Shalene's sister had a son who saw an amazing therapist—maybe she'd like to meet him. He also let it slip that they were taking a family trip to Europe around the Fourth of July and he'd love for her to come. Unfortunately, it wasn't possible until the custody situation was resolved.

And then he was asking how her mom was handling being back on the force. Evelyn didn't mention the incident last night with her pointing a gun at a delivery man. Finally, after a quick glance over at the oblivious Carla, he told her how worried he'd been about her and how he didn't blame her for what happened and knew that she'd only said and done what she'd said and done because her mom had turned her against him.

Evelyn stared at him, not sure whether to be horrified or angry. Was this the best he could do after not seeing her for three months? After she'd carefully rebuilt her life since trying to commit suicide? To dive right back into the same crap that screwed her up in the first place?

She looked at him, no longer hearing his words, trying to picture the man she used to cuddle up with to read at night before bed. Where had that guy gone? This man still looked a lot like that one. But it was like his soul had been sucked out and replaced by someone else she didn't recognize.

Her mom was a mess—a raw nerve of violent, hair-trigger emotion. But at least Evelyn still recognized her as the same woman who'd tucked her in at night and braided her hair and sang lame songs from the 1980s. This guy was a stranger.

And the next thing she knew, she was running down the hall away from him. And then she was in the locked bathroom, with her father banging on door, demanding she open it. She could hear Carla asking him to calm down even as Evelyn tried to call her mom. It kept going straight to voicemail so she called Mags, who picked up right away. She had trouble explaining the situation but Mags seemed to get it anyway.

"I'm on my way," she said. "I'll be there in fifteen minutes."

She was there in ten. Evelyn could hear her outside the door, using her honeyed inflection to try to soothe her dad, who seemed immune to her charms. Mags asked her to open the door but she wouldn't as long as her father was there and he refused to leave.

Then Evelyn got a text. It was from Mags. It said simply: "Called Ray. Here soon. Hang tight, darling."

Ten minutes after that, she heard Ray's deep voice. He sounded calm but she had gotten to know him well enough to realize that when he was this calm, it usually meant he was doing all he could to keep his anger in check. His voice resonated clearly through the door.

"This visit is over, Mr. Locke," he said, and Evelyn found it interesting that he didn't call her dad Stephen. "Margaret Merrywether will be taking Evelyn home, as has been agreed upon."

"But the visit is supposed to be two hours!" her dad insisted.

"It's being cut short," Ray said evenly. "Surely you don't want to force your daughter to stay if she isn't up to it. If that's a problem for you, take it up with the court."

"You better believe I will," her dad hissed. "Don't think that badge scares me."

"I'm sure it doesn't, Mr. Locke," Evelyn heard Ray say before his voice dropped nearly to a whisper. "Why would a badge scare a man who's blind to his own daughter trying to put her life back together, who's so concerned with his own needs that he can't be bothered with hers, who has her locked in a bathroom after less than an hour in his company? But you know what I bet does scare you? My fists. And they should, because if you ever make that girl feel unsafe again, you'll have me to deal with. Am I making myself clear, sir?"

There was no response, but a few seconds later she heard the sound of footsteps walking away.

"It's okay to come out now, darling," Mags said.

Evelyn opened the door and threw herself into her open waiting arms. After a long hug, she felt Ray scoop her up and carry her out of the house. She kept her eyes closed the whole time.

*

"I think this is the spot," Taylor said, pointing to a nondescript section of woods not too far from where Keri had found Tara's phone.

Keri pulled over and got out. Taylor was now pretty much completely sober and she could sense he knew he'd made a series of terrible mistakes by coming here and being so forthcoming along the way. She suspected he'd just picked a random section of trees in the hopes that Keri wouldn't find anything and they could be on their way. What he didn't realize was that she'd intentionally slowed down a half mile back so there was no way they'd overshoot this spot.

"This is the spot where you had sex or this is the spot where you dropped her off afterward?" she asked.

"Dropped her off, I guess?" he said, sounding unsure.

"So you had sex in the car then?"

"Right."

"Because you said you talked in the car, had sex, and then dropped her off so she could finish the challenge. So the sex was in the car? She definitely got in the car with you?"

"I think so," Taylor said. "I mean…to be honest, I had a little to drink that night and some of the details are a little hazy. Does it really matter?"

"It kind of does, Taylor. For us to pinpoint where best to search for Tara, we need to know the last place anyone saw her and it sounds like you were that last person."

"Wait, what are you saying?" he demanded. "Are you accusing me of something?"

203

"Have I accused you of anything, Taylor? Other than being a good guy who's trying to help find a missing girl? That's what you are, right?"

"I just feel like you've kind of started getting a bitchy attitude in the last few minutes and I don't think that's cool."

"I don't mean to sound bitchy, Taylor. I'm just trying to nail down the particulars," she said, leading him in the general direction where she'd found the phone. "Could you guys maybe have done it over here?"

She watched as his eyes followed her movements before involuntarily flickering to another spot just beyond the drop-off of a steep hill over to the right. He forced himself to look back toward her but Keri could sense his eyes being drawn back toward the drop-off, like they were being pulled by an invisible magnet.

"Maybe it was over here?" she volunteered, wandering in the direction he'd been trying not to look. She saw him stiffen as she approached the area. As she walked over, she made sure to keep an eye on both her destination and Taylor. She let her right arm drop casually, brushing against the clasp of her gun holster.

Glancing over the edge of the hill, at first she saw nothing. But then, in an area where a pile of leaves seemed to have accumulated, she caught sight of what looked to be clothes—a pair of jeans, a woman's top, and a pair of sneakers.

"Down there, Taylor?" Keri asked. "Does that seem about right?"

"I'm not sure. Like I said, I was pretty drunk. I don't really remember much at all, other than that she was really coming on to me hard."

"Okay, so maybe she took you down there so no cars with bright headlights would catch sight of what she wanted to do to you? Is that possible?"

"That sounds possible," Taylor replied.

"Well, let's go take a look, shall we?"

"It's kind of steep."

"You managed it once, Taylor. It shouldn't a problem for you. You're a lot younger than me, after all. You don't want to get shown up by some middle-aged lady, do you? What would your brothers say about that?"

"You said this was going to stay between us," he reminded her, a sharpness coming into his voice.

"I'm just teasing you, Taylor. I would never tell anyone an old lady out-hiked you."

That was enough to send him down the hill ahead of her. He stumbled a couple of times but never fell. Taylor was so focused on staying upright that he didn't notice Keri studying the clothes as they got closer. She didn't like what she saw. When they got to the bottom she directed him closer to them.

"Pick up the jeans by the cuffs at the bottom," she instructed.

"But then I'll get my fingerprints on them," he objected. "Won't that contaminate the crime scene?"

"Taylor, if you helped her take off those jeans to have sex, your fingerprints are already on them, so it's no big deal." She didn't draw attention to the fact that he'd used the term "crime scene." But she did undo the clasp on her holster. He picked up the jeans.

"Hey, Taylor, can I ask you something?"

"What?"

"Why is there blood near the crotch of those jeans?"

Taylor looked at the jeans and then dropped them back on the ground. When he looked back at her, his eyes were squinting in anger. Keri could tell that he was through playing her games.

CHAPTER THIRTY EIGHT

Keri breathed in the crisp, late afternoon mountain air, waiting to see how Taylor Hunt would react.

She was ready for him if he came at her. But she was hoping his arrogance and entitlement would get the better of him and he'd try to verbally bully her. As long as he kept talking, she was getting information that might save Tara.

"You're so smart, bitch, why don't you tell me? Maybe it's just that time of the month for her?"

"Wouldn't that have come up as you were discussing your upcoming sexual encounter, Taylor?" she asked. "Wouldn't Tara have mentioned it to you?"

"You got something to say, say it," he spat. "Because I don't like all the sweet-talk accusations you're making, lady. You act all into me but then you start throwing shade my way. You could hurt a guy's feelings."

"I'm not accusing you of anything, Taylor. I'm certainly not accusing you of stalking Tara. I'm not accusing you of forcing her down into this gully, ripping her clothes off and sexually assaulting her. I'm not suggesting that she tried to escape by clawing her way up that part of the hill right there in nothing but her underwear and bare feet."

Taylor looked over at a spot on the hill where the grass had been torn loose, leaving long streaks of indented dirt in its place. Then he looked back at Keri, half guilty, half perplexed. She didn't give him a chance to respond.

"Don't worry, Taylor. I would never suggest that you tried to chase her up the hill and she either kicked you back or you fell and landed in that spot of indented earth back there, where you probably got knocked out or passed out for a few hours before eventually waking up, crawling up the hill, getting in your car, and drunkenly returning to campus."

Taylor glanced at the spot she referenced with a sense of familiarity that made her certain she was right. She continued.

"Hell, you probably, never even noticed Tara's shattered cell phone up at the top of the hill that I'm sure slipped from her hand as she tried to call for help before deciding to just walk back down the road mostly naked. I wouldn't accuse you of any of that, Taylor."

"You are such a bitch," he seethed.

"And you are one of the dumbest criminals I have ever come across. Were you always this stupid? Or is it just all the brain cells you lost from the day drinking?"

Apparently that was the last straw. He came at her with surprising speed for someone hung over and out of control. But Keri had been expecting it, baiting him into it, in fact. She waited until he was less than a foot away before sliding to the left and thrusting her pointed kneecap into the meat of his thigh.

He grunted as he collapsed on his stomach into the leaves beside her. After a moment, he tried to roll over to pull her down. But she was already dropping to meet him, her right fist pinned to her chest so that her elbow formed a sharp point as her full body weight slammed it down against the right side of his rib cage. She felt a crack at the same time as she heard him cry out in pain.

While he was still gasping for air, she rolled him back onto his stomach, pulled his hands behind his back, and cuffed him. Confident that he wasn't going anywhere, she sat for a moment, catching her breath.

Then she stood and snapped a few photos of the scene. She didn't have any evidence bags and she didn't want to disturb anything for the forensic team she would call when she got back down the mountain.

"Time to go, Taylor," she said, hauling him to his feet.

"You are so screwed," he gasped through painful inhalations. "My dad runs the biggest investment firm on the West Coast. He's gonna run you out of town on a rail."

"Oh yeah, can investment bankers get their sons off on murder charges?" she asked, shoving him up the hill.

"I didn't kill her, you old skank!" he screamed. "Maybe I was little rough but she was into it. I could tell. I didn't do anything wrong."

"How do you know you didn't accidentally kill her by being so rough?" Keri asked. She hadn't actually arrested him yet and if he was willing to keep talking she was willing to listen.

"The last time I saw her, she was scrambling up this hill. I couldn't very well accidentally kill her from flat on my back, could I? You are such an idiot, I can't even stand it."

They reached the top of the hill. Keri looked at the guy, debating whether there was anything else useful he could offer her. He'd essentially confessed to raping her. The physical evidence to support the charge was down the hill below. She was pretty sure he hadn't killed her. Even if she didn't believe his story, Marla and Nicky from the campground supported the theory that she got away physically, if not mentally.

Nope, I'm pretty much done with Taylor Hunt.

"I'm sorry to hear you can't stand what an idiot I am, Taylor. Maybe you'd like to take a seat."

"Wha...?" he started to say. But before he got the word out she punched him square in his broken rib. He dropped to his knees involuntarily and began to whimper between gasps for breath.

"That's more like it," she said. "Now on to official business. You have the right to remain silent..."

CHAPTER THIRTY NINE

"A body?" Keri repeated, not sure she'd heard Hillman correctly as she watched the Sheriff's Department put Taylor Hunt in the back of their patrol car to be transported back to West LA Division.

She'd been on the phone with him nonstop since she'd gotten back in cell range, coordinating Hunt's return and the ongoing search for Tara, but this was the first she'd heard of a body.

"Yes, Locke," Hillman replied. "The report just came in a moment ago. The captain of a small sailboat coming back from Anacapa Island says he saw what looked like a female body on the rocks in the water near Point Dume."

"Has she been identified?"

"No," he said. "The Coast Guard says that with the weather changing, the waves are too choppy to get close to those rocks, especially with the light fading fast. They're going to coordinate to have some divers check it out. But that may take a couple of hours."

"Could the guy on the sailboat tell anything more? Was she in something that looked like underwear or a bikini?"

"All I know is that he thought it was a female."

"Then I say we proceed with the search in the mountains," Keri insisted. "The Coast Guard is right. The weather is changing. The last few nights have been in the low sixties but it's going to get into the mid-forties tonight. If she's out in those woods, she won't make it in that type of cold."

"Locke, we have to be realistic about this. It's late afternoon—too late to start a search tonight. And even if we did, I'm not confident we'd find anything good. We're approaching forty-eight hours missing. Even if that body in the water isn't her, I'm not sure I believe the girl really got away from that Hunt kid, despite what he said. I wouldn't be surprised if we found a shallow grave not too far from where you discovered those clothes. That's why I want to call in the cadaver dogs first thing in the morning."

"Cadaver dogs?" Keri repeated, incredulous. "What about what those campers said about seeing her in underwear and having her wallet and headband?" Keri asked.

"How do we know Hunt didn't take that stuff and pay them to say those things to throw us off the scent? That way we waste all our time trying rescue a living girl instead of hunting for a dead one."

"Lieutenant," Keri insisted, "with all due respect, I spent the whole afternoon with this kid. He's not capable of that kind of planning."

"You may be right. But we both know lots of stories of clever college kids deceiving overconfident cops. Let's not fall into that trap. Come back to the station. You can lead point on the interrogation. And if you want, you can lead point again tomorrow morning, right next to those dogs. Now I've got someone else who wants to talk to you so I'm going to transfer you over, all right?"

"Yes sir," Keri said, despite feeling deeply uneasy with his intended course of action.

"Keri," came Ray's voice over the line. "You okay? We couldn't reach you for a while."

"I'm fine. We were up in the mountains for a while. I lost reception. Did I miss a lot?"

"Kind of. Keep the line open. I'm going to call you right back on my cell."

He hung up before she could reply. Looking down at her phone for the first time since she'd called Hillman, Keri noticed a rash of missed calls—three from Evelyn followed by two from Mags, then two more from Ray and one from Castillo. All were within twenty minutes of each other earlier this afternoon. She saw there were several voicemails and was about to hit the button to listen when Ray called back.

"I just saw my missed calls," she began. "What's going on with Evelyn?"

"She's okay. Before I fill you in, just know that she's okay. She's with Mags right now at your apartment."

"What happened, Raymond?"

"It didn't go well at Stephen's. I was only there for the tail end of it—"

"You went to his house?"

"Yes. According to Ev, it started okay but then devolved into him badmouthing you and suggesting particular therapists, a new school. I guess it overwhelmed her. She locked herself in a bathroom. He was pounding on the door. She tried to call but you were out of range in Malibu. So she called Mags, who went straight over."

"Where was the court person during all this?" Keri demanded.

"She was there but apparently pretty useless. Anyway, Stephen was still big-footing things, so Mags called me. I was just finishing up with Jonas, who, as you know, only lives a few miles away. So I came over. After that, things calmed down. Stephen backed off for the most part. We got Ev out of there, went for some ice cream, and then Mags took her back to your place. She said she'd spend the night tonight to help out."

"What about her kids?" Keri asked as she pulled onto PCH and headed back toward the city.

"They're at her ex's for the week," Ray said. "Speaking of, she wanted me to make it clear to you that you are getting a new attorney, specifically her divorce attorney, the one who handled her custody issues. She stepped away to call him while we were having ice cream. She said to expect a call from him tomorrow."

"That's sweet, but I doubt I can afford any attorney Margaret Merrywether uses."

"She said you'd say that. And she wanted me to convey that she'd float the cost of his services until you write your memoirs. She said not to argue because it was already done. She also said this guy is a pit bull who will tear Stephen a new rectum, although her language may have been a bit more colorful."

"Oh, jeez," Keri sighed. "I leave cell range for a couple of hours and all hell breaks loose. I can't thank either of you enough. How's Ev doing?"

"Hard to tell," Ray admitted. "She was pretty traumatized when we left the house but after a double scoop she seemed okay. She was having fun imitating Mags's accent. I considered that a plus."

"I'll take whatever I can get, I guess."

"Well, don't relax just yet," Ray warned. "I have a little more news for you."

"What else could there possibly be?"

"Castillo got a hit from the personnel files," Ray said quietly.

"Are you serious?"

"Yes," he said, "and it didn't take long either. Only one person in the unit has anything close to a connection to a powerful local politician. Once she found the link, she checked to reconfirm and to see if they're still in touch. They are."

"Well, don't keep me in suspense. Who is it?"

"Keri," Ray said softly, "Garrett Patterson is the mole."

"Grunt Work?" Keri repeated, taken aback. "How does she know for sure?"

"One of his first assignments when he first started the job was as part of the personal protective detail for Carl Weatherford, the County Supervisor for the Third District. He was on his detail for about three years before he got transferred but they stayed in touch. In fact, they speak regularly, with dozens of calls in the last few years."

"Maybe they're just friends?" Keri said hopefully, not wanting to believe someone she had worked with so closely could have betrayed her so deeply.

"Maybe," Ray said skeptically. "It's possible they're just golfing buddies. But a lot of those calls are at odd hours, often in the middle of the night. And a bunch of them are clustered around times when you were pursuing leads about Evelyn."

"But why would he do this?" Keri asked.

"Castillo wondered that too," Ray said. "So after triple-checking to make sure no one else in the unit was connected to Weatherford, she came to me to ask if she could pull in Edgerton to check Garrett's financials. She couldn't reach you and she figured that if anyone could sneak a peek at them on the sly, it was him. So I okayed it. Hope you don't mind."

"No. It was the right call. What did he find?" she asked as she approached Pepperdine University. The Tuesday night rush hour traffic was agonizingly slow.

"The routing is a little complicated so I won't bore you with the details, but Patterson has been getting cash 'gifts' from an uncle of his starting around the second year he joined Weatherford's detail."

"How much?" Keri demanded.

"About ten grand annually, every year up until now—always just under the limit required to declare it for tax purposes."

"That hardly seems like enough to do the things he must have done," Keri insisted.

"But it's not the amount," Ray pointed out. "Once he took anything, he was on the hook. From the moment he took the first payoff, Weatherford could hold it over him, threaten to rat him out."

"But couldn't that work both ways?"

"I'm sure Grunt Work thought of that too. But clearly not or he'd have gotten out from under by now. I'm willing to bet the good Supervisor found a way to insulate himself and leave Garrett out in the cold."

"So Edgerton couldn't find anything sketchy on Weatherford?" Keri asked, trying not to let her frustration overwhelm her. She had a strong urge to honk at every car in her immediate vicinity for no particular reason.

"I didn't say that," Ray told her. "The guy may have insulated himself from Grunt Work. But that doesn't mean he was able to hide everything. Once Edgerton realized what kind of slimy bastard he was up against, he really started digging in. And he found a few things."

"Like?"

"All kinds of shell companies," Ray said. "You have to get through a few layers to find out the real connections. But let's just say Edgerton was incentivized. Weatherford has his hands in shady city construction deals and a liquor distribution business that gets surprisingly good rates from local watering holes. Not to mention a hidden bank account in the Cayman Islands. But I'm burying the lead."

"What's the lead?" Keri asked.

"He seems to have been tight with Jackson Cave. There are countless calls between them. Cave wasn't his lawyer but worked with Weatherford's firm all the time. And his personal financials have all kinds of sketchy payouts for things like 'team outings' and 'civic beautification disbursements.'"

"Sounds like a slush fund for drugs and girls."

"Agreed," Ray said. "And I'm betting Cave supplied a lot of both. I think it's pretty safe to assume this is who he was referencing as the higher-up before he died."

"I think so too," Keri said. "So what are the next steps?"

"We're prepping a warrant for everything now—his home, phone records, financials. Once we have all our ducks in a row, we'll go to Hillman. Edgerton's deep-dived his records and he has no connection to Weatherford so I think it's safe to fill him in. But I want to wait until we're set. I assume he'll authorize a warrant for Grunt Work's arrest and approve moving on the Supervisor. We'll probably wait until first thing in the morning to go to a judge."

"Sounds like you've had a busy afternoon, partner."

"All that and babysitting a movie star too," Ray conceded.

"Oh yeah. How did that go?" Keri asked as she inched past Pepperdine. She saw a strip center off to the left and debated pulling in for a bathroom break.

"There wasn't much to it. It was pretty clear he hadn't gotten any secret ransom calls. I think he mostly wanted to commiserate. He kept talking about things they did when she was younger—lots of stories about camping and hiking and stuff. He said he'd been thinking about suggesting a hike to that Sandstone Peak she liked the next time she visited, as a way to reconnect and maybe heal some wounds. Now he doesn't know if he'll ever get the chance. He hates how they left things. I really felt for him, Keri."

"Yeah, well. It's going to get a lot worse for him if that body off Point Dume is her," Keri said, immediately put off by the coldness in her own voice.

"I guess," Ray said, noticing it too.

"I'm sorry. I'm frustrated by this traffic and I have to pee really bad. I'm going to pull over and find a spot. I'll check in with you when I get closer to the city, okay?"

After they hung up, she navigated her way through the strip center and parked in front of a bookstore she hoped had a bathroom. As she walked through the aisles to the back of the store she passed a section titled *Malibu: Local Lore, Legends & Logistics*.

After she finished up, she walked back through the same section. She stopped in the middle of the aisle, thinking for a long time. She had that familiar itch in the back of her brain, the kind she couldn't quite scratch. Then she stepped over to the shelf with guidebooks, noting that the "Legends" subtitle was a clever reference to both folklore and maps.

She pulled out a book on hiking the Santa Monica Mountains and flipped to the page about Sandstone Peak. It listed the multiple trails leading to the top, including the grueling Mishe Mokwa Trail and the far less intense Sandstone Peak Trail. Both ultimately led to the 3,111-foot summit and the seemingly unimpressive reward of coming face to face there with the plaque of Herbert Allen, who had apparently donated a bunch of the land in the area to the Boy Scouts.

Herbert Allen. A thought flashed through Keri's head—something that the drunken camper Marla had told her Tara said: she was going to hook up with her old buddy, Herbie.

Could she really have been planning to walk all the way from the ocean to the top of this mountain in just her underwear?

It only took a second for Keri to decide that, yes, she could.

CHAPTER FORTY

Keri tried not to let excitement overwhelm logic as she pulled out her phone and did a quick search of the distance from the Leo Carrillo Campground to Sandstone Peak. It was well over nine miles using marked roads. But she suspected that if that's where Tara was headed, she wasn't using roads.

She tried to project herself into the girl's mind from two nights ago. She'd been recently assaulted. She was barely clothed. From Marla's description, she sounded disoriented and confused, possibly concussed or in shock—maybe both—after the attack by Taylor.

That might explain her seemingly unhinged desire to find her friend Herbie, to return to a place that held positive memories for her, before everything started to fall apart. As crazy as it sounded, it also made sense.

Keri looked at her watch. It was already after 6 p.m. and the sun was starting to dip in the sky. In a little over an hour it would be dark. She called Hillman, steeling herself to tell him what she needed.

"How did you hear so fast?" he asked before she could speak.

"Fill me in," she said noncommittally, not wanting to reveal that she no idea what he was talking about.

"The Coast Guard says the body off Point Dume isn't Tara Jonas. It was some spring breaker who got caught in a rip current near Zuma Beach."

"That doesn't surprise me because I know where Tara is," Keri said.

"Where?"

"Somewhere in the Santa Monica Mountains. She's trying to get to the top of Sandstone Peak."

"What?" Hillman asked, flabbergasted.

Keri quickly explained her theory and her plan. She wanted a Search and Rescue team to help her comb the area from the campground up to the mountain, following both the Yerba Buena Road path and the more direct route straight through the wilderness.

"That's a massive area, Locke. There's no way we can cover all of it, especially with darkness approaching."

"That's why we have to do it fast, Lieutenant. Like I said, the last few nights have been pretty warm but it's going to be really cold tonight, worse in the mountains. She won't survive out there dressed like she is."

"We don't have the manpower for a search like this, even if we called in County resources."

"Call in for helicopters then," Keri demanded, trying to keep her frustration in check. "That way we'll need fewer men."

"They won't authorize that kind of expense."

"That's fine, Lieutenant," Keri said, channeling her fury into a calm tone she didn't know she was capable of. "I'll just give Roan Jonas a call. I'm sure when I tell him we can't afford to pay for a helicopter search for his daughter, he'll be fine picking up the cost. Maybe he can send out a tweet to his followers to form volunteer search parties. I think that's the way to go. Let's get hundreds of untrained folks traipsing around in the dark mountains. I'm sure it will turn out great."

There was a long silence on the other end of the line before Hillman finally responded.

"I'll call the Chief," he growled. "We'll scramble a team. They should be onsite in less than an hour."

"Great," Keri said enthusiastically. "I'm going to buy some gear at the camping store across the street and head straight for the peak in case she made it there. It would be great if you could ask a team to meet me there."

"Locke."

"Yes sir?"

"I don't know if threatening your boss on your second day back at work is the best career advancement move."

"I'll take that under advisement, sir. Got to go now."

*

Things moved fast from there. First she called both Ray and Mags to let them know she wouldn't back any time soon. Mags reaffirmed that she'd spend the night at the apartment and said not to sweat it.

Then Keri loaded up at the nearby camping store, getting the clerk's recommendation on what she needed for a nighttime mountain hike and leaving with a trail map, a headlamp, a flashlight, a puffy jacket, and a small backpack. She filled that up with water, energy bars, a flare gun, and a personal locator beacon. She also threw in a thermal blanket, a pair of hiking pants, a sweater, and a second puffy jacket, all in case she found Tara.

She was at the Sandstone Peak trailhead a half hour later. According to the map she bought, it was only a mile to the peak from where had parked, but the 1,100-foot elevation was fast and steep.

She put on the headlamp, zipped up the jacket, threw the backpack over her shoulders, and started out just as the sun dipped beyond the Pacific Ocean. Almost immediately, she felt an increasing chill in the air. Looking at temperature on her phone, she saw it had already dipped into the mid-fifties. She could only imagine what it felt like at the top of that exposed, wind-swept mountain peak.

The climb was brutal. Within minutes her thighs were burning as she trudged upward at what seemed like a permanent forty-five-degree angle. Despite the headlamp and flashlight, she tripped multiple times on loose rocks and unseen notches in the trail.

Even though it had dipped to about fifty degrees, sweat dripped down her brow. She occasionally called out to Tara but gave up after a while, when she got no response and her throat became sore and hoarse.

After about forty-five minutes, she came to a sign that pointed her toward the actual peak. She looked in that direction and saw a carved-rock stairwell that turned into more of a sheer gravel scramble after the first fifty feet or so. She took several big gulps of water, retied the laces of her woefully inadequate loafers, which had turned into blister-creation machines, and started up.

She fell twice, once hitting her left knee so hard on a rock that she thought she might have cracked it. Branches just out of her line of sight ripped at her face as she pulled herself upward, using whatever semi-solid surface she could get a grip on.

Eventually, the trees and brush gave way, giving a clear view of the summit, only a hundred rocky, jagged feet away. There was no sign of Tara. Keri stood still, listening for a noise—crying, moaning, anything that might suggest a person was up there, maybe hidden among the rocks.

Keri briefly considered stopping there and turning around. But she decided to push to the top. She had come this far. And part of her knew there was a chance that Tara might yet be up here, just no longer alive. She steeled herself to find her body, maybe curled up in some corner, out of sight, where she'd hidden from the elements, hoping to find a place of safety.

After another ungainly five minutes she made it. Keri was at the peak, staring at Herbert Allen's plaque. He looked back at her with a severe, almost mournful expression that she knew she was giving more meaning than he intended.

After taking a moment to catch her breath, she noticed a mail slot at the base of the plaque and opened it. Inside was a summit register people could sign to indicate they'd been here. She flipped through to the end, debating whether it would be appropriate to add her name to the list. That's when she saw the most recent entry: Tara Justin.

Keri dropped the register and looked around. She seemed to be alone. But Tara had been here, and recently.

"Tara?" she called out.

There was movement off to her right. She shined the flashlight in that direction and saw a figure behind a rock about twenty feet away on what appeared to be the very edge of the summit.

"Stay away," a weak voice said.

Keri didn't make any attempt to move in her direction, instead pointing the flashlight off to the side so it wouldn't be directly in the girl's eyes. She didn't want to frighten or disorient her, especially when she looked to be so close to the edge.

"Tara, my name's Keri. I'm a police detective. I've been looking for you for a couple of days. People have been very worried about you. Are you okay?"

"Don't come close to me," Tara insisted, a wild edge in her voice.

"I'm not going to, Tara," Keri said, realizing that Tara's positioning on the edge of the mountaintop might not be accidental. "I'm just here to talk. Is it okay if we talk a little?"

"There's nothing left to say. There's nothing left at all!"

"Are you sure about that, Tara? Because I don't think your dad would feel that way. I think he might have some stuff he wants to say to you."

"My dad? What does he have to do with it?"

"How do you think I found you, Tara?" Keri asked. "It was your dad who told me how much you two used to love to hike these mountains, how this was your favorite peak to climb. He said he was hoping he'd get another chance."

"Not anymore he won't," Tara whispered hoarsely. "Not after this. Now he can be ashamed of me too."

"Oh, sweetie, he's not ashamed of you," Keri insisted, now fully aware that Tara wasn't just on the physical edge of a cliff but the emotional one too. "He's ashamed of himself. He told me what he did and how much it hurt you. He so desperately wants to make it right. And when he found out you were gone, all he cared about was getting you back."

"Does he know?" Tara asked, unable to ask the full question but not needing to.

"He doesn't know what happened to you yet. I only just found out a few hours ago. But if you think your father will be ashamed because of something that was done to you, you're wrong. Whatever mistakes he's made, he just wants to protect you, to keep you safe, to make you feel better."

"But he can't make it better," Tara said, her voice catching.

"No," Keri admitted. "He can't. What's been done to you can't be undone. But it doesn't have to define you, Tara. You can move on from it."

"How do you know?" Tara asked accusatorily.

"Tara," Keri said quietly, "look at me. Do you recognize me?"

She shined the flashlight so that it lit up her own face.

"A little. You look familiar. How do I know you?"

"You might have seen me on the news. My daughter was abducted."

After a moment of silence, Keri could see the recognition dawn on Tara's face.

"You're the detective who was looking for her daughter all those years. You rescued her a few months ago."

"That's right. I did. But that's just the news headline version of it, Tara. The truth is that, just like you, my daughter had terrible things done to her. But they were done over many years. She struggles with them every day. She's been through more in fourteen years than anybody should have to deal with in ten lifetimes. But she gets up every morning and faces whatever the day throws at her. So you ask how I know if someone can move on from something like this. It's because I see it every day, Tara. I see my daughter's bravery each time she steps out the front door to face the world. And I believe you have that same bravery inside you."

"I'm not sure I do."

"I *am* sure," Keri said firmly. "And your dad is sure. And your mom. And your little brother. And your friend Alice. You're stronger than you think you are. You just have to take that first step. And I'm right here to help you take it. Step over to me. Let me help you. I've got a sweater and a warm jacket in my backpack. Let's get you bundled up and off this mountain. What do you say, kiddo?"

Tara looked at her for a long time and for the briefest of seconds, Keri thought she'd failed and the girl was going to just let go and tumble off the side of the cliff. But she didn't. Instead, she gripped the boulder she was clinging to and pulled herself forward. She reached her hand out toward Keri.

"I need help," she said.

"You've got it," Keri said and started toward her.

CHAPTER FORTY ONE

By the time Keri got back to the apartment that night, she was so exhausted she could barely stand up. She peeked in Evelyn's room and saw that she was fast asleep. Mags had commandeered Keri's bed, assuming she wouldn't be home that night, so she crashed on the couch.

She looked at the clock. It was well after midnight but she didn't expect to see Ray tonight. He was prepping the early morning arrest of Supervisor Weatherford in conjunction with Castillo and Edgerton and expected to be busy all night. He'd said to go home, rest, and check out the fireworks in the morning.

She was more than happy to do it. After getting Tara down the mountain with the help of Search and Rescue, she's had to warn the Jonas family about her delicate emotional state, process paperwork on Taylor Hunt, and deal with Lieutenant Hillman's intermittent grousing at Keri's tactics. The whole thing had wiped her out.

When her alarm went off at six the next morning, she turned on the news. There was nothing yet about Supervisor Weatherford so she quietly checked on Evelyn, who was still sleeping.

After that, she headed into the bathroom to shower off the accumulated grime and dirt from Sandstone Peak. She washed herself carefully, cleaning the cuts and scrapes without rubbing too hard. Then she allowed the warm water to massage her shoulders for a good ten minutes.

When she finally got out, dried off, and got dressed, she saw that Mags was still asleep in her bed. Fighting the urge to wake her, Keri returned to the living room, where she saw there was now breaking news on the TV.

It was the Weatherford story. Video of him being marched out of his Hollywood Hills mansion in handcuffs was interspersed with file footage of him giving now-ironic speeches about law and order. The screen cut back to the anchor, who mentioned his ties to Jackson Cave and then made the obligatory reference to Cave's confrontation with Keri and his subsequent death.

Keri had seen enough at that point and turned it off. It was time to wake Evelyn for school anyway. She walked into her room. It was empty. She checked the bathroom but it was empty too. She poked her head into her own bedroom again. Mags was starting to stir but Evelyn was nowhere in sight.

She returned to her daughter's bedroom and looked around. Something was off. That's when she noticed her phone on the dresser. Evelyn wouldn't have gone anywhere without it.

Feeling panic start to rise in her chest, Keri looked around and saw that Ev's favorite shoes were gone, as was her school backpack. She rushed to the front closet and found her best jacket gone too. She glanced at the front door. It was unlocked. She was sure that despite her exhaustion, she'd locked it the previous night.

Mags poked her head out of the bedroom door and looked at her groggily.

"How's it going?"

"Have you seen Ev this morning?" Keri asked.

"No. I only just woke up. What's wrong?"

"I can't find her. She was in her room twenty minutes ago when I went to shower. Now she's gone, but her phone isn't and the front door is unlocked."

"Are you sure...?" Mags started to ask but stopped herself when she saw the look in Keri's eyes.

"Something's wrong, Mags. I can feel it."

She looked around the living room, desperately hunting for any clue as to what might have happened. Her eyes fell on her own phone, resting on the coffee table. She hurried over and checked it. There was a text from Evelyn. It said simply, "I'm so sorry."

"What the hell?" Mags said, when Keri showed her the message.

She darted over to her purse and checked the wallet. All her cash was gone. She didn't remember exactly how much she'd had in there but it was around sixty dollars.

"Why would she have left?" Mags demanded. "What happened from the time you got in the shower until you got out that would set her off like this?"

Keri stopped mid-stride and stared at the television set.

"I think I know."

"Care to share?" Mags asked.

"No time right now," Keri answered as she threw on some shoes and grabbed her coat. "I have to find her before she leaves town."

"What makes you think she's going to do that?" Mags asked.

"She's scared and she just wants to get away."

"From what?"

"Her own demons, Mags. She thinks she can outrun them if she leaves this place. But I've got to find her before it's too late."

"Too late? What do you mean?"

"I'm worried that when she finally realizes she can't outrun them, she might try to get rid of them the way she did last time."

"Jesus," Mags said. "What can I do, darling?"

"Please stay here in case she comes back," Keri said as she snatched her phone and purse and headed for the door. "I'll be in touch."

Without even a goodbye, Keri stepped outside into the cold morning air to find her daughter.

*

Keri Locke was a police detective with the LAPD and that's how she decided to start her search. So often in the past, she'd put herself in the mind of a missing, abducted, or runaway child, trying to determine how the kid might think in order to ascertain what might have happened to them. Just because this situation involved her daughter didn't mean the technique was any different.

She moved quickly, allowing her brain to ride the wave of instinct she imagined Evelyn would have followed. Her daughter had left the phone in the apartment, knowing it could be tracked. But she had taken the cash, likely in the hope of getting a ride somewhere. Unable to use a ride-sharing app without the phone and not wanting to risk hitching, she would have likely called for cab.

The closest, safest, currently open place to do that at this hour was Tanner's, the coffee shop at the corner of Culver and Vista del Mar Lane. Keri half-jogged there and pushed past the customers in line to get to the clerk.

"Did a teenage girl come in here in the last twenty minutes asking to use your phone?" she demanded.

"Hey, lady, there's a line," the guy behind her said, putting his hand on her shoulder.

Keri turned and stared him down.

"There's going to be a straight line from my fist to your nose if you don't back up right now."

He removed his hand from her shoulder.

She retuned her attention to the woman behind the counter, who fearfully pointed at the back office. Keri hurried past her and redialed the last number called. Sure enough, it was a local cab company. After identifying herself, she was given the destination of the service call from that location: the Greyhound bus station downtown.

After sprinting back to the apartment to get her car and speeding down surface streets to avoid the traffic-choked morning rush hour freeways, Keri got to the bus station in less than an hour. As she walked into the station, she got a text from Mags that said, "Looks like I'm missing $75 from my wallet too."

Keri called the cab company to find out how much the trip from the coffeehouse to the bus station had been and when it had arrived. They said drop-off had been at 7:14 a.m. and the trip cost $41 without tip. She looked at her watch. It was 7:47 a.m. now. She moved to the front of the ticket line and rapped on the window.

"I need to speak to a supervisor," she said, holding up her badge.

The agent buzzed her in and pointed to a haggard-looking older man in the back corner of the room. Keri walked over and explained the situation without preamble.

"I need a list of all the one-way buses that left in the last half hour or leave in the next hour and cost less than a hundred bucks."

The supervisor casually punched in a few keystrokes as if he got asked this kind of question every day.

"Three options," he said in a bland voice. "The seven seventeen to Sacramento cost fifty-two dollars. The seven fifty-four to El Paso is seventy-nine dollars. And the eight twenty-two to Vegas is eighty."

"How late do drivers pull out? Is there a grace period?"

"Door closes and bus pulls out at the appointed time. All bags and passengers have to be on board five minutes prior to departure or their seats can be given away."

Keri thought for a moment. There was no way Evelyn could have arrived at the station at 7:14 and made it onto a 7:17 bus.

She could ask them to hold the other two but she was pretty confident which route her daughter had taken.

"Thanks," she said. "Which lane does the El Paso bus leave from?"

"Seven," he answered without looking up.

Keri walked there quickly. She felt certain there was no way Evelyn would head to Las Vegas—another city known for its affiliation with the sex trade. Besides, she sensed her daughter was frantically trying to get as far from LA as she could, no matter where that was. El Paso met the requirement.

As she approached the bus, she looked at her watch again: 7:53. The driver, a heavyset guy in his fifties, was just reaching over to close the doors when she put her foot on the first step and flashed her badge. She seemed to be doing a lot of that.

"I need to check something. Won't take but a moment."

He nodded and she stepped on board, taking in the sea of people in front of her.

"You sold out?" she asked him.

"Uh-huh. Every seat," he said.

Keri looked up the left side of the bus and back down the right. Midway up on the right, in the window seat, she saw what she was looking for—an empty space. She walked back slowly until she reached the row.

Sure enough, crouched down low in the seat, hugging her backpack to her chest, was Evelyn. Her eyes were closed, as if willing herself not to be seen. Keri glanced at the older woman in the seat next to her.

"Can you let this one out please? Her passport's been revoked."

Evelyn opened her eyes and looked up at Keri.

"How did you find me?" she asked meekly.

"I'm a detective, sweetie. It's kind of what I do. Now come out of there and let's go get some breakfast."

*

They sat in the diner, neither saying much beyond ordering. Keri texted Mags to let her know everything was okay before calling the school to inform them that Evelyn would be in a few hours late today. Only when it became clear that her daughter wasn't going to initiate anything did she broach the subject.

"It was the guy on the news, wasn't it?" she said. "The Supervisor they arrested. That's the man who wore the mask and showed you the videos of me while he assaulted you, right?"

Evelyn nodded and sighed heavily before speaking.

"I heard his voice from the bedroom and I got so scared. When I came out, I saw that it was just the TV and that he was under arrest. But it didn't help. It just brought everything back. And after yesterday at Dad's, it was all just too much, Mom. I had to get away."

"I get it, sweetie. Really, I do. I still get nightmares when they flash that lawyer, Cave, on the screen, and I didn't go through anything close to what you did. But running away isn't the answer. That's when you come to me. And I make them pay."

"But what if you aren't there? I called you yesterday from Dad's and it just went to voicemail. I had to call Mags and she called Ray. It was a whole thing."

"I heard. And I'm so sorry, Ev. I was in Malibu up in the hills on a case and there was no cell service. I know that doesn't help you. But it really was a fluke."

"I know that," Evelyn said. "And I saw that you saved that girl. Just like I knew you would. I don't want you to feel bad about that. But Dad's not going to stop. And I can't handle it anymore. It's like he doesn't care what I want. He just wants to win. And getting custody of me is a win."

Keri sat quietly, sipping her coffee, uncertain how to proceed. Finally she decided to just lay it all on the line. Her daughter deserved that.

"Listen, Ev. I can't promise everything is going to turn out perfectly. But what I can promise you is that I will always fight for you. I will fight to make sure this Supervisor Weatherford pays for what he did. He'd be going to prison for a very long time even before anyone knows what he did to you. And I guarantee that you weren't the only girl he hurt. That part of his life is going to come out too. And one thing I know for sure, guys who hurt little kids, especially rich, corrupt politicians, don't fare too well behind bars. He's going to have a very ugly next thirty years or so."

Evelyn failed miserably at stifling a smile. Then something occurred to her and her face clouded.

"Will I have to testify?" she asked.

"I have a feeling there will be more than few other girls willing to come forward. Don't you worry about that too much.

But there is another situation in which you might have to testify, one I was hoping to avoid until now."

"What's that?" Evelyn asked, her brow still horribly furrowed.

"It's not a hard and fast rule. But in California, once a child turns fourteen, family courts give their preference a lot of weight in custody decisions. And as you may recall, you recently turned fourteen."

"Why didn't you tell me this until now?" Evelyn asked excitedly, her face brightening.

"Because it's not the route I wanted to go. I was hoping your dad and I could find a way to make this work. But it sounds increasingly like he's not willing to do that. And after yesterday, on top of what happened in January, I'm not sure *you* should have to."

"I don't want to see him anymore, Mom. He's not the same person he was. And I don't think he's even interested in trying to understand who I am now. Being there is depressing. I can feel the ulcer start to come back every time I think about it."

"Okay, well, Mags gave me the name of her lawyer and I'm going to talk to him today. Apparently, he's the worst—in the best possible way. But it could get kind of rough. You need to be prepared for that."

"You don't think I can handle rough?" Evelyn asked skeptically.

"I know you can. I just wanted to warn you. But here's the thing. I can handle rough too. That's my job. To handle the really bad stuff so you don't have to. And I won't ever bail on you or let you down. But you have to trust me. You have to come to me when you're having problems, okay? Because the only way we're going to get through this mess is if we stick together. We're a team, you and I. Sound good?"

"It sounds good, Mom. Even though that's really cheesy, it sounds good."

CHAPTER FORTY TWO

ONE MONTH LATER

Keri pulled into the police station parking lot and gulped hard, surprised at how nervous she felt. It was late afternoon and the spring sun was still high in the sky. Forcing herself to stop procrastinating, she got out of the car and walked into the lobby, where the desk sergeant gave her a goofy half-smile. She returned it.

It seemed like everyone was friendlier to her these days. Well, maybe not everyone; certainly not Stephen. After she'd hired Mags's lawyer, Porter K. Frendlehaus, Esq., as her family law attorney, he'd actually gotten very nasty.

But Keri let Porter handle all that, including prepping Evelyn for her testimony stating her strong preference to live with her mother, as well as establishing that her suicide attempt had come immediately after, and likely in part due to, her time in her father's company.

The judge had granted Keri temporary sole custody with zero visitation for Stephen. And even though the final determination wouldn't come down for another five months, he seemed to have lost interest in the fight once it became clear he would likely lose.

Former County Supervisor Carl Weatherford wasn't all that friendly either, especially after learning Keri had tracked down over a dozen underage girls he'd assaulted in the last year alone, all while wearing his mask. They each identified him by his voice and distinctive markings on his body. Evelyn wouldn't have to testify or even come forward as a victim if she didn't want to.

Prosecutors estimated that with those charges, along with the public corruption, embezzlement, and racketeering ones, even with good behavior, he would spend somewhere between forty and sixty years behind bars. Since he was currently sixty-six, it was likely he would die in prison. And because of the sexually violent nature of some of the allegations, he would be placed in a maximum security facility, which Keri especially liked. He would have lots of touchy-feely friends there.

Garrett Patterson—he'd been informally stripped of the affectionate nickname "Grunt Work"—had fared better. By pleading guilty and turning state's evidence against Weatherford, he was expected to be sentenced to between six and eight years. He'd probably get out in less than three. But he was persona non grata for life in law enforcement.

And apart from Frank Brody, who had just retired and seemed to have developed a soft spot for the kid immediately thereafter, no one in the Missing Persons Unit would even speak to him. Ray had been warned by Hillman on more than one occasion that attempting to mete out any form of personal justice could complicate Patterson's sentencing and put his own freedom at risk. Brody had given Keri a letter Patterson wrote her. And while she hadn't burned it or thrown it out, she couldn't bring herself to read it.

Maybe one day...in a decade or so.

The good news was that after his good work helping with the Vista bust, former mall security officer and current police trainee Keith Fogerty, who was in high demand, had been promised to West LA Division as a replacement for Patterson upon his graduation next month. He wasn't a detective. But he'd already proven he had the skill set to do the grunt work.

Far more friendly these days were the folks at Internal Affairs, who had formally dropped their investigation into Keri a few weeks ago. No one was really pushing the case after Weatherford's arrest anyway. But it had truly become moot after California Governor Gregg Macklin, at a campaign event announcing his reelection bid, pardoned her for any offenses related to her work investigating the disappearance of her daughter.

Nothing formal was ever said. But Keri couldn't help noticing that Roan Jonas, along with his wife, son, and daughter, Tara, were all standing near the governor onstage when he made the announcement.

Keri knew Hillman was glad to have the weight of the investigation off his shoulders. With her name no longer under a cloud, Brody now retired, and Jamie Castillo recently promoted to detective to join Ray, Manny Suarez, and Kevin Edgerton in the Missing Persons Unit, he seemed to have a little extra spring in his step.

That was, until Keri told him she was stepping down. Maybe that's why she was getting all the goofy half-smiles. Everyone in the division had to know this was her last day and that she was really only stopping by to pick up her box of personal effects. Goodbyes were awkward, so she was getting those half-smiles instead.

It had been a tough decision. Part of her still wasn't sure she was doing the right thing. Even in this last month she and Ray had solved seven of the nine cases they'd been assigned and returned two kids to their homes. Victories like that made her think she should stick around.

Of course, they'd also found two other children dead, as well as three adults, one of whom had been chopped up by her own husband. Those were the cases that tore her up. And with a vulnerable, recovering teenage girl in the house, she couldn't afford to be any more torn up than necessary.

So she'd reached out to a few universities—UCLA, USC, not LMU—about returning to Criminology. They'd all jumped at the prospect. A bidding war had even broken out. Eventually she chose UCLA because they were more amenable to her continuing to consult for the LAPD whenever she wanted.

Porter K. Frendlehaus, Esq., had also been a big proponent of the move. In his direct style, he'd pointed out that the court would look favorably upon her switching from a job where she might get shot in the head every time she went into work to a job where her biggest risk was sleeping with coeds.

Ev never said it, but Keri knew she was excited about the move too, if only because it meant her mother would work more regular hours, possibly be able to pick her up from school on occasion, maybe even go to a PTA meeting here and there.

She also sensed that Ev felt a little guilty, as if it was her fault her mom wouldn't be rescuing people anymore and some kids might die as a result. Keri kept a close watch on that, ready to address it if the topic ever came close to coming up. That's the last thing her daughter needed to be piling on herself just as she was finally starting to climb out of the pit of darkness that had been her life for six years.

Keri chose not to think too much about the question herself: would kids die because she wasn't on the job? It wasn't productive. And she'd come up with an answer that was at least somewhat satisfying—recently promoted Detective Castillo would be Ray's new partner.

Keri couldn't think of anyone better to step into her shoes and keep those kids safe. Jamie was sharp as a tack, street smart, and unbelievably tough. She'd also proven loyal, hardworking, and relentless in pursuit of justice for victims. Those were the qualities that really mattered in the end.

Keri knew Ray was glad to have Jamie on board. But she could tell it was complicated for him. He wanted to embrace his new partner. But he also wanted to keep her on her toes so she wouldn't get too cocky.

Beyond that, he wanted Keri to know he was happy for her and the choice she'd made (he had suggested it, after all) but not so happy that he wouldn't miss having her around. He was in kind of an impossible situation. But he was handling it with his usual grace.

He didn't even mind her ribbing him about how she was now crushing him in the salary department. With the UCLA professorship salary, her substantial retainer as a consultant for the police department, and the advance on her memoir, she was pretty flush these days.

She'd thought the memoir thing was a joke when Mags had mentioned it. But when an agent friend of hers (at Stephen's rival agency, no less) pitched Keri on the idea, it was hard to turn down. And best of all, Mags was going to co-write it with her, this time under her real name. "Mary Brady" would have to take a backseat on this one.

One additional plus of all the added income was that she and Ev had gone from the tiny two-bedroom apartment to a much more spacious three-bedroom townhouse. It was still in Playa del Rey, so Ev could go to the same school and see all her friends regularly. But it was gated, with a real security system. It even had a homeowners association.

Of course, Ev didn't care about any of that. She was more excited that her mom had agreed to become a foster parent to Susan Granger, which meant she would have a sister of sorts. Keri had been reluctant at first when Rita told her that Susan had reached the limit of her stay at the group home and would be going into the foster care system.

But the more she thought about it, the less she could think of a reason not to do it. Susan adored her and she'd grown to love the girl back. And she genuinely thought she might be able to make a difference in her life.

Furthermore, even though she was a year ahead of Ev in school, they had grown very close. Keri knew that it helped for both of them to have someone to talk to who understood the depths of what they'd been through. As much as she hated to admit it, sometimes a mom just wasn't enough. Sometimes a girl needed a sister.

Keri had been mulling that over a lot. And though she didn't dare mention it to Evelyn, there was the very real possibility that she might have a sister for real. If the foster care situation worked out, Keri was seriously considering making things permanent and adopting Susan.

With her head full of these thoughts, Keri stepped through the station lobby doors into the bullpen to find the entire workforce of LAPD's West Los Angeles Pacific Division standing silently at attention. The Missing Persons Unit was standing in a tight group by her desk.

Every cop saluted her in unison. Stunned, she managed to remind herself to salute back. After a second, everyone broke into loud applause and raucous cheers and whistles. The next fifteen minutes were comprised of officers coming up to shake her hand or give her a hug.

For a second, Keri thought she saw Chief Beecher in the back of the room, behind a crowd of people. But when she tried to get a better look, whoever had been there was gone. Maybe she'd imagined it.

Ray held back as the Missing Persons Unit got their turn. Hillman was last. As he squeezed her tight he whispered in her ear.

"I can't believe I'm saying this, Locke. But you're not technically retired, so if you get bored in the world of academia, let me know. I'm sure we can find something for you."

"Thanks, Lieutenant," she said, not mentioning that the same idea had occurred to her.

Eventually she walked out with Ray beside her, carrying her box of things. She gave one last wave, and then turned to the door, refusing to look back, intentionally directing her focus on what was ahead of her.

*

Evelyn ran ahead of Ray and her mom as they casually strolled along the path that led from where Culver Boulevard ended to Toes Beach. They'd just had a celebratory dinner at Playa Provisions, her mom's favorite restaurant (and one she

233

said she could actually now afford) and were planning to watch the sun set over the Pacific Ocean.

Evelyn stopped where the path met up with the Ballona Creek bike path just before the sand and sat on a bench to wait. She was giddy but doing her best to hide it. Everything had changed so much recently. And if things went as planned, even more changes were on the way.

Ray and her mom finally caught up just as the reddish-orange sun started to dip behind the horizon. Evelyn saw her mom shiver slightly. Ray immediately took off his jacket and wrapped it around her shoulders. He looked over at Evelyn.

"You okay there?" he called out. "Mind if your mom and I go in the sand for a minute?"

"Yeah, I'm fine," she called back, her legs swinging up and down enthusiastically. "Go for it."

"Take off your shoes," Ray said as he kicked off his own sandals.

"I don't want to go in the sand," her mom said. "It'll be cold."

"Don't be a wuss," he said.

"Yeah, Mom, you're such a wuss!" Evelyn called out from the bench.

"I'm a wuss—the woman who's a walking, talking, bullet-riddled human scar?"

"You're stalling," Ray said, stepping into the sand and reaching his hand out for hers.

"Yeah, stop stalling," Evelyn called out, enjoying the teasing immensely.

"Oh, fine," her mom said and took Ray's hand. She slid off her shoes and stepped into the sand and stifled a gasp that suggested she really did consider it especially chilly.

Ray led her out a few steps so that they were atop a small dune, where they had a better view of the sunset. The sun was dropping fast. It was now only halfway visible and hints of pink and purple were starting to appear.

"Beautiful evening," Ray said.

"It sure is," her mom agreed.

It was a little hard to hear her over the waves crashing in the distance but Evelyn was paying close attention. She didn't want to miss any of this.

"Beautiful girl," Ray added nonchalantly, glancing over at her mom.

"Who, me?" she replied playfully.

"Yes, you; the kind of girl you could spend the rest of your life with."

"What?" her mom said and Evelyn noticed that her tone wasn't playful anymore. It sounded serious; almost scared.

And the next thing Evelyn knew, Ray was down on one knee. He had pulled a small black box out of his pocket and opened it. Ev could see it glint in what was left of the evening light.

She couldn't hear what Ray was saying. But she could see tears running down his cheeks as he spoke.

Her mom wasn't saying a word. She was just staring at Ray with her eyes wider than Evelyn had ever seen them. And then Evelyn saw something else.

It was something she'd seen in her head many times during all those years away, when she was suffering, when she'd closed her eyes and needed something to hold on to, something to keep her going when she didn't think she could anymore.

She saw her mom smile.

Blake Pierce

Blake Pierce is author of the bestselling RILEY PAGE mystery series, which includes twelve books (and counting). Blake Pierce is also the author of the MACKENZIE WHITE mystery series, comprising eight books (and counting); of the AVERY BLACK mystery series, comprising six books; and of the KERI LOCKE mystery series, comprising four books (and counting).

An avid reader and lifelong fan of the mystery and thriller genres, Blake loves to hear from you, so please feel free to visit www.blakepierceauthor.com to learn more and stay in touch.

BOOKS BY BLAKE PIERCE

THE MAKING OF RILEY PAIGE SERIES
WATCHING (Book #1)

RILEY PAIGE MYSTERY SERIES
ONCE GONE (Book #1)
ONCE TAKEN (Book #2)
ONCE CRAVED (Book #3)
ONCE LURED (Book #4)
ONCE HUNTED (Book #5)
ONCE PINED (Book #6)
ONCE FORSAKEN (Book #7)
ONCE COLD (Book #8)
ONCE STALKED (Book #9)
ONCE LOST (Book #10)
ONCE BURIED (Book #11)
ONCE BOUND (Book #12)
ONCE TRAPPED (Book #13)

MACKENZIE WHITE MYSTERY SERIES
BEFORE HE KILLS (Book #1)
BEFORE HE SEES (Book #2)
BEFORE HE COVETS (Book #3)
BEFORE HE TAKES (Book #4)
BEFORE HE NEEDS (Book #5)
BEFORE HE FEELS (Book #6)
BEFORE HE SINS (Book #7)
BEFORE HE HUNTS (Book #8)
BEFORE HE PREYS (Book #9)

AVERY BLACK MYSTERY SERIES
CAUSE TO KILL (Book #1)
CAUSE TO RUN (Book #2)
CAUSE TO HIDE (Book #3)
CAUSE TO FEAR (Book #4)
CAUSE TO SAVE (Book #5)
CAUSE TO DREAD (Book #6)

KERI LOCKE MYSTERY SERIES
A TRACE OF DEATH (Book #1)

Made in the USA
Lexington, KY
13 June 2018